DEATH IN ROOM FIVE

ALSO BY GEORGE BELLAIRS

Littlejohn on Leave
The Four Unfaithful Servants
Death of a Busybody
The Dead Shall be Raised
Death Stops the Frolic
The Murder of a Quack
He'd Rather be Dead
Calamity at Harwood
Death in the Night Watches
The Crime at Halfpenny Bridge
The Case of the Scared Rabbits
Death on the Last Train
The Case of the Seven Whistlers
The Case of the Famished Parson
Outrage on Gallows Hill
The Case of the Demented Spiv
Death Brings in the New Year
Dead March for Penelope Blow
Death in Dark Glasses
Crime in Lepers' Hollow
A Knife for Harry Dodd
Half-Mast for the Deemster
The Cursing Stones Murder
Death in Room Five
Death Treads Softly
Death Drops the Pilot
Death in High Provence
Death Sends for the Doctor
Corpse at the Carnival
Murder Makes Mistakes
Bones in the Wilderness
Toll the Bell for Murder
Corpses in Enderby
Death in the Fearful Night Death in Despair
Death of a Tin God
The Body in the Dumb River Death Before Breakfast
The Tormentors
Death in the Wasteland
Surfeit of Suspects
Death of a Shadow
Death Spins the Wheel
Intruder in the Dark
Strangers Among the Dead Death in Desolation
Single Ticket to Death
Fatal Alibi
Murder Gone Mad
Tycoon's Deathbed
The Night They Killed Joss Varran
Pomeroy, Deceased
Murder Adrift
Devious Murder
Fear Round About
Close All Roads to Sospel
The Downhill Ride of Leeman Popple An Old Man Dies

DEATH IN ROOM FIVE

AN INSPECTOR LITTLEJOHN MYSTERY

GEORGE BELLAIRS

NEW YORK

ISBN: 978-1-5040-9267-8

This edition published in 2024 by Open Road Integrated Media, Inc.
180 Maiden Lane
New York, NY 10038
www.openroadmedia.com

The patron shrugged his shoulders.

'The usual.'

The Chief Inspector didn't quite know what he meant. He rose, screwed up his napkin, which his wife immediately straightened and slipped in the wooden ring engraved with a number One. The best bedroom!

Next door the argument was still going on.

'But I tell you, we've hardly enough to pay the hotel bill.'

The two men were standing patiently in the hall. The usual. Littlejohn understood. The kind one saw on conducted tours. Both had *Englishman* written all over them. A bit shy and a bit suspicious, bothered by the currency and the language, working out the sterling equivalent of the labels on goods in the shops for the benefit of their wives, and now and then touching their passports in their inside pockets to make sure they were safe.

Littlejohn was the same himself and his heart warmed to them.

These two, however, looked worried and deflated. A tallish young man with a handlebar moustache, dressed in a blazer and flannels, and a small, middle-aged man perspiring in a Harris tweed sports coat and white shorts. He wore white shoes, too, and a white canvas cap. He looked as if he'd started for the South heavily clad and had shed some clothes when he got there. They were obviously relieved when the Inspector's massive form filled the doorway and hurried to meet him.

'You tell him, Leslie.'

The younger man spoke. A warm, friendly, cultured voice. He turned out later to be the conductor of a private coach-tour from England. A sports master at a Grammar School, adding to his income during the recess.

'Sorry to bother you, sir, but we're in a spot of trouble. I'm here with a party from the north of England and last night one of them was stabbed in Cannes. He's in hospital there and he's in a poor way. He's asking for *you*.'

Littlejohn slipped on the light jacket he'd been carrying over his arm. The little man in the white cap thought he ought to speak.

'There's a party of us come by coach from Bolchester. We're doing a round trip back through Switzerland. This 'as put paid to it, by the looks of it.'

'But this is surely a job for the French police. I'm here on holiday as an ordinary British citizen. I'll do all I can, but I've no standing.'

'Oh, but Alderman Dawson has. He's a JP.'

As though Alderman Dawson's judicial authority stretched all over the earth!

'Alderman Dawson?'

'Yes, he's the man as 'as been stabbed. He's an ex-Mayor of Bolchester. He speaks French. Got a medal from the French in the last war. Work with the Resistance. Parachuted into France not far from here. That's why he's come. He wanted to see the place again...'

The young man thought it well to intervene.

'You see, sir...'

But white cap hadn't finished.

'Alderman Dawson won't have no truck with the French police.' He said it proudly and took off his white cap as he did so, as though someone were hauling up the flag. Then he nodded his head to show he'd finished.

'You see, sir,' said the man in the blazer, 'we saw the other day in the paper that you were staying here. The Alderman remarked when I showed the notice to him that he'd met you once somewhere. Then, when he was stabbed, the first thing he said when the local police arrived at the hospital was "Get Chief Inspector Littlejohn. I want to speak to him." We thought that seeing...'

'That's all right. I'll come with you.'

'We've got a taxi waitin'.'

The little man was on the run for the door right away.

The taxi driver was a little dishevelled man and hurled them through Golfe-Juan and straight into the stewpond of traffic on the Nice road without a pause. They had hardly recovered their breath before they were through Cannes and on the Grasse road. They passed an 'H' sign, then another, *Hôpital. Silence*. The taxi driver hooted furiously to show it didn't apply to him and pulled-up dead.

A pair of beautiful wrought-iron gates, open beneath a stone arch. *Clinique des Petites Sœurs de la Miséricorde.*

'I think it's a Catholic place,' said the little man apologetically. 'But they say it's one of the best nursing-homes on the Riviera. I don't know what Alderman Dawson will say when he comes round properly and sees his nurses are nuns. He's a Baptist himself.'

They made their way along the loose gravel drive between palm trees and hedges of mimosa and hydrangeas. The young man tugged the chain at the side of a massive oak door and a bell clanged above their heads.

If complete silence was a part of the treatment, the patients would certainly get it here. A handsome building, with a broad, white stuccoed front, a long row of windows with neat green shutters, a wing on each side. Smooth lawns with beds of red geraniums and four revolving sprays at the ends of hose-pipes casting feathers of water on the grass. The chapel clock struck ten. The sky was clear, cloudless blue and it was hot for the time of day. The sight of the water-jets on the lawns made you more parched and stifled and you longed to lift one and let the water cool your head.

A panel in the big door opened, revealing a wrought-iron grille, behind which appeared a coiffed face.

'Bonjour, ma sœur.'

The young man evidently knew his way about. The door opened silently to admit them.

A wave of cool air met them as they crossed the threshold and, faintly mingled with it, the smell of incense from a distant chapel. As they moved farther inside it became lost in the more powerful odours of iodoform and ether.

The doorkeeper led the way, her hands folded in her large sleeves.

The place must have been a private château before the nuns took it over, for it was too lavish for their simple utilitarian purposes. The floor was of mosaic and a large, broad staircase of white marble swept upward to a balustrade beyond which the corridors stretched into other parts of the building. At the foot of the staircase, a small cabin of wood and glass, occupied by another sister busily writing in a large book. The doorkeeper glided ahead of Littlejohn's party without sound save the flutter of her clothes, and handed them over to the second nun.

A woman in the late forties, by appearances, although in the frame of the white coif, with her smooth pale cheeks, she had an ageless look. It must have been the eyes which dated her, the wrinkled eyelids, the expression of experience. The two hooded figures spoke in whispers, their *cornettes* touching. The Alderman's visitors were passed from one to the other and the second acknowledged them with a slight inclination of the head.

'Your passports, *messieurs*. It is not that I need your credentials, but that I can better spell your names if I see them written down. I have to put them in my book.'

She spoke in perfect musical English.

All the time nursing sisters were passing to and fro and it gave you a shock to find them so near, for their movements were noiseless. A tall man in a grey suit, probably a doctor, rapidly descended the staircase, raised two fingers at the presiding nun and was let out by the sister at the door.

Leslie Humphries, Schoolmaster, Bolchester.
Frederick Jackson Marriott, Wine Merchant, Bolchester.
Thomas Littlejohn, Chief Detective Inspector, London.

The receptionist raised her head and gave Littlejohn a shrewd look through her round gold-rimmed spectacles, smiled very faintly by simply dilating her nostrils, bracketed the three names together, and beside them wrote a large 5.

'You wish to see *Monsieur Cinque?*'

The Alderman, however great he might be in Bolchester, had lost his identity here. He was plain Mister Five, the number of his private ward.

The sister rang a handbell and from the balcony above, her counterpart of the first floor descended rapidly down the staircase, her light silent feet scarcely seeming to touch the steps.

A younger nun this time, with a rosy face without a wrinkle. A pretty girl with a clean complexion, polished like a ripe apple.

'Monsieur Cinque.'

The younger sister said nothing, but Littlejohn detected in the drooping of the mouth that something was wrong. With a gentle wave of the hand the nun indicated that they must follow her.

The Chief Inspector began to capture the old lost feeling of more than forty years ago when he had been a choir boy in the parish church at home. The large, silent building, the crucifix on the wall of the staircase where the steps turned, the stray whiffs of incense floating above the hospital smells and then fading away, the hollow echoing sounds of his footsteps on the bare tiled floors. He caught himself walking on his tiptoes.

The little man, Marriott, must have felt the same. He looked over-awed, his eyes wide, glancing all over the place, his slight disapproval at the religious atmosphere. He was presumably a Protestant and a bit out of his element. He made no bones about walking on his tiptoes and lifted his feet like a trotting-horse the better to move quietly. Humphries, the schoolmaster, was a step ahead. He must have known the ropes, for he made no attempt to speak to the nun leading them, not even to ask how the patient was.

They reached a corridor containing four numbered doors and the sister halted at the first, bearing a 5 in white paint. She tapped and the door opened silently, revealing a woman who was obviously not of the rank and file. She was dressed in the usual habit, but it was either of a better cut or she wore it with better grace. She was tall, middle-aged, slim…an obvious aristocrat and one in authority. She had an aquiline face and beautiful hands. The sister leading the party was deferential. The older woman spoke quietly.

'Oui, ma mère.'

Littlejohn felt a bit at a loss. At home, he would have taken over easily on account of his authority. Here, he was a nobody, a visitor without standing. Something was obviously wrong. The mother superior herself had opened the door to them. Either the Alderman had been kicking up a fuss and demanding to see the head of the hospital, or else…

The young nun had effaced herself and the older one was addressing them in good English.

'You wished to see *Monsieur Cinque*. I am sorry to tell you that he died half an hour ago.'

It must have been the atmosphere of the place and the serenity of the striking woman speaking that prevented them all from expressing surprise or asking questions. Instead, the three men stood there like pupils before a headmistress.

'You may come inside. The police will wish to see you.'

She opened the door wider and they entered the room, still without a word. It was large and airy with a broad window on the sill of which stood a box with geraniums growing in it. One side of the window was open and, at first, the silence was so intense that they could hear the swish of the water from the hoses in the garden and the hum of the distant traffic, with the militant horns of the motorists blaring now and then at one another.

There was a simple iron bedstead with a crucifix on the wall at the head of it, a wardrobe, a chest, and a bedside table from which the doctor had not yet removed his stethoscope and instruments. On the bed lay a form covered with a sheet.

The ward seemed full of people. A surgeon in a white smock; a silent gendarme in summer uniform; two men in civilian clothes; a clerk, obviously dancing attendance on them; another nursing sister and the mother superior; and the visitors she had just brought in.

The taller man of the two in civilian dress looked at the newcomers. Tall and slim, middle-aged, with a skin like parchment and a high bald forehead. He was dressed in a black coat and striped trousers and his long neck emerged from his white collar like that of a bird. His features were aquiline and he wore black-framed spectacles. But you first noticed the shrewd, black, humorous eyes, which seemed to miss nothing. He was fastidious and gentlemanly to his fingertips.

'Permit me, *ma mère*.'

The mother superior nodded.

'If you will excuse me, I will leave you together.'

The tall man moved like a cat in the direction of the door and held it open for her.

'I will see you later, with your permission, *ma mère*.'

After she had left them, the tall man became active. He looked keenly at the three Englishmen and singled out Littlejohn.

'You speak French?'

'Yes.'

'You were a friend of the deceased?'

'No. The other two are his friends; they come from the same town. After he met with his accident, they called to ask for my help.'

'You are a doctor?'

'No. I am a police officer. I am here on holiday and they had heard I was at Juan-les-Pins and called to say that the dead man wished to see me.'

The eyes behind the black shell frames suddenly lit up and all the officious sternness in the man's manner vanished. 'You are Chief Inspector Littlejohn?'

'The same, sir.'

The man looked ready to fling himself upon Littlejohn and embrace him. Instead, he calmed himself, seized both the Inspector's hands in his own, and shook them warmly.

'Charmed to meet you, Chief Inspector. Honoured to welcome you to Cannes. I am Marcellin Joliclerc, *juge d'instruction*…examining magistrate. Things are a little different here, you know. In your cases in England, you are in charge as detective. Here, the detective works under the examining magistrate. Allow me to introduce my colleague, Commissaire Dorange, of the Brigade Mobile, Nice…the Nice Flying Squad.'

The Inspector from Nice didn't look like a detective at all. He was on the small side, thin and wiry, with a keen hatchet face and dark eyes which reminded you of black shoe buttons. His skin was baked mahogany colour and deeply furrowed, although he must have been on the right side of fifty. He wore a pearl-grey suit of material which looked like nylon, a red tie, and brown snakeskin shoes with holes punched in the uppers which made them almost sandals. There was a red carnation in his buttonhole, as though he'd picked it up from one of the stalls of the Nice flower market and stuck it in out of light-heartedness. He shook Littlejohn's hand warmly. His fingers were sinewy and like small vices.

'Delighted to meet you.'

They might have been getting ready for a wedding or a first communion instead of presiding over the dead body of Alderman Dawson of Bolchester.

The other two Englishmen stood silently near the door. Marriott coughed behind his hand.

'What's it all about, Inspector?'

It pulled Littlejohn up with a jerk. The atmosphere of the hospital, combining as it did religion, healing and death, coming on top of the holiday feeling and hot sun of the Riviera, had got to his head.

'I'm sorry, Mr Marriott.'

He introduced his two companions and explained how he came to be there.

'The Alderman wouldn't have anything to do with the French police. Have you told him that?'

Marriott was holding up Dawson's end even in death. He said it in a cocky, defiant voice, as though by shouting and gesture he could translate the Alderman's sentiments into good French.

The examining magistrate bowed Marriott and Humphries into two of the fragile-looking chairs of the room. Then he took Littlejohn and introduced him to the surgeon who was still scribbling notes at the bedside. A busy little man with a fair complexion and pale blue eyes. A ragged moustache crossed his upper lip and he wore old-fashioned pince-nez clipped on his nose and held for safety by a chain which hooked round his ear.

'Doctor Murols, the resident surgeon here. He has been attending to Mr Dawson since he was admitted.'

Murols was a little fusspot. He seemed reluctant to part from his fountain pen and official forms. As he wrote he made little grunting noises and kept sitting back to survey his handwriting as though anxious that it should be legible. He told Littlejohn as they shook hands that he had once been to England as a student and had spent a year at St Barnabew's Hospital, which left the Chief Inspector wondering whether it was St Bartholomew's or St Barnabas'. In any case, it didn't seem to have done Dr Murols much good. Littlejohn found himself thinking he'd rather trust himself to his wife than to Murols in an emergency.

'He died of internal bleeding. The knife had passed between the ribs and punctured the lung. We could not stop the haemorrhage. I called in Dr Matthieu, but he was of no avail.'

Matthieu. Littlejohn had heard of him. One of the best surgeons on the Coast. Dawson had, therefore, had the best attention. And he had died, nevertheless, refusing to have any truck with the French police.

'Did he make any statement, doctor?'

Murols looked at Joliclerc to see if it was all right for him to answer Littlejohn's question.

'No,' he said after the magistrate had nodded assent. 'Shortly after he was brought here, he lost consciousness. His friend, the one over there, was with him. He spoke to him.'

Littlejohn turned to Marriott and translated what Murols had said.

'That's right. The Alderman told me then to get you.'

'Did he say anything else?'

'He was ramblin' a bit. He said somethin' in what might have been French...Wait a minute. I put it down to the best of my ability...'

Marriott fumbled in his pocket and brought out a soiled envelope.

'Val O'Ree,' he read. 'Val O'Ree, it sounded like. That's all I got. It might have been a man's name. It sounds like one. That's all. He was gaspin' when he asked for you. He wanted a word with you. Then he started to ramble and the doctor sent us out. We came for you right away. Seems it wasn't much use. I don't know what they'll say in Bolchester when the news reaches them. To die abroad and from foul play. I don't know...'

Marriott shook his head gravely as though anticipating serious diplomatic repercussions.

'How did it happen? I forgot to ask in the rush.'

The doctor and the police officials were busy with their forms and Littlejohn took the opportunity.

'We're stayin' at an 'otel just off the prom here, called *Bagatelle*. Reminds you of the old game we used to play, doesn't it? But here it means somethin' else, I gather. However, after dinner last night, the Alderman said he was goin' out for a breath of air. I said I'd go with him, but he said straight he'd rather go on his own. He was here in the war, you know, and might have wanted to look up a few of his old friends. So, I didn't press it. I went to bed soon after.' Marriott had protruding eyes and these eloquently searched Littlejohn's own as though he wondered if his tale were being believed.

'We was got up about three in the mornin'. The Alderman had been picked up outside the Palm Beach Casino, at the end of the promenade. At first they thought he was dead drunk, but when they touched him, they found him covered with blood. He'd been stabbed in the back and left…'

'Who found him?'

'One of the kitchen staff from the Casino. The Alderman was lyin' in a quiet part and it seems the man who found him was just havin' a stroll and a cigarette. He brought help and they got the police and an ambulance. Then they sent for us, because the Alderman's travel tickets and his passport were in his pocket.'

'Had he been robbed?'

'No. Not a thing missin'. Watch, wallet, passport, gold cigarette-case, all untouched.'

'He was unconscious when you got here?'

'He'd just come-to, but was in a very bad way. He spoke to me and Humphries and it was then he asked for you.'

'Well?'

The examining magistrate called across the room. He had been listening to Mr Marriott's spate of English, which he understood but dimly, and was getting impatient.

'Sorry, sir,' said Littlejohn. 'Mr Marriott was just telling me how the body was discovered.'

'I can't understand it,' said Joliclerc. 'But then we haven't begun the investigation yet. All the party who came with the dead man will, naturally, remain here until the inquiry is over.'

Littlejohn translated to Marriott, who was very put out. 'It might go on for months. I've my business to see to.'

M'sieur Joliclerc was speaking again.

'Did the deceased say anything to his friends before he died?'

Littlejohn told him what Marriott had said about Val O'Ree.

The examining magistrate paused. He mouthed the expression.

'Val O'Ree…Vallouris…That's it. Vallouris. That's the name of a village just outside Cannes.'

Then, suddenly, M'sieur Joliclerc grew excited. He spoke sharply to the doctor, who thereupon removed the sheet from the dead body.

It gave Littlejohn quite a shock in more ways than one. Here was none of the portly Aldermen of fiction, but a lean, long-faced figure, the death-mask of which showed a high intelligent forehead, a thin almost ascetic face, and features of taste and refinement. Littlejohn had been mistaken. He'd imagined Alderman Dawson to be the usual pompous stage clown.

''Ere. What are *you* doin' ? Have you no respect for the dead?'

Mr Marriott was outraged, for the doctor had pulled the body of the dead man into a sitting posture and was examining the back in the region of the left shoulder.

'Yes, M'sieur *le juge*, it is here. A bullet wound of long-standing. It is as you thought.' Beneath the old cicatrix the doctor was indicating, Littlejohn could see the fatal wound still bound-up.

Littlejohn couldn't follow what was going on. With the new turn of events and Mr Marriott's strange information, the whole atmosphere of the room had suddenly changed from cordiality to chilly reserve. Even the gendarme, who had hitherto stood mute and deferential, began to mumble things under his moustache.

'Chief Inspector. A word with you, if you please.'

M'sieur Joliclerc had lost none of his politeness, but the smile had gone from his face. He took Littlejohn to the window.

'The case is as good as closed. It will be quite impossible to solve it, either you or I. Things have happened in France over late years which are different from those in your country. We are only just establishing law and order again after years of war and confusion. This is such a case. Circumstances will make it quite impossible for us to finish it satisfactorily. I shall therefore recommend it remain unsolved. Your friends will be free to go their way as soon as certain formalities have been gone through. Two days at most. That is all.'

Littlejohn was first dumbfounded, then annoyed. Whatever Alderman Dawson had done, he was an Englishman and he had sent for Littlejohn on his deathbed. Dawson had been murdered, stabbed in the back, and here was the case already going in the unsolved files. He couldn't believe his own ears.

'Do you mean that, sir?'

M'sieur Joliclerc raised his thick black eyebrows.

'Certainly, I mean it.'

He smiled again, ingratiatingly this time.

'I know how you feel, Inspector. He is a fellow countryman and at Scotland Yard...well...the British bulldog does not let go until the murderer is brought to justice. But this is not Scotland Yard, Inspector. This is France, recovering from her wounds of a long unhappy war and occupation.'

'All the same, sir...'

'All the same...'

The examining magistrate issued sharp orders and his retinue and the doctor started to gather together their things for leaving. One by one they left the room and then M'sieur Joliclerc bowed out Humphries and Marriott. Finally, only he and Littlejohn were left and then he turned to the Chief Inspector.

'Tomorrow, I will arrange for the body to be handed over to the dead man's friends. They may take it home or inter it here, as they wish.'

'I still don't understand, sir. I'm afraid I can't let it rest there. I shall have to get in touch with my consulate and report to Scotland Yard. It doesn't seem fair that after...'

The magistrate threw up his hands.

'Fair, fair. Is it fair that a man on whose treachery rest the lives of a score or more good Frenchmen during the Resistance should escape his dues? But there. I cannot explain it all now. My address is *Solitude,* Avenue Charles de Gaulle. I shall be very pleased to see you there for an apéritif at six this evening, if you will do me the honour. We can then talk about what you call fair play.'

The sister led them to the head of the stairs, where the nun who seemed to be in charge of the route down the staircase took them in hand and descended with them, to turn them over to the custodian in the glass box below. Then the doorkeeper let them out. In the wide hall, an old woman in black was sitting with a young consumptive-looking man who wore yellow gloves. Someone else rang the outer doorbell and Littlejohn saw two old men about to begin the passing-on ceremony he and his companions had earlier been through. The hoses were still spraying the grass, and on a tree near the gate a blackbird was singing.

2

HANDLE WITH CARE

Littlejohn and his two companions were standing outside the clinic with the main door closed behind them before they knew quite what was going on. They had the humiliating feeling that they'd been chucked out and that what had happened to Alderman Dawson was no affair of theirs.

'I'm not goin' to stand for this.'

Little Marriott was digging his heels in. He put on his white canvas cap, which was just a shade too big for him, and looked at the closed door as if ready to rush and break it in.

'I'm goin' straight to Nice. There's an embassy or a consul or whatever you like to call it, there, and I'll see to it that we get our rights. What do you say, Inspector?'

Littlejohn quite agreed. It couldn't end like this. But he grew hot under the collar at the idea of discussing the problem in the blazing sun and right on the hospital doorstep, like a trio of waits who'd been told to go and sing in the next street.

'We'll have to talk it over. Let's find a café in Cannes and discuss what we'd better do.'

It couldn't end there, however much the examining magistrate might want to hush it up. Dawson was a British citizen and he'd been murdered in France. Although the arm of English law couldn't stretch out and avenge his death, the powers-that-be in London would want a full explanation and assurance that the crime was being thoroughly investigated. In that case…Littlejohn sighed at the thought of it. If Scotland Yard hadn't already been on the telephone to *La Reserve* asking him to look into things, there would be a call as soon as the news reached England.

Littlejohn could almost repeat word for word what the message would be. Tactful approach… Be discreet… Handle with care…

'I've kept the taxi waitin'.'

But they didn't reach it.

First M'sieur Joliclerc's little Citroën passed them. The examining magistrate was driving himself and by his side sat the uniformed police officer from Cannes they'd seen at the bedside. In the back seat lolled the magistrate's clerk, who reminded you of a floor-walker in a big shop, intently poring over a dossier. M'sieur Joliclerc solemnly raised his hand in salute, accelerated as he reached the gates, and tore into the stream of traffic on the main road, hooting furiously as he did so.

Then somebody blew a police whistle. Littlejohn and his companions were within a stride of the waiting taxi and it was funny to see all the rushing motorists on the road slow down at the sound of the whistle; some even stopped and looked out anxiously in case the police were on their tails.

Littlejohn turned to see Inspector Dorange waving excitedly after him and indicating his own car which was standing in front of the hospital. He'd evidently blown his whistle as the only way of attracting attention. Dorange jumped in his car and drew up beside Littlejohn.

'Going my way?'

From the friendly light in the eyes of the officer from Nice,

Littlejohn knew that here was probably a solution to his problem. He made excuses to Marriott and Humphries, promised to ring them at *Bagatelle,* and he and his French colleague drove off.

'You're staying at Juan-les-Pins, sir?'

'Yes…'

'I'll drop you off on the way back to Nice.'

The little Inspector smiled, baring his white, even teeth. 'But I think we ought to have a talk before we part. I'm not really on the case. It's a matter for the Cannes police, but as you've doubtless gathered, M'sieur Joliclerc is a nervous man. He asked me to come over just in case of developments. Nice, is, of course, the capital of the department, and at the *Súreté* there we're at the beck and call of anyone who wants any help.'

They had left the suburbs of Cannes behind and now they were in the town again. Dorange seemed well-known among the force there. As they reached the crossing at the Rue d'Antibes, the lights were at red, but the agent on duty altered them to green to let the Inspector through and smartly saluted as they passed him.

The town was bathed in clear sunshine. People in light clothes looking in the shops and then, as they reached the waterfront, all the luxury yachts on parade there, their tall masts like lances and their paintwork shining white. A motorboat was just starting out to the Lérins and opposite the casino the sailors supposed to be touting to take you on a sail across the bay were so warm and comfortable that they looked as if they couldn't be bothered with your custom. A sumptuous Rolls-Royce passed in the direction of the harbour.

'That's Sir Clarence Hobhouse. His yacht's in the basin there.'

Littlejohn caught a glimpse of the English banker as he passed, sitting between two women and wearing a yachting cap.

Dorange was more like a guide than a policeman. He started to point out the various large yachts and tell Littlejohn who owned them. Then he turned round and showed Littlejohn the villas on the hillside and across the bay.

'Hartpole Keith, the British novelist, has taken that place there, for the summer.'

Littlejohn had never heard of him, but he nodded.

Dorange indicated another building which reminded Littlejohn of a caramel cream — brown roof and custard coloured sides — across the bay at La Napoule.

'...and Sir Bowley, your famous film producer, is living there...' Dorange apparently specialised in English nonentities.

Littlejohn nodded again drowsily. He could hardly take his eyes from his companion's nylon suit and red carnation. At home something would be said about a detective in such a get-up. At least, it would earn Dorange a nickname, *Carnation Joe* or *Flash Dick*. And as for Sir Bowley... He turned over all the names of film producers he knew, but it didn't fit. 'Who the hell's Bowley?' he felt like saying. It must have been the sun. He was in real holiday mood in spite of Alderman Dawson and the telephone message which was sure to be waiting for him over in Juan...

'What about a drink? You look hot. Is the sun affecting you?'

Dorange looked very solicitous and sympathetic.

Behind them was a charming shady square with trees round and a lot of cafés with coloured awnings. Dorange led the way to the terrace of the *Café des Champs Elysées.*

'Deux Pernods.'

They just sat there relaxed and saying nothing until the apéritifs arrived and they'd diluted them with iced water. 'Here's to you.'

'Is this your first visit to the Riviera, Inspector?'

'Our first to this part.'

As a matter of fact, it wasn't Littlejohn's first trip. He and Letty had spent their honeymoon at Beaulieu, in August twenty years ago, and the mosquitoes had been such a pest that after three days, they'd packed up and cleared off to Evian where they were nearly as bad. All the same, that was years ago. Come to think of it, they ought to take a trip to Beaulieu, just for old times' sake.

'I thought I ought to explain things to you about the Dawson affair.'

Littlejohn jerked himself back to realities again. All this holiday feeling was all right but… Dawson… *L'affaire Dawson*. That's what it looked like becoming. An international scandal. Handle with care.

Littlejohn was smoking a cheroot Dorange had handed him. The little inspector had put up his snakeskin shoes on a chair and looked settled for the day.

'*Encore deux*.'

Two more drinks! Littlejohn's fingers were hot and sticky and as he thrust them in his trousers pocket to get out the money to pay, he pulled the lining inside out.

An Algerian hawking rugs and jewellery half paused to pester Littlejohn. Then he spotted Dorange, and beat it hell for leather.

'It's a bit difficult you know, *cher collègue*.'

The Pernod was beginning to act. Dear colleague. They'd soon be buddies now!

'Joliclerc says you're going to see him this evening. I don't want to interfere and tell you things in advance, but Joliclerc was in the *maquis* and that makes a difference. I was a prisoner of war all the time. You understand how it is?'

Littlejohn didn't understand at all, but he nodded. Sooner or later it would come out. Dorange untied his tie and let it hang loose. Next thing he'd be taking off his snakeskin shoes! All the same, thought Littlejohn a bit dimly through the fog of *anis*, all the same, he's got all his chairs at home. I wouldn't like him on my trail, especially at one of those police interrogations he'd read about in French thrillers. The *passage à tabac*, where the detective smoked and every now and then slapped the victim across the face.

'Did you ever hear of the eight men of Menton? They held the St Louis bridge against the Italians when they invaded us in June 1940 until Pétain threw up the sponge. I was one of them. I was a prisoner of war for the rest of the time.'

Dorange made light of it and dismissed it with an airy wave of the hand. A pretty girl passed and the French detective paused to admire her.

'With men like Joliclerc it was different. He and a lot more started the Resistance here and then when it came time to take the offensive, they cleared off into the hills behind. Did you fly to Nice? Well then, if you looked down as you passed over the hills, you'd see what I'm getting at. The enemy couldn't have found them there if he'd searched till doomsday. They were drilling and getting ready for the day. Joliclerc was a Colonel, although you wouldn't think it to see him now. A good man.'

Cars of all descriptions tore past, their tyres hissing on the hot asphalt. A man led a dog to the fountain opposite and lifted it in his arms to get a drink, and a horse hitched to an open carriage neighed. It wore a white bonnet against the flies and gave Littlejohn a droll look.

'Up there in hiding, always on the *qui vive,* with none of the distractions of the town and above all, nursing a hatred of the enemy…well…it gave them a peculiar outlook. It took some of them politically. They brooded on the sort of world they were going to make when they got back. Some turned communist. But above all, they were madly loyal to one another. Remember that in the Dawson affair… Joliclerc's attitude towards it will seem clearer if you remember that.'

L'affaire Dawson! They were back again on that. What had Dawson to do with the Resistance? Littlejohn said as much to Dorange.

'Ah! I ought to let Joliclerc tell you. All I wished to say was that, if you have to investigate the Dawson affair for your own police, it might be difficult for you. I just wanted to tell you that you could count on me for any official help you might require.'

'That's very decent of you, Dorange. I'm very grateful.' The bell of Nôtre Dame de Bon Secours, nearby, clanged.

'It's lunch time. They're clearing out the visitors and penitents. What about going inside the café for a meal?'

'Thanks, old chap. If I can ring up my wife at Juan and tell her not to expect me, I'll be very glad.'

'I thought as much,' his wife said when he got her on the line at length. 'No matter where we go, you always get a busman's holiday, Tom. By the way, you went off without leaving me any money. I had to borrow some from the landlord. I've been doing a bit of shopping.'

'Don't forget we've only our allowance between us and starvation.'

'Oh, that will be all right now. Scotland Yard have been on the line and want you to ring back.'

'Already?'

'Yes. You'll get a business allowance of money now, so you needn't worry!'

When the Inspector got back to the table, Dorange was sitting before a large bottle of *Château de Selles* and the cloth was covered with hors d'oeuvres dishes. Prawns, crayfish, mussels, good black olives, egg mayonnaise... Dorange shovelled them on Littlejohn's plate and then for himself, insisted on cardoons, which were served with anchovy and garlic sauce. The latter was kept on a plate-warmer and Dorange dipped his cardoons in the sauce and ate them like asparagus.

Littlejohn resisted *bouillabaisse* and finally, in a hospitable gesture, the officer from Nice ordered roast beef, which called forth a small charcoal furnace and the grilling of barbecue steaks.

All the time the *Château de Selles* flowed.

'I may as well tell you what all this Dawson affair's about, old chap…'

That again!

They had finished the barbecue, cheese, and some *fougassettes* from Grasse, made from a sort of heavy pastry flavoured with orange water. Dorange had insisted on the *fougassettes*. And now over the coffee and Calvados, *l'affaire Dawson* had cropped up again.

'Don't think we're going to let the matter drop. Once Jolicerc gets his teeth into a thing, he sticks, believe me. But he wants to handle it privately. That's why he told you at the hospital the file's closed. It's closed, or he wishes it to be closed, as far as you're concerned.'

'Whatever for? I shall have my report to make, and if I don't get it officially, where do I stand?'

'You get it unofficially, and that's where I help you, old man. I've got the key that will unlock a lot of doors for you.'

Littlejohn was smoking another of Dorange's cheroots. The talk was entirely in French and lubricated by the *Château de Selles* and the Calvados, Littlejohn felt how proud the Depatys, who'd taught him, would be of his fluency if they'd only been there. He found himself using outlandish words and gesticulating to emphasise his points.

'It's this way…'

Another Algerian selling bags and bracelets thrust in his head, looked hopefully at Littlejohn, and vanished hastily when he rolled his eyes to Dorange.

'... Dawson was in the *maquis*.'

So that was it! It was an international affair after all. Dawson was in the *maquis*, returned to the scene of his former triumphs with a charabanc party, and got bumped-off for his trouble.

'You'd have expected he'd get a great welcome after all this time.'

'Yes, if he'd been loyal, but something happened to make him unpopular. In fact, more than unpopular.'

Littlejohn threw away his cigar and started to fill his pipe. Lunch time was over and people were making for the Croisette again. Bronzed skins, coloured bathing suits and wraps. Money no object! Two little girls on their way to their first Communion held up the traffic. They looked solemnly excited and self-consciously aware of themselves, like little brides going to church. They were followed by a small procession of female relatives.

Dawson. Yes, Dawson.

'It all came out through the remark of the little man... Marriott...Vallouris, that's what he said. Vallouris is the name of a village just outside Cannes. But it gave Joliclerc a clue. You see, some of the prominent leaders of the *maquis* concealed their identity behind the names of places. Vercors, Gap, Manosque. And Dawson was called Vallouris.'

'But Dawson wasn't a prominent leader, was he? They were all Frenchmen.'

'At first. But as time went on, it became necessary for liaison to be established between the isolated troops of the *maquis* and the rest of the allies. Furthermore, arms were parachuted. As the more modern and complicated weapons — mainly from England, at first — arrived, there was need for someone to explain them and generally act as go-between. Dawson was dropped into the mountains behind here and joined with the *maquis*. There was a small landing-ground, too. He returned to England and came again, twice.'

It was close inside and they moved with their drinks under the awning again. Even then the air was shimmering with heat and the asphalt and the water of the harbour nearby seemed to vibrate with it.

'When Marriott mentioned Vallouris, Joliclerc became suspicious right away. He said when he saw Dawson, that he was sure he'd seen him before. The wound in his shoulder…the old one, I mean, settled it.'

'The old wound?'

'Yes. When they first parachuted Dawson into the resistance area, some highly-strung recruit, or else one who didn't know, mistook him for a German and took a shot at him. It went through the shoulder. Joliclerc recognised the old scar.'

'But why was Dawson murdered, assuming he *was* Vallouris?'

'He was taken into the confidence of the commanders. They shared their secrets with him and even took advice from him. Then…there was a girl. Many of the women fled with the men to the mountains. This one was a trained nurse, with whom Dawson seems to have fallen in love. She looked after him when he was wounded. He passed on to her certain information. It turned out she was in touch with the other side. Her lover, a Frenchman, had thrown his lot in with the collaborators. Twenty of our men on a mission were surprised and killed. This happened after Dawson had been flown out for the last time. The girl was interrogated and shot. She betrayed Dawson.'

'And there was a price on Dawson's head after that?'

'Naturally. You and I cannot understand the burning hatred the *maquis* could bear. We were not confined with our broodings like they were. I was a prisoner, I admit, but that was a different thing.'

Dorange shrugged his shoulders.

'The relatives of those twenty men, to say nothing of their comrades, must have longed to lay hands on Dawson. Now, he has come back. Very foolish of him.'

'Perhaps he hoped he wouldn't be recognised after all this time, or that the passage of years had softened the thoughts of revenge.'

'Someone must have recognised him and taken vengeance, although M'sieur Joliclerc says he wouldn't have known him except for the two clues, Vallouris and the old bullet wound.'

In the harbour they were starting a yacht race. A maroon was fired and you could hear someone announcing through a microphone the details of the race and the direction of the course.

'It will be properly investigated, of course. I can assure you of that, old man. Only, old Joliclerc is a bit touchy about these *maquis* murders. There have been one or two, you know. Old wrongs remembered. A few traitors put away. Only a few months ago, a man was found in the harbour there, with an anchor tied to his ankles. He'd been strangled. Same thing. An old traitor. He'd have been there still if one of the yachts hadn't had propeller trouble and they sent down a diver who found himself face to face with the corpse...'

'All the same, you can't hush-up a thing like that over here, can you?'

'No. But it will be an enormous job investigating it. You can't expect Joliclerc to keep all the motor-coach party in Cannes until he's found out who's to blame. There were twelve hundred men in the *maquis* squad concerned, either directly or indirectly, and not one of them wouldn't welcome the opportunity to see Dawson brought to book. Not that the whole lot would want to knife him. But it will be a big job.'

'And the examining magistrate wants me and Dawson's English friends out of the way whilst he carefully investigates the crime. In other words, he might have a hundred or more suspects to interrogate.'

'Yes.'

'And when he finds out the guilty party?'

Dorange shrugged his shoulders.

'There will be an arrest and a trial, of course, if the culprit is ever found.'

'What sort of a sentence would he get?'

The Frenchman's eyes were fixed on the old cab horse standing opposite, still patiently waiting for the right type of fare to come along and want a jog-trot in an open carriage along the Croisette.

'All…or most of the magistrates and judges were either in the Resistance or away with the Free French.'

'Hm. And where do I come in? I obviously can't butt in and insist on following in the footsteps of the *juge d'instruction*, can I?'

'No. But you will doubtless be asked to keep an eye on things. Your authorities will communicate with ours and we shall be instructed to give you every assistance. That's why I've already offered to help, old man. You might not find everybody here so cooperative.'

'I'm very grateful, Dorange.'

They lapsed into silence again. The delightful lethargy which comes after a good meal followed by good brandy in the warm sunshine, was taking hold of both of them. They lolled in their chairs talking slowly with long pauses in between. Time seemed to stand still. An afternoon quietness had fallen on the place. Things seemed softened and a bit blurred. This little square mile surrounding the church of Nôtre Dame de Bon Secours was known by the locals as the 'village' of Cannes. The restaurants and cafés, the church, the old waterfront, the flower and vegetable markets, the town hall. And now, with the fashionable world basking on the nearby beaches or else out on the busy roads, the place seemed to have fallen asleep in the hot sun, just like many another village all over France.

'The usual formalities have been gone through about the murder?'

Dorange lit another cheroot.

'Yes. The kitchen-hand who found him has made a statement. The scene of the crime has been photographed and a search is going on for the weapon which hasn't been found. Then, as a matter of form, all the members of Dawson's party will be interrogated. Joliclerc will be seeing to that now. He'll have been at it all morning. He's very thorough.'

'Will the dossier be available?'

'Certainly. As soon as your authorities communicate with ours, the Prefect at Nice will issue the necessary instructions. Here, of course, M'sieur Joliclerc is in charge of the case and the police act under his supervision. He is the official of the department of public prosecution, the *Parquet* as we call it here.'

'You'll be around then until the case is closed?'

'Yes. And at your service. I recommend that you start a private investigation of your own among Dawson's companions on the tour.'

'I was thinking that myself. It doesn't follow that because he was knifed in France, one of the members of the trip didn't do it.'

'I see we think alike. Well… I must be getting back to Nice. We'll meet again. If you need me in a hurry, ring up the area at Nice. I'll come along.'

They drove back to Juan-les-Pins along the busy Nice road. From Golfe-Juan the beaches were crowded. Half-naked sunbathers, physical culture classes, with instructors drilling young people and older women anxious to lose weight. Beach chairs and coloured sunshades, gaudy wraps and parasols. A whole wealth of colour and happiness. Two motorboats tugging water-skiers behind them, large cars dashing madly along, and smaller ones buzzing in and out of them like a lot of little mosquitoes. Everybody having fun except William Dawson who'd come to his old haunts for a holiday and had finished up in the morgue at Cannes.

Mrs Littlejohn met them in the garden of *La Reserve*.

Littlejohn introduced his new friend. They were both smiling and feeling that life was good, in spite of Alderman Dawson.

'You two seem to have been enjoying yourselves.'

She said it in English and then in French for the benefit of Dorange.

'After pleasure comes work,' she added. 'London have been on three times. They didn't sound so pleased the third time. I told them you were already on the case. They want you to ring back at once when you get in…'

'Could you wait, Dorange, and I'll tell you what it's all about?'

He left them in the garden. Dorange was ordering some more Pernods.

After ten minutes he returned.

'It's as I thought. Keep a watching brief and do what I can at this end. Scotland Yard have spoken to Paris and Paris have been in touch with Nice. They say they're sorry to interrupt my holiday but that I'm used to that sort of thing.'

He turned to his wife.

'They think of everything. They've even fixed-up for the necessary money. The Bank of England have been hastily consulted…'

And then to Dorange.

'…and I'm to use the utmost discretion. It's to be treated with tact and handled with care. They don't seem to know all there is to know about Alderman Dawson. They say he was a hero of the Resistance. He was decorated by the President and he's written a book about his adventures in the *maquis*.'

3
THE EXAMINING MAGISTRATE

The Littlejohns had left London on the Wednesday, William Dawson had been stabbed on the following Monday evening, and now it looked as if the rest of the holiday was going to be spent finding out who did it. Tactfully, of course... Scotland Yard had insisted on that.

Dorange had no sooner left than the telephone rang again. It was Marriott, the little man in the white cap.

'...Me and my fellow guests here would be glad if you and your wife would come over to dinner this evenin', if you can. It'll give you a chance to get to know all of us who were on the trip with Alderman Dawson. Mister Joliclerc's only just left. He's been questionin' the lot of us all day. He's given us a 'ell of a time, to put it mildly...'

According to what Marriott said, *Bagatelle* wasn't exactly a hotel. It was a holiday home run by some sort of an association in England, called the TTA...whatever that meant.

'...It's a villa. Easy to find. *Bagatelle,* Rue des Martyrs de la Resistance. You take the main road to Nice from Juan-les-Pins...'

Marriott went into an intricate route map, pronouncing all

the roads and streets in English fashion. He seemed to have somebody at his elbow prompting him.

'You turn left at Avenue de l'Observatoire…what's that? No; I mean you turn right…'

Like an actor getting his lines from the man in the wings! Littlejohn was quite exhausted when he returned to his wife in the garden. The landlord, anxious to make them at home, had served tea in a pot with a sieve hanging by a wire from the spout.

'I wouldn't drink too much Pernod if I were you, Tom. Have a cup of tea instead.'

His wife seemed to read his thoughts.

'Too much of it isn't good for you. They passed a law in France against absinthe drinking because it drove people mad and was bad for the birth-rate, and then people started drinking Pernod, which is very potent if you take too much. I heard that a man who'd drunk seven Pernods the other week, undressed himself stark naked on the promenade here, and thought he was at home in his bedroom. When the gendarme interfered the man accused him of stealing his pyjamas.'

'Good Lord! Who's been educating you?'

'It was a man I met in the Post Office while you were in Cannes.'

'Sounds like a dirty old man, too.'

'As a matter of fact, he was very nice. He was about your age and looked like you. A professor of Sanskrit, he said he was, at Montpellier.'

Littlejohn eyed his wife, who was still good-looking, and felt a strange pang of jealousy. It was absurd. The sun and all the *anis* drinks of the morning. He felt irritated and off-colour with everything.

'I think I'll get myself some snakeskin shoes like those Dorange had on. They looked light and cool.'

He'd no intention whatever of buying snakeskin shoes with

the dossier in my office at the town hall. You may see it if you wish.'

Littlejohn took a good swig of his Alsatian beer.

'I'm dining with them this evening. I'll question them, too, and then, if you don't mind, I'll compare my own with your notes. That should help. Needless to say, my findings are at your disposal, too, *M'sieur le juge*.'

'Thank you. That will be a great help. I'm afraid some of the people at *Bagatelle* didn't quite understand our methods in France. They were a bit timid in some cases and, in others, obstructive. Especially the ladies and Monsieur Marriott, who kept asking for the English consul to be there.'

Littlejohn could imagine it. The aggressive official questioning, the solemn face of M'sieur Joliclerc, the fact that in France the examining magistrate was all-powerful during his inquiry which was made without lawyers or any outside help for his victims. 'We, Marcellin Joliclerc, Chevalier of the Legion of Honour, Examining Magistrate appointed by the Parquet de Cannes...' He was the boss and the Inspector could see him trying to intimidate the obstinate teetotallers at *Bagatelle*. Especially any middle-aged spinsters of independent means who happened to be among them.

The English party at the next table were paying their bill and gathering up their traps. The boy, who looked about fifteen, took a photograph of the rest standing with the bay in the background. Littlejohn could imagine them later in the year showing the picture. 'That was us at Theoule...'

'Goodbye,' he shouted after them, and they looked surprised and replied. As they entered their car, the Inspector heard the boy say, 'I'm sure I've seen his photograph in the paper somewhere...' and he kept looking back until the car turned the corner and was gone.

They returned the way they had come. Although the sun had not quite set, there was a cold breath in the evening air. People were beginning to pack up from the day's pleasures. Bathers putting on their wraps, children protesting as their parents yanked them from their business on the beach, fishermen taking in the nets which had been drying in the sun, men going home on bicycles holding fishing rods aloft and with strings of livid fish hanging from their handlebars. Through the windows of the restaurants on the way home you could see the empty tables with clean cloths ready for the evening meal.

'What time did Dawson die, *M'sieur le juge*?'

Now that the ice had been broken and his ideas and purposes confessed to Littlejohn, Joliclerc talked quite freely.

'I got the report just before I left to meet you. Dinner at *Bagatelle* takes place about nine; Dawson left there about ten, according to what his compatriots say. His body was found by the workman at the casino at just before eleven. Dawson could not have been there long, for, although very ill, he was conscious and groaning. Had he been there any length of time, he would have died from loss of blood and shock. That is as near as we can get to when Dawson was stabbed.'

The magistrate pronounced it 'Dayson', and only then with difficulty. It would have been discourteous to correct him, but Littlejohn instinctively wanted to do it.

'I'll show you where they found the body, Inspector.'

They were back in Cannes, and there was the Croisette. Expensive cars gliding along, people taking a quiet stroll before dinner, a few late birds drinking on the terraces of the elegant hotels. The little Citroën dodged its way past the limousines and stationary cars to Palm Beach and the magistrate parked in front of the gardens there.

A little square with a roundabout sprouting palms in the middle. A neck of land jutting out, with the sea on its two flanks, the one nearest Cannes more elegant than the other. Cafés along one side and the trim and fashionable Palm Beach casino on the remaining one. The bars were just lighting up.

BOB'S BAR...CHEZ SAMMY...LA POTINÈRE. The beach farthest from Cannes was a homely affair, a bit shabby, but a place where you could bring the family and sunbathe and sport around without having to pay for the fun as you had on the expensive pitches adjoining the Croisette. Between the beach and the casino, a stony plot of land used for parking cars and where they unloaded goods for the side door of the restaurant.

'It was here they found Dawson.'

Just under the casino wall which adjoined the plot. The sort of place where in England you'd find a notice, *Tip No Rubbish.*

'The place was thoroughly examined, but the knife was not found. Dawson may have been brought here by car after the crime had been committed elsewhere.'

'Is it likely he might have been involved in a quarrel, say with the rowdy element of the town, and got killed that way?'

M'sieur Joliclerc shook his head emphatically.

'No, Inspector. Cannes is a very orderly place, even in the poor parts. There might be some quarrelling and even blows, but no knife-play, I assure you. The police have the place properly cleaned-up and under control.'

The magistrate seemed jealous of the reputation of his town, as anxious as the *Syndicat d'Initiative* to assure you that Cannes was the spot to come to for a safe holiday.

'But what was the Alderman doing here at that time of night? It seems a long way out of town, M'sieur Joliclerc.'

'Not really. *Bagatelle* lies on this side of Lower Californie and this is one of the nearest beaches to the villa. About half an hour's good walking from *Bagatelle*. It is quite reasonable to assume that Dawson was followed here. He might just have stepped off the road to look at the water-edge. It is dark and quiet where they found him. Would you like to speak to the man who discovered the body?'

'Yes, I may as well.'

They entered the sumptuous hall of the casino. Thick carpet

on the floor, bright lights, and masses of flowers all over the shop. The air was thick with the exotic scent of them.

The rooms were empty but lit up and waiting for the night's visitors to the gala dinner and the gaming tables. A large dining room all ready, set with shining glass and napkins folded like bishops' mitres. A dais at one end with music stands and a big drum. *Jimmy Madden's Band.*

The officials were in dinner suits and made a big fuss of M'sieur Joliclerc. *Oui, M'sieur le juge. Non, M'sieur le juge. Mais certainement, M'sieur le juge...* Joliclerc had them running round like a lot of small boys. Eventually they brought in the kitchen-hand who'd found Dawson's body. A small, wiry chap, like an Italian, with a pale face and dark eager eyes. A decent workman of the type whom foreign visitors frequently mistake for an *apache* ready to slit their throats for a franc or two. He was dressed in ill-fitting dungarees and had dirty hands and a streak of soot across his cheek.

'He looks after the boilers.'

The sub-manager of the casino thought some explanation was necessary. It was obvious that the workman wasn't at his ease on the public side of the place after opening time. He tried to appear familiar with it, but it didn't quite come off.

'You found the body of William Dawson last night?'

'Yes, *M'sieur le juge.*'

M'sieur Joliclerc started a real interrogation again and showed Littlejohn how they did it. The man who looked after the boilers slowly degenerated from a cocky, almost insolent swagger to a frightened whimper. He thought M'sieur Joliclerc was trying to pin it on him just because he'd found the body.

'I didn't do it, *M'sieur le juge.*'

His breath smelled strongly of garlic and wine. He'd just been eating his evening meal before stoking-up for the night.

Having reduced his victim to a decent state of respect for

authority, the examining magistrate turned him over to Littlejohn.

'What's your name?'

'Jean Bassino, *Monsieur le Commissaire de Scotland Yard.*'

That was how Joliclerc had introduced Littlejohn and everybody started to give the Chief Inspector his long-winded title.

'How long had you been out of doors when you came upon the body, Jean?'

'I walked right out of my boiler-house into the open air, lit a cigarette, and stumbled over the body.'

'Do you always go that way?'

'Yes, *Monsieur le…*'

'Plain *monsieur* will do, Jean. Why do you go that way?'

'There's often a breeze from the sea. I go under the wall to light my cigarette.'

'Was anyone else about? Did you hear footsteps or a car starting?'

'There were cars passing on the road, but none about where I was. There was nobody else there and I didn't hear anyone around.'

'And you got help right away. That would be eleven o'clock?'

'Yes, *monsieur*. My usual time for taking the air.'

'Has there been much talk about the crime among your friends? It will have caused a sensation and a lot of talk, Jean. What is said about it among the natives round here?'

Bassino looked at the examining magistrate and then at Littlejohn. He was the kind who doesn't like getting in the hands of the police. The sooner his business with them was finished, the better he'd feel.

'Nothing much has been said…'

Littlejohn turned to Joliclerc.

'Will you excuse us a minute? I would like to see just where Bassino went last night. I won't keep you waiting long.'

And before Joliclerc could reply he had taken the stoker by

the arm and was leading him back to where he'd come from. The door closed between them and the rest.

'Now, Jean, what are they saying about the crime? You can tell me and I won't tell the magistrate.'

'But...'

'I'm not the French police. I want to know, and if you tell me, you won't suffer for it.'

He took a thousand-franc note from his pocket and flicked it with his finger to make it rustle. Bassino's eyes glowed with cupidity.

'I don't want to get mixed up in a police investigation, *monsieur*. It is not a good thing. They either fix you, or else one's friends suspect one of becoming informer and involving them as well. If you won't...'

'I'll say nothing.'

The note changed hands.

'All I know is, that Sammy at the bar opposite stands at the door of his place most of the night, greeting customers and friends. I ran over to Sammy's as soon as I found the body to telephone for the police and help. The head waiter here said that afterwards, Sammy said he'd seen someone come from near where I found the body and start running like mad in the direction of the main Nice road.'

'That's in the opposite direction from the way back to the Croisette?'

'Yes, *monsieur*.'

'Why wasn't the magistrate told this?'

'The head waiter passed it round later that Sammy didn't want it to be told. He didn't want to get involved.'

'I see.'

Probably Sammy had good reasons for keeping the police away!

'You won't say anything. It's as much as my job's worth to run afoul of the head waiter.'

'That's all right. I'll see you don't get implicated. Anything else?'

'No, *monsieur*.'

It was dark when they got outside. All the illuminations were on and a chorus of frogs was croaking. You could hear them from all over the place, like a lot of ducks. The last of the daylight hung in a thin rim over the Esterel range and on the other side of the casino, the lights of Juan-les-Pins and Cap d'Antibes shining over the water and the Antibes lighthouse winking in and out.

Monsieur Joliclerc took Littlejohn back to his jeep near the town casino, which was closed for the summer. Lamps bobbed over the harbour and across the forest of masts and the coloured neon signs of the expensive restaurants on the quayside shone red and blue.

'Any time you need me, please telephone. You can get me at the town hall,' said the magistrate. Dawson had probably said the same thing over and over again back home in Bolchester.

All the noise of the day had died down and now it was quiet and peaceful. People strolling round before dinner, lovers embracing in the dark spots under the trees, dance-bands and little orchestras starting to tune-up. Overhead a plane droned its way to Nice airport. Last night it probably all seemed the same to William Dawson.

At Juan-les-Pins Littlejohn found a taxi waiting at the gate of *La Reserve*. Inside, little Marriott was talking to Mrs Littlejohn in the lounge.

'I thought I'd get a taxi and come for you both, Inspector. *Bagatelle* might be a bit hard to find in the dark. It's not a hotel, you know. It was the villa of a wealthy ironmaster of Bolchester. 'E had one at Lucerne, in Switzerland, as well. When he died, he left them in trust for natives of our town and neighbourhood, to spend cheap but 'omely holidays there for the purpose of gettin' to know foreigners in the interests of peace. Good idea, eh? The two villas is run by the Turnpike Trust Association. That was the name of our benefactor. Benjamin Turnpike. The TTA… You'll enjoy it tonight. 'Ome from 'ome, as you might say.'

Mr Marriott breathed a blast of *Dubonnet* over Littlejohn in his enthusiasm.

So, it wasn't teetotal after all!

Littlejohn felt so tired after the day's efforts that he didn't even smile about it.

4
ROUND DOZEN

'It was good of you to come, Inspector. We've no right to be spoiling your holiday, but we're all desperate. You know what it is. A foreign land and all that. They look at you as if you weren't telling the truth.'

Littlejohn couldn't get rid of the woman. Marriott had introduced her as Mrs Beaumont. Small, fat, and sixty or thereabouts, with a thin black moustache, clear, blue pop-eyes, a button nose, and rouged pink cheeks which hung like little bags from her cheekbones. Her hair was quite white and she'd had a blue rinse because she was going on holiday. She wore a long, billowing blue gown and a lot of bangles and gold chains. She seemed to think that Littlejohn had come specially for her peace of mind and before he'd been there ten minutes, he knew all about her. Her husband had been a dentist in Bolchester, he'd been dead ten years, and he'd been the first to drive a motorcar in the town. She fished a photograph out of her bag to prove it. A man standing beside a crock of a car, swathed in mackintosh driving clothes and nothing else showing but whiskers and goggles.

The Littlejohns had driven from Juan-les-Pins to *Bagatelle* and as soon as the front door of the villa had opened to admit them, it had felt like being in a stew pond. People milling round trying to prove they'd nothing to do with Dawson's death. Mrs Beaumont had taken charge of them at once and elbowed Marriott out of the way.

'I don't know why that common little man, Marriott, keeps pushing himself to the fore, I'm sure. He was never fond of Alderman Dawson when he was alive. Now that the Alderman is dead, you would think they were bosom friends.'

'They didn't get on well together?'

'They were political opponents on the council at Bolchester. Marriott was a councillor once and then when the war ended and Alderman Dawson came home, he put up against Marriott and defeated him. Marriott never got over it. I don't know why he's fussing round now, I'm sure.'

'How came this touring party to be formed, Mrs Beaumont?'

'The late Benjamin Turnpike, a benefactor of our town, left two villas, here and in Switzerland, and the money in trust to keep them up for the benefit of the burgesses of Bolchester. That was after the first war. He said it would help people to understand one another in an international way.'

She talked on and on, beginning fortissimo and ending pianissimo as her breath ran out; then she gulped in more air and started full blast again.

'My late dear husband, John Stuart Beaumont, was one of the first trustees of the fund. Places, which number fifteen twice every summer, are balloted for. By letting the two guest-houses to tourist agents the rest of the year, the trust, with the aid of its investments, pays for the holidays. What that common little Marriott is doing here I don't know, I'm sure.'

She was always sure. It came over and over again, like the passing bell.

'On the death of my husband, I was appointed a trustee in his place. My husband was Mr Turnpike's dentist. They were very good friends. They would turn in their graves if they knew Marriott was benefiting by the trust, I'm sure. Something for nothing, he's after.'

'The trustees accompany each trip?'

She nodded.

'Always one of us. As a rule, I come every summer. It is a bit tying, but one must do one's best for the memory of the two good men who formed this benefaction before they passed on.'

Mr Marriott appeared waving a bottle.

'Now then, you two, just time for what the French call an aprateeve before we start our meal. I bet you've never tasted anythin' like this before, Inspector. Or you, Mrs Bewmont. Just a little one, Mrs Bewmont. 'Armless, but nice. You let it down with water, so it's quite 'armless.'

'No thank you, Mr Marriott. You know I never *touch*.'

'But this is Pernod, Mrs Bewmont. You let it down with water.'

He stood pathetically there with his bottle.

'What about you, Inspector? Tell Mrs Bewmont it won't do her any harm.'

'Just a little one won't.'

He wondered what they'd say if he told them about the man who started to undress out of doors at Juan-les-Pins after potations of Pernod!

'I never *touch*, Mr Marriott, and I must ask you to remember again that the name is *Bow-* not *Bew*mont.'

And with that she sailed away and collared Mrs Littlejohn.

'If you'll excuse the word, that woman's a proper bitch. Her husband drank himself to death to get away from her. She's only here to get somethin' for nothin'. She's a Turnpike trustee and gets all paid for.'

None of the other Turnpike beneficiaries seemed to be about.

'The gong goes for the first time at half-past eight. Then they start comin' down from dressin' themselves and we start the meal about a quarter to nine. Funny time, but when in Rome, do as Rome does, eh?'

'The winner of the ballot gets two tickets, my dear. A very wise idea, suggested to Mr Turnpike by my late husband. It enables a man to bring his wife; a widow or unmarried woman to invite her companion. A very good scheme, I'm sure. I, myself, only have one ticket. I'm a trustee, you see, officially accompanying the tour to see that the terms of the trust are fulfilled.'

Non-stop, Mrs Beaumont, was pumping information into Mrs Littlejohn, panting as she reached the end of her long tale, inflating herself, then off again. As she paused for breath, they could hear the frogs croaking in the pond in the garden of *Bagatelle*.

'I'd sooner hear the frogs than old Bewmont,' said Marriott out of the side of his mouth. 'And, by the way, while we're waitin', I thought this would be useful.'

He took from his pocket a double sheet of notepaper smoothed out into a large one.

'This is a list of all of us on this trip…'

1. *William Dawson*
2. *Marie Ann Blai*
3. *Leslie Humphries*
4. *Jeremy Sheldon*
5. *Irene Sheldon*
6. *FJ Marriott*
7. *Mary Hannon*
8. *Elizabeth Hannon*
9. *Mrs Beaumont*
10. *Jocelyn Mole*
11. *Lola Mole*
12. *Peter Currie*

13. *Martin Currie*
14. *Isabel Currie*
15. *David Gauld*

'...I've put 'em down by numbers, which represent their places in the charabanc, you see, and the large gap between say, two and three, represents the passage between the seats. The two on the left are doubles, and the one on the right, a single. It's a luxury coach, with seats for fifteen and the driver in a separate cab at the front. Mr and Mrs Mole, an accountant and his wife, aren't with us, but their places are held. She was taken ill the day before we left. We go on to Lucerne from here in three days' time, and if Mrs Mole's better they'll fly there and meet us then.'

'Thirteen and the driver?'

'Yes. Unlucky, wot? Now there are twelve of us, for the time being.'

Outside, the night train thundered past in the dark. Through the French window they could see the neon signs of the hotels glowing on the promenade.

'When did you start from Bolchester, Mr Marriott?'

'Last Saturday mornin'. Stayed the night at Dover, crossed by the ferry next mornin', and spent another night at Lyons on the way here. Got here on Monday evenin' and Dawson, as you know, sir, was stabbed a few hours after. It seems weeks since they first told us of the crime.'

'Did Dawson leave the party much and go off on his own?'

'No. It was late when we got 'ere. Today, we'd planned a run to Nice and Monte Carlo and get back here for dinner. That's why dinner's later here than at home. Gives us a long day.'

In the hall, the gong boomed and almost at once they could hear people descending the stairs as though they'd been sitting in their rooms waiting for the call.

'You were all friends together. I mean, you all got on well? No quarrelling or differences?'

Marriott was pouring out a third Pernod, adding the water, childishly watching the liquid turn cloudy.

'You'll have another, Inspector?'

'No, thanks.'

'Mind if I do? It seems silly stuff. Tastes like the aniseed balls we used to suck when we were kids. But, somehow, it leaves you feelin' good. Must be medicinal, eh?'

Once again, Littlejohn could barely resist the tale of the man who thought he was in his bedroom, when all the time he was on the prom at Juan!

'You were sayin'? Did we all agree? Of course we did. We all came from the same town and knew one another. A 'omely, compact little party in a special luxury coach, with all laid-on by the Trust. What more could we ask for?'

'Did you like Dawson, sir?'

'Eh? Me? Why not? Has Mrs Bewmont been talkin'? She's a trouble-causer, if you like. When they told me and one or two others *she* was coming, we said we'd chuck in our tickets if they didn't find her a seat to herself. They put her in a single behind me. Too near, I admit, but she doesn't interfere with me. You see, she's hot temperance and disapproves of wine merchants. All right by me. Suits me.'

'Did you like Dawson?'

Marriott regarded Littlejohn dubiously.

'Didn't have much to do with him. Matter of fact, a political opponent on the Bolchester Town Council. I'm not a councillor now, but we differed politically. That's all. Ah... Here comes the belle of the ball. Come along, Miss Elizabeth, and have a li'l of this aniseed drink. Buck you up. Makes you feel fine.'

There were two women, both around thirty, and sisters by the look of them. One was dark and the other fair; one was good-looking and the other plain; one had a good figure and the other was chubby and a bit shapeless.

But there was no mistaking their relationship, for one of

their parents had made a proper job of passing on to them both exactly the same nose. Slightly concave, rather bulbous at the end, with wide nostrils like a horse.

The dark, chubby, plain one was evidently the object of Mr Marriott's mild flirtation. The kind who would jump at the familiarity of the unattached wine seller. She was even prepared to put up with his white cap and sly insinuations during the excursions, in spite of the fact that she came from an old, well-bred family in Bolchester. She tittered and left her sister behind in her eagerness to please Marriott.

'Miss Elizabeth Hannon, Inspector. This is Chief Inspector Littlejohn, of Scotland Yard, Miss Elizabeth. He'll soon have us all out of this mess.'

Miss Mary Hannon didn't mind her sister's desertion, for behind her was a man at her beck and call. A tall, ginger-headed fellow, with large hands and feet and a craggy, heavy face with a livid scar down one cheek. His tired grey eyes lit up at the sight of the better-looking of the two sisters.

'Can I get you a glass of sherry, Miss Mary?'

Marriott was pouring out the drink for his lady friend. 'This'll do you good, Elizabeth.'

She blushed at the use of her Christian name.

'Watch it go cloudy as I pour in the water. Funny, eh? Drink it up, now. I see your sister's got a new boyfriend now the Alderman's out of the way.'

It probably slipped out on account of the amount of *anis* Marriott had put away. Both he and Miss Hannon paused and stood silent for a minute. Then they tittered self-consciously.

'Has the Alderman been looking after your sister, then?' They both looked sheepishly at Littlejohn.

'They've known one another for a long time. He sort of took her under his wing on the trip until...until...'

'Bottoms up, Elizabeth. No morbid talk before dinner. Drink it down.'

'Come on and be introduced, you two.'

At the sound of Marriott's voice, the red-haired man and Mary Hannon started from their whispering, looked a bit guilty, and slowly approached.

'Meet Inspector Littlejohn, who's helpin' us out of our present troubles, Miss Mary. And this is Mr David Gauld. Miss Mary is the sister of our friend 'ere, who's enjoying her Pernod, I see.'

There was a titter again as Elizabeth sipped her drink like a hen.

'…And Mr Gauld is an engineer in our biggest steelworks in Bolchester. He won the draw for this trip, Inspector, for himself and his wife, but as his missus was away nursin' a sick mother, he very kindly gave her ticket to the Curries so they could bring their son along with them. You'll be meetin' them later. They're always last down.'

Gauld turned crimson at the mention of his wife. Marriott seemed to have fired the shaft deliberately to remind him and his lady friend that their attraction was not unnoticed.

'You should drink French stuff when in France, not sherry. Try a drop of this, you two.'

'No, thanks.'

Mrs Beaumont was still chattering to Mrs Littlejohn, of whom she'd taken complete possession.

'My husband was the only qualified dentist in Bolchester at the time. All the rest were quacks. He worked himself to death at his profession and died in his early fifties. I have never looked at another man since. A fine man, he was. Ha! Come and meet Mrs Littlejohn…'

She addressed the Misses Hannon, who sauntered across, followed by Gauld.

'Gauld's got a wife, you know. I don't like the way him and Mary Hannon are carryin' on. There's been talk about them back at home. Gauld's not in her class at all, but she seems smitten. He's only a sort of mechanic. Dawson mentioned it to me. That's why he interfered, so to speak, and took Miss Mary in charge. To keep Gauld away from her. Not that I blame him. She's a good-looker…'

Littlejohn looked across at Gauld. A fine, well-set-up man just in middle-age. He seemed a bit shy and out of his element, but he hung around Mary Hannon like a devoted dog.

'Not that his wife's much good to him. One of these intellec-shules. Runnin' all over the place with dramatic societies and dancing groups and surrounded by a lot of sissy young men. Leaves Gauld to get his own tea and do the housework, I'll bet. Still, right's right. He's married. We don't want no scandals on the Turnpike trips.'

Marriott downed another Pernod, his fourth. Littlejohn wondered what would happen at the seventh.

'So Dawson put a spoke in his wheel?'

Marriott drew himself up in alcoholic dignity.

'Yes. And with my full approval, sir. Here come two more. Two more love-birds.'

Littlejohn looked in the direction of the door. Old Turnpike, whoever he might have been, must have been a match-maker as well as an internationalist. Leslie Humphries, the schoolmaster Littlejohn had met earlier in the day, was opening the door for a pale-faced, dark girl of striking beauty. Everyone turned to look at them, except Gauld, whose adoring eyes still rested on Mary Hannon.

'That's Marie Blair, Alderman Dawson's niece, who came with him. I'm sorry for Marie. This 'as been a sad blow to her. She's been in bed all day. Passed out, poor girl, when we broke the news.'

Marriott, under the influence of his drinks, had grown all sloppy. He hurried to meet the newcomers and bring them over to the Inspector.

'This is Chief Inspector Li'ljohn, Marie, who's come to get us out of our troubles. You'll find him a big 'elp, my dear.'

In normal times, her skin must have been pink and white; otherwise Marie Ann Blair had a classic, Italian type of beauty, dark, with finely chiselled features and a gentle dignity. She was young — in her early twenties — slim and graceful and, judging from the full generous mouth and the poise of the head, naturally impetuous.

Humphries was a changed man from the bewildered schoolmaster who'd called at *La Reserve* that morning. He was obviously head over heels in love with Dawson's niece and saw and heard nothing but her.

They had no sooner exchanged greetings than Mrs Beaumont was wobbling across, with Mrs Littlejohn in tow.

'How are you, Marie Ann? You oughtn't to have got up. What did you let her get up for, Leslie?'

As though Humphries could help it! Mrs Beaumont gave the young schoolmaster a melting, stupid glance. He was obviously one of her favourites.

'I always said thirteen was an unlucky number. When the Moles didn't turn up, we ought to have got two more. You may laugh at me if you like.'

Another pair arriving. An elderly man with a bald head and a woman with long earrings. Those were the first things you noticed about the Sheldons. He was tall and well-built, had a smart grey moustache and wore tweeds and a bow-tie. A tea planter from Assam, who had lost his wife there and who had rushed home to marry his childhood sweetheart when he heard she was a widow. And there she was, mutton dressed up as lamb, tall and slim and pallid-looking through dieting to keep her figure, and her hair dyed and her face painted to make her look younger.

'I said you shouldn't have put on those tweeds.'

She looked at the suits of all the other men, which were dark ones, with a frowning glare which changed to a smile when they met her gaze. Her fine hands, with long tapering fingers, were never still.

'But you know I haven't a dark suit with me.'

'Hush!'

They'd evidently been quarrelling. Their faces were set and Sheldon was red around the ears.

Mrs Beaumont took the Littlejohns from Marriott's care.

'Let me introduce Chief Inspector and Mrs Littlejohn, who have kindly come along to help us out of our predicament.'

Littlejohn was sick of it already. Here they were, standing about, waiting for the meal to be served, getting to know the kind of people they'd normally avoid on a holiday. It was even worse than that, for over all hung the constraint and suspicion caused by Dawson's death. Everyone was a bit afraid. Marriott with his drinks, Mrs Beaumont with her over-confident manner and edgy voice, and two men in love dancing protective attendance on two women. To say nothing of Mrs Sheldon, taking it out of her husband. M'sieur Joliclerc's examination must have shaken them all up. In the exceptional circumstances, nobody seemed to know what expression or attitude to adopt.

Dawson! He'd evidently come between Gauld and Mary Hannon. He'd thrown little Marriott off the local council in Bolchester and made a fool of him. Had he also made love to the bejewelled Mrs Sheldon, whose husband obviously adored her and who, in return, publicly wiped her feet on him?

'Go and take off that coloured tie. You have a black one somewhere. And don't be long.'

Sheldon almost ran out to hide his humiliation. That was his wife's way of working off her nervousness.

'Have a drink of Pernod, Mrs Sheldon?'

'I'd rather a Cinzano, if it's all the same to you, Mr Marriott.'

She rolled her eyes at him and Marriott ogled her back.

'A good-lookin' woman,' he said to Littlejohn, who helped

him find the bottle which, in his confusion, he missed from under his very nose.

'Did Dawson think so, as well?'

'If Dawson's wife hadn't been alive at the time, it's said he'd have married Irene Sheldon before Sheldon got home. Mrs Dawson died some years ago. Irene's a good singer. Gives concerts in Bolchester.'

Littlejohn could imagine what would have happened had Dawson still been alive. After dinner, Mrs Beaumont would have gathered together a party at bridge and Mrs Sheldon would have sung ballads at the piano. Sentimental mush, probably, with a moist eye in Dawson's direction.

Marriott handed over the drink to Mrs Sheldon with a gallant flourish and she smiled sweetly in reward and turned away to Mrs Littlejohn.

'What are we waiting for? Is it those Curries again? They're never in time. I'm famished and shall start if they don't come in a minute.'

Mrs Beaumont was baying again. She'd obviously taken over Dawson's mantle as the bully of the party.

'That's all right, Mrs Bewmont.'

She turned her back on Marriott.

'Just a minute, Mr Marriott.'

Littlejohn drew the little man aside.

'What's this about Dawson and Mrs Sheldon?'

'Ours is a small town. Full of gossip, sir. Everybody knows what everybody else is doin'. After his wife died, Mrs Sheldon set her cap at Dawson. She was a widow, on the look-out for a second. She actually got Dawson on the run. At first he was flattered and responded a bit. Then, he got scared and avoided her. She married Sheldon for spite, then, if you ask me. But there was something between her and Dawson, though. Perhaps Dawson was carryin' on with her, hopin' to get what he wanted without leadin' her to the altar, if you get me. Then when she started to grow awkward, he took fright. Now and then, you'd see her and Dawson exchange a queer look or a smile as if they'd some secret in common. You know what I mean. Let's join the others.'

'Just a minute. Miss Blair and Humphries. They're in love, aren't they? Did Dawson know?'

'Of course. He was Marie's guardian till she came of age. Trustee for her father's money, too. The pair of them aren't engaged. But there was no reason for Dawson objectin'. Humphries is a decent lad. No money, of course, but a decent lad. Marie should come into quite a packet when she marries. Now, I believe, she enjoys the income.'

'At last!'

Mrs Beaumont said it loudly and it struck the party entering like a shot from a gun. They looked surprised. The man pulled out his watch, looked more surprised, and then apologised.

'We're so sorry. My fault. Stayed in the bath too long. Hope we've not kept you waiting.'

'*Only* twenty minutes. Somebody please ring the bell.'

'Certainly, Mrs Bewmont. Come over here, Mr and Mrs Currie, and meet our guests.'

Again! More handshakes, only this time the newcomers were refreshing. A jolly, buxom, middle-aged woman, with greying hair, and a tallish, ordinary, homely-looking man.

'Where's Peter?'

'In bed. We sent him off with the housekeeper's little boy to get him away from this atmosphere. He's learning French at school and it's good practice for him because Henri can't speak English. They ate too much cassata ice-cream and Peter was sick... He'll be all right.'

The soup was coming in and Mrs Beaumont had already fallen-to. She had captured Mrs Littlejohn and was sitting with her at a table for four. The Inspector joined them and Gauld, obviously ill at ease, made up the fourth. His eyes kept turning to Mary Hannon. Mrs Beaumont took this as a signal to pester him for attention. The salt, the bread, the water, a clean fork...

They ate the roast beef and two veg, and then ice-cream and peaches. Nobody seemed to bother about the food. The meal went on in silence, punctuated by a whisper now and then or the loud demands of Mrs Beaumont.

'We always try to get English cooking. It agrees with one better,' explained Mrs Beaumont. As Marriott had said, a proper 'ome from 'ome. Littlejohn wondered why the TTA-ites came abroad at all! He looked down the room at the other tables, making guesses at what these people were like in everyday Bolchester. It was difficult, under the cloud of Dawson's death and the emotions it had caused on top of the holiday feeling, to get them in proper focus. Sheldon, for instance. What was he like at home? Or Marriott in his wineshop? Gauld, in his engineer's overall, supervising the mechanics in the engineering shop...?

'And now, sir,' said Marriott. 'Want to get to business?' Coffee had been served and under the influence of the dinner wine, conversation was breaking out on all sides.

'I heard what you said. It's no use denying it. I shan't listen.'

Mrs Sheldon, still bullying her husband, *sotto voce*, which they all heard.

Littlejohn felt more like putting on his hat and going home. The incessant conversation of Mrs Beaumont over dinner, crescendo and diminuendo as her breath waxed and waned; the moody silence of Gauld, preoccupied with his lady-love at the next table; the almost indecent frivolity of Marriott, lubricated by Pernod; the loud and spiteful rebukes of Mrs Sheldon against her husband, who did everything wrong; the worried faces of the Curries about the boy who'd stuffed himself with ice-cream until he'd passed out. Littlejohn grew moody himself and wished he'd never come to the Riviera at all. This sort of thing might go on indefinitely.

And now Marriott, wanting him to start an investigation of some sort, ask questions, check alibis.

'Did the examining magistrate take statements and alibis this morning when he came?'

'Yes. A proper inquisition.'

'He's promised to lend me his files. I think that will be all I want. I only came here to meet you all.'

'I thought you'd be interested. Besides, it would be a change to have a decent, gentlemanly English inquiry.'

So that was it! Littlejohn was expected to provide entertainment for Marriott and the rest. A sort of stage turn of detection!

'It's too bad to put them through it all again, sir.'

'But I've told them what to expect. They're all ready to help.'

He was saved by the telephone. The maid entered all of a flurry.

'Al le Commissaire Littiezhon…? Téléfon!'

It was Dorange of the Nice police. His cheerful, energetic voice was a pleasant change. His news was a change, too, but it wasn't pleasant.

'There's been another murder on almost the same spot where they found Dawson. Another stabbing. Only this time, the man's quite dead. You won't know him, but I think you might be interested, so come along if you can. A man called Sammy, who owns a bar opposite the casino at Palm Beach. We're there now.'

'I'm wanted by the French police,' was all he told the party at *Bagatelle*, and he ordered a taxi to take his wife home to *La Reserve*. As they waited for it, there was another call. M'sieur Joliclerc, this time. The guests must not leave Cannes until further notice. They could, of course, make excursions in the motor coach, but in that case, a police officer would accompany them.

'It's scandalous. I shall wire to the embassy tomorrow.'

'A fat lot of good that will do, Mrs Bewmont!'

'No need to be common, Mr Marriott.'

More handshakes all round. This time they clung to Littlejohn like swimmers out of their depth and floundering.

It was very quiet as the Littlejohns left and, above the hum of traffic in the town below, they could hear the bell of the abbey on the Ile Saint-Honorat in the bay, calling the monks to service.

5

CHEZ SAMMY

Chez Sammy.

The name in blue neon met Littlejohn as he turned the corner of the square at Palm Beach. Someone had forgotten to switch it off in the confusion, although Sammy was now out of business. Elsewhere, however, things were going on as usual. The casino was brightly lit, crowds of people in evening dress arriving in expensive cars, the uniformed doormen helping them in and out. Every time the door opened, you could hear the drums and saxophones of Jimmy Madden's band. The other bars were doing a good trade. The headlights of passing cars kept the whole place in a state of constant illumination and momentarily floodlit the forms of embracing couples among the trees.

The door of Sammy's was closed, but when Littlejohn knocked, a gendarme let him in. Dorange came forward to meet him.

A rather flashy chromium and plastic affair of the American bar type. A long counter with a string of stools with round tops of red leather. A coffee machine and a lot of little tables.

Behind the counter, shelves with bottles of all kinds of

drinks, glasses of all shapes and sizes, a cash register, and some piles of cigarettes, including the stiff yellow packets of an English make. Notices on the walls. *Cassata. Bacon and Eggs. Hot Dogs. Visitez le Moulin Rouge…* Sammy had fancied himself as a cosmopolitan. His name wasn't Sammy at all. Henri Cristini, born in Marseilles, according to his papers. They showed Littlejohn his body in the room behind.

A door led from the bar into the rear premises. It was like stepping into a different world after the flashy frontage. A few comfortable easy chairs and a couch, a table with dining chairs, pictures on the walls, most of them photographs, including one of Sammy dressed in tights. He'd been an acrobat until he twisted himself and had to give it up. The room had a domestic cosiness about it. At the table sat a pale woman in her late twenties, with the clear olive complexion of the South and large dark eyes that stared unseeing into space. She wore a shabby flowered wrapper and leaned her elbows on the table. Both her breasts were visible, but nobody bothered. They were too busy with Sammy.

Cristini was lying on the couch ready for his journey to the medico-legal dissecting room or the morgue. A small, thick-set, strong-looking type, with brushed-back, long black hair, a Roman nose and a large mouth with thin lips. No doubt, the hidden teeth were white and flashing when he was alive. Now, in death, much of the stuffing had gone out of Sammy. Only a few hours ago, he'd been the uncrowned king of the locality, a man to be feared and, if he was your friend, you boasted about it. One who would buy and sell anything as well as drinks. Tickets for galas when the casino was booked-up; dope if you could pay for it; foreign currency; even a new passport.

The room seemed packed. Dorange and the police; the officials of the *Parquet* at Cannes headed by M'sieur Joliclerc; a doctor, photographers, fingerprint men…

M'sieur Joliclerc shook hands with Littlejohn. He'd done a

lot of work already. Two of his victims were sitting on chairs by the wall, smoking disconsolately. Bassino, the stoker from the casino, and another man in a dinner suit, presumably the head waiter of whom Bassino had spoken to Littlejohn earlier in the evening. The man to whom Sammy had talked about the figure who ran away about the time Dawson was stabbed. And then Sammy had told him to keep his mouth shut. M'sieur Joliclerc had worked well and fast. Bassino looked dolefully at the Inspector, shrugged his shoulders and, as he did so, a policeman tapped him and his companion and hauled them roughly to the waiting police van. Littlejohn felt a bit sorry for Bassino. He was obviously off to the police station for a *passage á tabac* and wouldn't get much sleep that night. Just a room full of tobacco fug and the incessant questions of relays of officers until he told all he knew and more besides.

'And now, mademoiselle…'

M'sieur Joliclerc signed a long official form with a flourish and turned to the woman at the table. She pulled herself up, drew the wrapper decently round her shoulders, revealing in doing so that she hadn't a stitch of clothing on underneath, and turned the large eyes on the examining magistrate.

'Name, surname, age?'

'You know them.'

The girl seemed to wake up.

'No cheek, my girl. Answer, either here or at the police station.'

'Toselli, Georgette, twenty-nine.'

'Profession. Come on…'

'Waitress.'

The magistrate's clerk, who was taking it all down, cleared his throat menacingly and smiled by twisting his upper lip.

'Address…'

'This is my address. I live here.'

'Home address, I mean.'

'My mother's. Rue des Capucins, 12*bis*, Nice.'

Dorange rose.

'Come in the bar, Inspector. There's nothing here to help you.'

They rose and entered the empty public room. A gendarme was sitting by the door smoking a cigarette.

Dorange went round the counter and took down a bottle.

'Whisky?'

He poured two fingers in each glass, opened two bottles of Perrier, and filled them up.

'*A votre santé*.'

'Good health.'

'Sammy must have been killed around eight o'clock. His body was found just near where Dawson's was discovered. Stabbed in almost the same way and place. No knife. M'sieur Joliclerc, who has a way of his own, at once had Bassino, who found Dawson, brought in. Bassino was suspiciously uneasy. Under pressure from Joliclerc and myself, for whom the examining magistrate immediately sent, Bassino told a story of Sammy seeing the murderer of Dawson running from the scene of the crime. He also said that Hugat, the waiter at the casino, had heard it from Sammy, who later told him to keep his mouth shut. There may be more. They will get it from them at the commissariat of police very soon.'

Dorange smiled confidently.

'It seems to me that Sammy not only saw the assailant of Dawson, but recognised or followed him. Then, perhaps, he tried to put on the screw. Sammy would do such a thing, you know. We used to keep an eye on him.'

From the room behind voices were raised. M'sieur Joliclerc's like a bassoon and Georgette's screaming arguments and abuse.

'Georgette is a hopeless case. Started here as a waitress nine years ago. Crazy about Sammy. He became her protector. You understand the term...?'

'Yes.'

'When we came to tell her of the death of her friend, she was in bed with the door locked. Someone scrambled through the window and off through the back.'

Dorange shrugged his shoulders, handed Littlejohn a cheroot, and lit one himself.

'We shall get him if we want him.'

It all sounded so easy and confident. Dorange seemed to have all the local wrongdoers on the hook ready for hauling in.

'I'm quite sure the murder of Cristini is tied up with that of Dawson.'

They were interrupted by a policeman hustling Georgette unceremoniously through the bar and into a waiting car.

'She's getting rough, this one,' he said on the way. 'She won't talk and she won't get herself dressed, so we'll see what she does in clink.'

He was trying to hold a jumper and skirt and some underwear as well as Georgette, who would presumably be vigorously and properly dressed by the women at the police station.

M'sieur Joliclerc stood in the doorway polishing his glasses. He'd had a very busy day, but didn't look much different than early in the morning. That was presumably because he wasn't much to start with. Dark bags under his eyes and a swarthy complexion which didn't register much fatigue, except that the existing lines between nose and mouth and down his cheeks were folded deeper.

'I've got the dossier for you, Chief Inspector. You may take it and peruse it at your leisure.'

He handed over a large folder full of typewritten dispositions, medical and experts' reports, police routine, all strung together by flexible wires running through punched holes. Littlejohn opened and closed the file automatically. All he saw was a sheet presumably headed for Mrs Beaumont's evidence. It was a conglomeration of French and pidgin-English.

BEAUMONT, Emmeline, Penelope.
60. Born Chetleman, England.
Widow of John Stuart Beaumont, Dental Surgeon,
Domeotter, Wawrick Road, Bolchester.

He smiled. Someone had been having some fun with the addresses. No wonder! They'd all presumably had to be spelt out to the *greffier* who took them down, and after about the third effort, he'd got fed-up and spelt them in his own way.

'...I would be most grateful, however, if you'd interview them all one by one with the dossier before you. There was an interpreter at the examination this morning, of course, but it was all very difficult. Especially the spellings. Some of the witnesses, as I told you, were not very cooperative.'

Littlejohn groaned inside himself. The international complications were turning out graver than he'd bargained for. Until all the trippers at *Bagatelle* were in the clear, it looked as if he'd have to take charge of their side of the case.

'If you wish it that way, M'sieur Joliclerc, I'll be happy to cooperate. I'll take the file, then, and if there's nothing else, I'll be getting along. I'll report to you at the Town Hall as soon as I get through with checking the depositions.'

He looked at his watch. Half-past twelve. Outside, there was no slackening in the traffic or the night life at the casino. The band churning it out, people coming and going, the bars open and doing a roaring trade, the Croisette a blaze of lights, moving people and vehicles. Littlejohn felt fagged-out. They'd packed an extraordinary amount of experience and work in the past fifteen hours and yet, when he looked back, the bulk of the time seemed to have been spent in eating and drinking. Dorange himself looked bright and fresh as a daisy, his cheroot cocked at a jaunty angle between his teeth, his carnation still in his buttonhole, and his snakeskin shoes and synthetic fibre suit...

'I'll take you to Juan on my way.'

It was two o'clock when the Chief Inspector got in bed. His wife had retired already. Outside there were a lot of comings and goings. The casino, cars, people walking along the promenade, shouting and talking.

'It makes you feel like a child who's been sent to bed early whilst the grown-ups finish their fun,' said Letty, but her husband was already asleep.

At eight the following morning they knocked on Littlejohn's door.

Téléfon!

It was Marriott.

'We thought of goin' to Vence today for a short run in the motor coach. We'll get our lunches there. That is, unless you think we'd better not. There's a plain clothes chap arrived to keep an eye on us. Quite a nice civil fellow. We'll take 'im with us. How would it be if you and your wife came along?'

'I'm sorry, Mr Marriott, but I've work to do this morning. Perhaps you'll get back to *Bagatelle* for lunch and I'll call there about two. I want to see you all.'

'How did things go last night? Did you get any further?' Littlejohn shuddered and felt like taking the next plane home.

'Nothing to report. See you later.'

He hung up before Marriott could speak again.

They went for a bathe and had breakfast. Then they ran out to Eden Roc at the end of Cap d'Antibes and parked the jeep. Mrs Littlejohn read a library book and Littlejohn set about the dossier. *Dossier Dawson*. That's how they'd labelled it.

At first, it was interesting.

DAWSON, William.

Aged 58. Coal Merchant.

So that was what Dawson did. Coal. Littlejohn hadn't

thought of that. He'd seen him in his mind's eye purely as an Alderman, robes and all.

Then, the anthropometric squad had been busy on the body. Details of measurements from head to feet, skull as well, back and front. And it stated that Dawson was only five feet ten inches in height. At the hospital he'd looked taller than that. There were a lot of grisly photographs, too, taken in stark black and white, with Dawson on the slab of the morgue in his birthday suit. Back and front again, with the wound showing, and the scar from the war by which they'd recognised him as Dawson, or Vallouris of the *maquis*.

The medical report. Nothing new in that. Details of Dawson's work with the Resistance.

The depositions of the travelling party were a bit of a bore. Translated into French they were stilted and completely devoid of character. For example, you had to know Mrs Beaumont to appreciate her statement fully. 'I was positively playing bridge from ten until midnight. Then I retired to my room. I locked the door and you can hardly imagine I climbed down the drainpipe and got out. In any case, why should I kill William Dawson? It's absurd.'

They'd got it all down in black and white translated by the interpreter into good French.

And Gauld. It seemed he'd got into a scuffle with the police because he'd said they were bullying Mary Hannon.

Another character appeared on the scene as well; one Little-john had forgotten. Alfred Fowles, the driver of the motor coach.

Alf Fowles, *né* Alfred, as the document described him.

The man with the perfect alibi. He'd been drinking with a lot of Frenchmen in a bar behind *Bagatelle* until two in the morning. He'd gone there just after nine and didn't remember when they brought him home, but the owner of the bistro did.

As for the rest, they'd all been intent on establishing alibis, covering one another, trying to prove they'd been indoors all the time the crime was going on. Not very successfully, in some cases. One or two had gone to bed...

It was half-past eleven when Littlejohn awoke. The sun had been shining on his face and his wife had covered it with a handkerchief. Even then, he felt dry and feverish.

'Let's run home for lunch, Letty. I've a big afternoon before me.'

He was right. When he got to *Bagatelle,* it reminded him of an examination for a piano diploma or a matriculation *viva.* Marriott had taken things in hand and they'd established a private room for Littlejohn in a sort of cubby-hole where the manageress did her books. The day before, M'sieur Joliclerc had ensconced himself in the drawing room and kept his victims hanging about on the stairs and in their rooms. Marriott had tried to do things a bit better for the travellers.

'Quite informal, we all 'ope, Inspector. The ladies get so put out and nervous when...'

'Quite, Mr Marriott. Suppose we start with you.'

Aged 52, although he looked much older. Probably through drinking and good living. An unhealthy, flabby sort of man who had to be throwing his weight about wherever he went.

'It says here, Mr Marriott, that you were in the drawing room all the evening, from after dinner until after midnight.'

'That's right. I was tired and stayed watchin' the game of cards and havin' a quiet drink or two with Sheldon and Gauld, till Sheldon went to bed. His wife made him go at eleven. Wears the trousers and treats him like dirt. Not good enough.'

'So you can give alibis to all the rest?'

'Mrs Bewmont, Mrs Sheldon, and Miss Elizabeth Hannon were playin' bridge... and yes, Mr Currie got roped in the party, too. Mrs Sheldon took off Sheldon to bed at eleven and Mrs Currie took her cards for an hour then.'

'What about the rest... Miss Blair, Humphries, Miss Mary Hannon and Gauld?'

'Marie Ann Blair went for a stroll with 'Umphries as soon as her uncle's back was turned. They're smitten on one another, as you'll gather, but it was enough to spoil the whole outing for Dawson to get to know.'

'Were they out long?'

'Just after dinner, after Dawson left on his own, till about eleven. Then Humphries had a drink with me and Gauld, and Marie Ann went up to bed.'

'Gauld and Mary Hannon?'

'Here all the time. In the lounge, talkin' together. There's somethin' between those two, as I told you before. He can't keep away from her, though they didn't go out as far as I know.'

'That's right. They say so in their testimonies.'

Marriott evidently had something on his mind. He kept licking his lips and eyeing Littlejohn as though trying to find out if he might raise some ticklish point.

'Will this questioning last long, Inspector?'

Littlejohn laid down his pen and looked straight at Marriott. 'Why?'

'Well... None of us had anythin' to do with Dawson's murder. It doesn't seem right that the whole holiday should be spoiled on account of it. After all, most of the party can't come to France every year. Much if they ever get here again. And here's this murder ruining the whole shootin'-match. It hardly seems fair...'

'Fair! What about Dawson? Do you think it's fair to him to leave the case in the air, go gallivanting off on pleasure jaunts, and abandon him on a slab in the morgue? After all, he was one of your fellow citizens. Do you all feel like this?'

Marriott started to sweat freely.

'Don't get me wrong, Inspector. I'm only watching the interests of my friends...'

'Perhaps you'd better send them in, one by one, then. I think I'll see Miss Blair…'

Humphries brought in Marie Ann, who, after a good night's sleep, had recovered her colour. She was very beautiful and the Inspector didn't blame Humphries, but…

'I'd like to speak to Miss Blair alone, please, Mr Humphries.'

The schoolmaster flushed red.

'But…'

'Please wait outside.'

'I'll be around if you need me, Marie.'

She didn't require an escort. Marie Ann was very self-possessed and knew her way about.

BLAIR, Marie Ann.

25. Radiographer, Bolchester Hospital.

'Alderman Dawson was your uncle, Miss Blair?'

'Yes. My guardian, too, until I reached twenty-one. My father and mother were killed motoring when I was fifteen.'

'Did you live with your uncle?'

'Yes, until I got a job when I was twenty-two. Auntie died about that time. I got a little flat then and have lived there since.'

'Had your uncle any enemies who might have done this to him?'

She turned pale. The thought of him, lying dead from a knife wound, must have returned.

'I'm sure he hadn't. He was a most popular man in Bolchester. An Alderman, prominent at the Baptist Church to which he gave a lot of money, treasurer and things for charities. He was well-liked.'

'By everyone?'

'Well…yes…'

'You have some reservations?'

'Not really. He was a man who wanted his own way. He liked

to be in charge of whatever he was doing, if you understand. It sometimes annoyed people. But, after all, that happens everywhere, doesn't it?'

A very attractive girl indeed! And quite different from the clinging, distressed nearest-relative-to-the-deceased of the night before. Marie Ann had resisted Dawson's wish that she should come and live with him after his wife's death. And now, in spite of the bereavement, she was wearing a light summer frock with a low-cut neck, and showing her very shapely arms and legs, most likely to the greater confusion of the bemused Humphries.

'Did your uncle sit next to you in the coach?'

'Yes. He didn't get his tickets through the ballot. They were won by one of his coalmen. Everyone who's a ratepayer in Bolchester is eligible. The coalman didn't want to come to France. He'd booked rooms at Blackpool and had a family of five. So, uncle bought his tickets and asked me if I'd come with him.'

'Did he say anything to you about being in danger here, or fear of enemies?'

'No. Not a thing.'

'He knew this coast well from wartime experiences, I believe.'

'Yes. He served with the Underground here in the war. He wrote a little book about it. Actually, it was a reprint of some lectures he gave to Rotary Clubs and the like. They persuaded him to print them.'

'He was trustee for your money, Miss Blair?'

'Yes. My father left me all his money and it yields me an income of almost a thousand a year. When I marry, I get the capital. Till then, my uncle was trustee, along with the bank.'

'And now?'

'I don't know. I expect there will have to be arrangements for another trustee till I marry.'

'Are you engaged or attached to anyone?'

She looked him straight in the face without a blush. 'No. I like my work, and until I find the right man...'

If she was as frank about her trust income to everyone as to Littlejohn, she'd not be long without a string of suitors, quite apart from her extreme attractiveness.

'You told the French magistrate that you were out taking a walk with Mr Humphries at the time your uncle was assaulted. Is that right?'

'Yes. We walked right into Cannes and back.'

'Did you pass Palm Beach?'

'No.'

'Thank you. You might send in Mr Humphries on your way out.'

Humphries was dressed in his flannels and blazer again. He was a bit aloof at first, probably annoyed at being kept out of Miss Blair's interview.

'You're really in charge of this party, Mr Humphries?'

'Yes. Though I can't take responsibility for what's happened.'

'Nobody said you could.'

He was dark and strongly built with a handlebar moustache and sleek hair. The kind the schoolboys would think the world of, especially if he showed great prowess at games, which, judging from his physique, was probably the case.

Littlejohn understood, however, why Marie Ann Blair hadn't fallen for Humphries in spite of his attentions. He thought a lot of himself. Worshipped by the boys in the gymnasium and on the playing fields, he expected everybody else to do the same. Added to this, Humphries was lacking in sense of humour. He took himself too seriously.

'How did you come to take on this job ?'

'It was going and I thought, as it coincided with school vacation, it would bring me in some nice pocket-money and get me a good holiday as well. I stood a good chance with being in Bolchester. The Trust always hires a courier, you know.'

He looked straight at you, but his eyes didn't stay still. Just a little bit shifty, especially now, when he wasn't quite telling everything. He'd joined the party to be near Marie Ann Blair. That was obvious. And Marie Ann was flattered by his attentions, but that was all. There was perhaps some young doctor at Bolchester Hospital…

'You liked Alderman Dawson?'

'He was a governor of Bolchester School, where I'm on the staff.'

'That's hardly an answer.'

Humphries flushed. Not from shame, but in the same way he'd do at home if one of the youngsters ragged him or doubted his prowess.

'What do you want me to say? He's well-liked in the town and he's a popular man on the governing body of the school. "Give the boys a half holiday," so to speak. I don't have much to do with him.'

'You seem to have some reservations about him.'

'Oh, my views don't count for much. He was of the sort who *buy* popularity. Half holidays, school treats and such like, subscriptions to charities, board of the local hospital, Alderman, etcetera, etcetera…'

'And yet?'

Humphries' eyes began to gleam.

'And yet… He'd bully the head of the school about something and nothing. He just had to be in the limelight all the time. He couldn't stop showing off in front of a nice looking girl. He liked them young and pawed them about. The sort of man who'd put a pound in the collecting box for cruelty to animals and kick the next dog he met in the ribs because it happened to be in his way. All the same, wherever he went, you'd hear them all bleating "Isn't Alderman Dawson nice?", "Isn't it just like Alderman Dawson to be so good?"'

He halted for breath. And then, having fully delivered himself in a burst of rage, he turned to the door to see if the Alderman's niece had heard him. He looked relieved to find it closed.

'You didn't like the Alderman, did you, Mr Humphries? Had it anything to do with his niece?'

Humphries almost ground his teeth.

'No; and don't you make insinuations. If I think Miss Blair is a fine girl, it's my own damned business.'

'It might be mine, too. Did Dawson object to your attentions?'

'No. He never got a chance and I'll trouble you…'

'Were you present with Marriott when he visited Dawson on his death-bed?'

'Yes.'

'Did you hear the conversation… The Vallouris business?'

'No, I didn't. Neither did Marriott, if you ask me. I wasn't as near as Marriott, but, at the time, neither Marriott nor anybody else could have made out what Dawson was saying. He was too far gone.'

'Thank you. That's all.'

Humphries hesitated.

'Well, sir?'

'Sorry I lost my shirt a minute ago. I'm officially in charge here and I'm worried stiff. It isn't helped by Marriott and that old baggage Beaumont trying to boss the show. I wish you good luck in your efforts.'

'Thanks. I'd like to see Gauld now.'

'The Beaumont's outside on the rampage. She thinks she should be first in order of precedence. If you have Gauld in, it'll set her back a bit. Wait till I tell her.'

'You can tell her I won't need her at all. I have it all down in the examining magistrate's file.'

'Oh, boy. I wouldn't miss this for anything.'

Gauld made his way in to a loud accompaniment of Mrs Beaumont's disapproval, like a Greek chorus chanting-in a leading actor.

'I shall report it to the Lord Lieutenant when I get home. I never heard…'

And the door closed.

'Sit down, Mr Gauld. You were in all night when the crime was committed?'

'Yes.'

Tall, well-built, and normally exuding vitality, Gauld must have been good at his job and among his own sort. Perhaps at the works, he was hearty and a bit coarse-grained and plebeian. Here, where he had to mind his P's and Q's with people like Mrs Beaumont and to please Mary Hannon, he was out of his element.

'How did you come to be mixed up with this lot, Mr Gauld?'

Gauld jerked his head in surprise and his red hair seemed to stand on end.

'I won the draw. I'd never been abroad before, except in the forces in the war. Then it was only Northern Ireland. I'd a right to the tickets. But it seems working men aren't welcome among this gang of snobs. I'm not good enough for them.'

A man with an inferiority complex. Without any but an elementary education and self-educated after that. But when it came to skill with his hands, he could soon show his superiority. Yet Mrs Beaumont probably looked down her nose at him and the little drunken Marriott patronised him.

'You won two tickets?'

'Yes, but my wife wouldn't come. Her mother's not well and she made that an excuse, but really she wanted to stay behind because in three weeks she's taking part in a play and would have had to give it up if she'd come with me.'

'You're enjoying this trip?'

He twisted his large useful hands and shuffled from one foot to the other.

'I can't say that I am. I'm like a fish out of water. The only working man in the lot. The Curries are decent enough and so is Sheldon, if his wife would let him be. She fancies herself a cut above me. But I'll show her one day! Marriott thinks he's doing me a favour somehow. As for Mrs Beaumont; she actually said in front of the lot, that Turnpike would have been glad to know that the *poor* were getting their share of his bounty. And she looked at me and smiled. The only one I feel at home with is Miss Hannon... Mary Hannon. She's a lady and we knew one another before this. We were at a university extension course together.'

'What about Dawson?'

Gauld was breathing heavily after his outburst. He'd been nursing his grievances for days and now he'd boiled over to the large homely Inspector from Scotland Yard. Gauld's father had been a policeman; a constable who'd pounded the beat all his life and died just when his pension was due.

'Dawson... I only knew him as a local bigwig. Or mainly that. Our political party's working itself into gradual control of the council at Bolchester, and when we've got it, Dawson and his likes will go out neck and crop. They think they own the town, instead of which they're the servants of those who elected them. To see the local papers, you'd think Dawson was the cat's whisker. Opening bazaars and Sunday School sales of work; talking about the need for a religious revival; and even preaching in churches when there's something big on and they can draw a crowd to spout to. It makes me sick...'

He thumped the table.

'Do you know that even before his wife died, Dawson was carrying on with other women…'

Then he stopped. He must have remembered his own feelings for Mary Hannon.

'…His wife was one of the best. Everybody liked her and she made Dawson what he was in town life.'

It sounded a bit mixed up and ambiguous, but then Gauld's emotions were confused. The holiday feeling, a strange country, the company of a lot of people trying to patronise or snub him because he wore overalls at his work. Then, Mary Hannon, under the romantic Riviera sun, played the gracious lady and got him all moonstruck.

'You were in all night when Dawson was stabbed?'

'Yes; anybody'll tell you that. I was having a drink with Marriott from eleven to twelve; before that we'd just been chatting together. We were all a bit tired…'

Littlejohn looked straight at Gauld and spoke slowly. 'Had you any grudge against Dawson?'

'I told you, I wasn't anywhere near him when he met his accident. I'd no grudge against him really, except that I objected to his hypocrisy. He's the largest coal merchant in Bolchester and poses as a public benefactor. They ought to see some of the good he's done himself in business with coal contracts by being on the council. But he saw to it that they couldn't pin a thing on him…'

M'sieur Joliclerc's assistant had excelled himself this time. He'd got it down as Sheldoh!

SHELDOH, Jeremy.

60. Retired tea planter.

Darjeeling, The Close, Bolchester. And his wife,

SHELDOH, Irene.

41. Married.

That explained quite a lot. If Irene Sheldon had given the correct age, she probably thought she'd married an old man, had the right to bully him for the sacrifice, and seek a few diversions into the bargain. She came in with her husband, for whom Littlejohn sent next.

'I'd like a word with your husband alone, please, Mrs Sheldon.'

Her jaw dropped. This was something new! As a rule she was the spokesman.

Mrs Sheldon wore large crescent shaped earrings, a black flared skirt, and a nylon blouse through which her underclothing and the uncovered parts of her arms and chest were visible. She was heavily made-up and entered with a gust of exotic scent. She gesticulated nervously with her painted nails. Some men would find her very attractive; especially the middle-aged ones the younger women wouldn't look at.

'But we are in this together, Inspector. I'm sure you'll allow me to stay with my husband.'

She gave him an arch smile.

'Later, madam. I want him alone at the moment.'

She showed a flush beneath her paint and banged from the room without even a glare for the two men.

'You must excuse her, Inspector. She's highly strung and you'll admit, sir, this damned business has been a bit of an ordeal for her.'

'That's why I asked her to go. No sense in upsetting the ladies.'

'Damn good of you. What can I do for you, Inspector? Damn' relief to have a decent police officer about the place. The fellah who came up yesterday… Jolliboy, or somethin' silly…was a bounder. Shelterin' behind his authority and bullyin' the women shockin'ly.'

'You were all in *Bagatelle* except Dawson on the night he was killed. I know that Humphries and Miss Blair went for a stroll. The rest, you can vouch for, sir?'

'Certainly. Vouch for 'em all. Wife and I retired at eleven, but they were all here then. Little woman was tired after the journey, so didn't wish to keep her up, or wake her if I went up later.'

'You knew Dawson well, sir?'

'Yes, moderately well. Matter of fact, he used to come up to our place now and then for a drink. Friend of the wife's when they were younger. Bit quiet for Mrs Sheldon just livin' alone with me. Dawson used to buck her up a bit. Talkin' of old times and such. Decent enough chap, except…'

There it was again. Dawson, a good fellow, charitable, public spirited, local preacher and bazaar opener… Except… Always some sort of qualification.

'Except what, sir?'

'Funny sense of humour. Got the idea he sometimes laughed at me. I know I'm a bit of a queer fellah. Spent a lot of time alone workin' in India and a bit set in my ways. Once caught him winking at my wife behind my back. Irene, of course, wasn't amused. Loyal to me…'

His bald head might be empty of thoughts or jammed full of dark forebodings and secrets, but his kindly face showed solicitude for his wife and he was anxious to get her out of the whole sorry business.

'Sorry I brought the little girl on this silly jaunt. But we won the ballot and Dawson came and said it would be a pity to lose the chance. He'd bought the ticket off a fellah who couldn't go. I'd rather have brought my wife myself, just the pair of us, later, but she seemed set on it. Hope you'll see she's not bothered.'

A big man to allow himself to be bullied by his bitter little wife. He must have been someone to reckon with when he was bossing around in India. Now, he stood anxiously there, dressed in a neat tweed suit, and the whole spoiled by the silly black tie his wife had made him put on.

'She's not very strong and I'd go to extremes to save her from trouble.'

'I'll do my best to help you, sir.'

'Appreciate it, Inspector. Want to call the little woman in now?'

'No, sir. In view of what you say, we'll not bother her.' She was outside waiting for him and as their steps receded in the passage, Littlejohn could hear odd words.

'Never so humiliated. And you allow me to be insulted… Don't care for my feelings… I'll never forget…'

There only remained the Hannons and the Curries, and they had alibis. And, of course, Alf Fowles, *né* Alfred, as the dossier said. He'd better have a word with them as well. But first…

He rang up his wife and talked with her.

'I'm only working on the surface here. If one of the party did it, the truth will lie in Bolchester. I'd better go. I could get the 2.50 plane early tomorrow morning. I'd be in Bolchester before noon. Then, I'll try to get back within two days if I'm successful.'

'You'd better come back here as soon as you can and get a bit of sleep, then. I'll ring up Var airport and get your tickets from Nice.'

'If you've any trouble, let me know. Dorange will be able to pull some strings, I'm sure, even if they have to chuck somebody from the plane to accommodate me.'

He rang up Joliclerc and told him of his plans. The magistrate was almost tearful in his gratitude. He'd tell Dorange. So far, nothing had developed in connection with the murder of Sammy. The stoker and the waiter from the casino and the prostitute from Sammy's had been freed without giving much help.

When it was over, Marriott entered.

'Mrs Bewmont's in a rare tantrum. She says you're avoiding her. She's threatening to take it up in 'igh quarters when we get back. Says you're deliberately prolonging the case.'

'Perhaps you'll tell her then, that I've other business which will keep me away from you all for another couple of days.'

Marriott chuckled.

'I'd like to see her face when I tell her. Here; I brought you a drink of Pernod. Buck you up. Say when…'

He poured in the iced water.

'And now I'd like to speak to the Curries please…' Nothing about his trip to Bolchester. He thought it best to keep the lot of them in the dark.

6
DOSSIER DAWSON

Martin Currie was a strange type, difficult to classify. Littlejohn found himself trying to guess what his job was before he looked it up in the dossier. Average; that was it. No predominant features at all. Neither young nor old, handsome nor ugly, tall nor small. The sort you'd forget. A nonentity.

CURRIE, Martin.
52. Manager of Building Society, Bolchester.

When Littlejohn saw Currie's profession, it all tied up. A nice, courteous fellow, one you could trust, and yet he had to be all things to all men to get business and because he served such a varied lot of clients and was responsible to his directors for every one of them.

He was neatly dressed in a flannel suit and had got himself a black tie in keeping with events.

'Was Dawson a director of the Bolchester Building Society, Mr Currie?'

'Yes. They're mostly local men.'

A pleasant voice. In fact, a pleasant chap. Thin face, large ears and nondescript grey eyes. You'd pass him any day in the street and never give him a second look. His wife was with him, but she was different.

CURRIE, Isabel.
46. Married, née Shakeshaft.

She was small, well-built, vivacious and didn't by any means look her age. Her husband was far from a nonentity to her; she obviously thought the world of him. A happily married couple, content with each other and the son who'd been born late in their lives. Then, they'd drawn a winning ticket for the *Bagatelle* trip and here they were, reluctantly up to their necks in a murder case. They were facing it as they probably faced any other crisis in life. If they were in it together, they were confident of coming through.

'Did you like Mr Dawson?'

The Curries looked at one another understandingly. They'd expected this one.

'To be candid, Inspector, I've no reason for liking him, but I'm sorry he's dead. He was highly respected in our town and, if I hadn't had a glaring example of how he carried on, I'd probably have thought him a fine fellow, like most of the others do.'

Mrs Currie simply nodded in confirmation. Littlejohn found himself wondering if this dark, vivid, attractive little woman had stimulated the Alderman to make passes at her, as he seemed accustomed to doing whenever he got a chance. But it wasn't that…

'You see, I've been with the Building Society ever since I left school. I rose to be assistant manager and expected to get the head job when my boss retired, which he did three years ago. Dawson was a prominent director and he always said he'd see me right. "You're sure to get it, Martin," he must have said a dozen times or more.'

'He told me, as well,' chipped in Mrs Currie. 'We just couldn't understand…'

'You're getting on a bit too fast with the tale, mother. Let me tell it.'

'Yes, do.'

'Unknown to me, Dawson tried to get another of his protégés the job over my head. To my face he was as nice as pie; behind my back he was trying to do me down. Luckily, two of the other directors liked me, supported me, and carried the day for me. One of them told me after, that Dawson had said I wasn't good enough for the post. Short of *go*, he said. I never liked him after that, however much he tried to play the friend to me. I was loyal to him as a director, but I couldn't trust him out of my sight.'

'He seems to have led a sort of Jekyll and Hyde existence, as far as I can make out, sir. Everybody says how well he was thought of in Bolchester by the general public, and yet… There's always a fly in the ointment.'

'That's right, Inspector. You can only take a man as you find him. Some must have seen his better side and judged him accordingly. Don't let my views influence you.'

'Did Dawson have much to do with your Building Society?'

'Yes. To tell you the truth, he was a bit of a nuisance.' Mrs Currie's cheeks began to glow.

'A *bit*, did you say, Martin? You know he was a perfect pest to you. Interfering in the office and throwing his weight about.' Currie smiled wryly.

'That's over now and I'm almost tempted to say "thank God". But we shall miss him coming in every other day, telling us how to run the business, bullying the staff and pretending all the time it was for their own good. If there hadn't been other directors who were jealous of Alderman Dawson and saw to it that he didn't chuck his weight about too much, life in the office wouldn't have been worth living.'

'There were other prominent men in the town who disliked him, then?'

'Well… You know what it is in a small provincial town like Bolchester. All the jockeying for position and prominence that goes on every day and everywhere…'

'I see.'

Littlejohn was glad he'd made up his mind to go to Bolchester. Perhaps the answers to a lot of questions, if not the solution to the crime, would lie there.

'What sort of a place is Bolchester? I've never been there.'

'A bit stuffy, but we like it there, don't we, Bella? It's a bit ecclesiastical, too. We've got a Minster, you know, and a very good public school, where our boy, Peter, goes…'

'I suppose Dawson was a governor of the school.'

'Oh dear, no. The local Secondary School was his pet hobby. Bolchester Edward the Sixth School was anathema to him. He was a big nonconformist, you see, and couldn't stand the Minster set. I think they must have looked down their noses at him some time or other and the Canon and the Rural Dean, who're big shots at the King Edward School, are like red rags to a bull with Dawson. When a new Mayor's elected and makes the usual procession to church on Mayor's Sunday, Dawson always stays away if they go to the Minster. You'll excuse me talking as though Dawson were still alive. It's difficult to think of Bolch-ester without him, you know.'

'And you've no suggestions to make regarding Dawson's death?'

The Curries looked at one another a bit puzzled.

'Not a thing. We were indoors with the rest when it happened.'

'Thank you very much, both of you. Are the Misses Hannon in?'

HANNON, Mary.

30. School Teacher.

HANNON, Elizabeth.

28. Librarian.

Spinsters living together with the sands of matrimonial chances running out. Mary was good-looking and fair, and she knew it. They both looked well-bred and Mary had good taste and a trim figure. Her sister, on the other hand, was a bit nonde-script and plain and given to giggling to attract attention. Mary faced Littlejohn with her nose in the air; her sister was arch about it.

'I hope you're not going to arrest us, Inspector. We had nothing to do with it.'

'Don't be silly, Elizabeth. Of course he isn't.'

Littlejohn spread out the dossier in front of him and tried to make it look as if he *had* to have the information.

'You both live together?'

It didn't make any difference where they lived, but he felt he would like to know a bit of the history of this queer pair. Why hadn't the good-looking one got married, for instance?

'Yes. Since dad died we've had the house to ourselves.'

Elizabeth was so anxious to ingratiate herself with Littlejohn that, if the other didn't interfere, he'd soon have the story behind their lives.

'You were born in Bolchester, Miss Elizabeth?'

'Yes. My sister is a mistress at the girls' school there and I'm first assistant in the library.'

'You've known Alderman Dawson long?'

Mary Hannon looked hard at her sister. In spite of her good looks, hers was a hard face. The lips were too thin and set in a bitter line.

'Yes. He was a friend of dad's before dad died. They were both natives of Bolchester and went to school together.'

'Your father worked in Bolchester?'

Mary was getting impatient.

'Is this really necessary, Inspector?'

'If it weren't, I shouldn't be troubling you, Miss Hannon.' Elizabeth was nodding her head jerkily.

'Yes, of course I'll tell you. He was the borough treasurer of the town. He had a breakdown and died. Mother had died two years before and it's just four years since dad died.'

She sniffed slightly as though stifling a tear. Her sister gave her a look of contempt.

'This is the first time we've been abroad and we won't want to come again in a hurry.'

Elizabeth tittered this time.

'Dad never let us go away on holidays alone. He always went with us. He was a very strict man until mother died. Then, he seemed to go all to pieces.'

'There's no need to tell all the family history, Elizabeth. The Inspector's not interested in us and the narrow life we've led.'

Mary was bitter about it. You could almost fill in the gaps of the tale. The strict father domineering his brood, probably kicking out the suitors. Then the death of the mother; the girls at home; the old man hardly able to let them out of his sight. Then he'd had a breakdown...

'Did Dawson enter much into your family life? Did he keep up his friendship with your father?'

The two women looked at one another. Mary was anxious to keep quiet; Elizabeth wanted to talk and didn't wish her sister to be annoyed or butt in.

'He wasn't very nice to dad in his later years. Dad's breakdown made him have to stay away from the office. You'd have thought that after forty years in the service of the borough, they'd have been a bit easy. But Alderman Dawson — Councillor, as he was then — was the chairman of the finance committee, and he said dad ought to resign. He was pensioned off on a miserable pittance.'

Littlejohn wondered if the old man had taken to the bottle and his peccadillos were called a breakdown and hushed up. His two girls might have been brought up a bit above their station. The way in which the younger was perpetually called Elizabeth… not Betty or Lizzie, but the full length of it. The Inspector could almost hear the old man calling her. Elizabeth! do this or that. And the girl had probably obeyed in her good-natured way and gone a bit soft from the repression. Mary, on the other hand, had been rebellious, but to little purpose. Now, she was dallying with a married man.

'You were with Mr Gauld at the time Alderman Dawson was attacked, Miss Mary?'

Elizabeth gave her sister an arch look this time. Mary's nose went up in the air and she flushed.

'Yes. What of it?'

'Nothing. It gives you an alibi…and gives Gauld one, too.'

'We're not suspected, are we? We'd have no motive. In any event, a knife is absolutely repulsive…it's cruel. Neither my sister nor I, nor Mr Gauld, for that matter…'

'We couldn't kill a chicken. When dad kept hens in the war we had to send for a man to wring their necks.'

'Oh, do be quiet, Elizabeth. The Inspector isn't interested in when we kept hens. Have you done with us?'

'You were a friend of Mr Gauld?'

More arch looks from one and angry blushes from the other. 'We know each other in Bolchester. We attend the same classes in psychology.'

Littlejohn felt like asking if Dawson was the psychology tutor, or at least the class secretary. The Alderman seemed to have a finger in every Bolchester pie.

'You won seats in the ballot of the Turnpike Trust?' There was a pause.

'Not exactly...'

Elizabeth was volunteering the explanation again, with Mary looking uneasy and self-conscious this time.

'The girl under me in the library won it. She had hoped to take her mother, but her mother is a semi-invalid and they were a bit anxious about bringing her so far by motor coach. Mary wanted to come abroad this year, so we bought the seats from Ada and she took her mother to Cleethorpes with the money. I wish we hadn't now. Not that I wish Ada... Well, you know what I mean.'

She wandered off into shoulder-shrugging and giggling.

So, it had been Mary who'd cooked up the trip. Probably to be with Gauld, who, even if he'd wanted her with him, could hardly have offered her his wife's ticket in the full limelight of a coachload of Turnpikers. But when they'd heard that Ada had tickets and an invalid mother, it had been a godsend. Elizabeth, a twittering chaperone, making things respectable for Mary and Gauld. And Dawson... What had he had to say about it?

The rest was interrupted by the sudden arrival of Mrs Beaumont. She wore an ugly hat and carried a large reticule. Her face was flushed and her jaw set.

'If you want to speak to me, Inspector, you'd better hurry. I'm going out. I'm not staying cooped up here for anyone, police or no police. I would have thought that as a Turnpike Trustee, I'd have been the first to be interrogated.'

Littlejohn didn't turn a hair.

'All right, Miss Mary and Miss Elizabeth. That'll be all for the present. Thank you for your help.'

Mrs Beaumont followed them out with a jealous, flashing eye.

'Much use will those two be to you! One too big for her boots, the other a silly giggling little hussy. Librarian, indeed! All she's there for is to roll her eyes and flirt with the men who come in. It's a disgrace. As for the other... Ordinary decent

Bolchester boys aren't good enough for her. She wants married men. Scandalous! I shall report her carryings-on to the trustees when I get back. In future, we shall carefully scrutinise all the lists of winners. We want no scandal. My late husband…'

Her breath thereupon gave out and as she gulped in more air, Littlejohn was able to get his word in.

'I didn't ask to see you, Mrs Beaumont, because we'd already had a long talk. You were, you said, in bed when it all occurred. There seemed little more to be said.'

Mrs Beaumont beat her handbag on the desk.

'I am the official representative of the Turnpike Trust. It was only courtesy to deal with me first on the *official* list. I could have told you quite a lot about the various parties on this trip.'

I'll bet you could, thought the Chief Inspector.

'The father of the two hussies who've just left *drank* himself to death. If it hadn't been for Alderman Dawson, he'd have been carrying on a lot of *drunken* accounting in the borough books. Until he died, he practically kept those two girls prisoners in the house. He was a strict old puritan who saw seduction in every young man who smiled at them. Well, time told. He wasn't so good himself when it came to temptation and the *bottle* mastered him…'

Everything relating to Mrs Beaumont's pet aversion, alcohol, was heavily scored in her speech and she spat out the word in contempt.

'That's why they never married and the elder one seems to have a preference for married men herself.'

'Has she had some affairs, then?'

He almost held his breath, anticipating news of more wrong-doing by the ubiquitous Alderman Dawson!

'There's the way she's behaving with Gauld. Disgraceful!'

'But that's only one.'

Mrs Beaumont drew herself up and her heavy bosom

ballooned upwards under her rustling silk frock as she breathed indignantly.

'Isn't one enough! Really, Inspector, I'm surprised at you. Very surprised and disappointed. I thought…'

'If you'll excuse me, Mrs Beaumont, I've another…' He almost said 'customer', but changed it in the nick of time. '…I've another suspect to interview and time's passing.' In her curiosity, she overlooked the polite dismissal.

'And who may that be?'

'Fowles, the driver.'

'Ah! The *drunken* sot. To think that the trustees took on a *drunkard*. Unfortunately, our usual driver was booked in advance for another trip. I always suspected Fowles of *the habit,* but never caught him red-handed. I shall see that he doesn't get the job again. He is, of course, only the paid driver. Mr Brewer, of Bolchester, owns the coach… Mr Brewer is a big temperance man.'

'Indeed!'

She looked hard at Littlejohn, but he was looking at the dossier.

'And now, Mrs Beaumont, if you don't mind…'

'I know when I'm not wanted, Mr Chief Inspector. But I'm glad we think alike. I have always suspected Fowles and I hope you will give him a thorough examination and prove his guilt. I know the late Alderman remonstrated with him at Avignon on the way here. Fowles had actually been *drinking* when we stopped for lunch. Disgraceful, and with a load of passengers and their lives in his hands.'

'What did Dawson say to him?'

'*Alderman* Dawson told him he'd see he lost his job when he got back to Bolchester. He wasn't fit to drive. Fowles began to whine about his wife and four children, but the Alderman was adamant. Nobody who takes *drink* ought to be allowed a driving licence, he told Fowles and I fully endorsed it. He made Fowles drive slowly all the way to Cannes after that.'

'Fowles has an alibi, of course, for the night of the crime.'

'A *drunken* alibi, Inspector. An alibi given by *drunkards,* which isn't worth the paper it's written on. You understand that, I'm sure. And now, I'll go, but I rely on you to see that Fowles doesn't touch another *drop* until he gets us all safely home to Bolchester. Good afternoon to you.'

FOWLES, Alf né Alfred.

37. Motor Driver.

47. River Bottoms, Bolchester.

The *greffier* had taken it all carefully down.

'It was jest my joke, sir. River Bottoms. It's reely River Street, but I was always a one for…'

'This is too serious to be funny, Fowles. What was the cause of the row you had with Alderman Dawson at Avignon?'

Fowles was a little strip of a man with bad teeth. Although he knew he could get cheap dentures, he was afraid of the dentist. He'd only had one tooth extracted in his life and he and the dentist had ended rolling on the floor. All the same, Fowles was a bit of a humorist. The life and soul of any party; but not the Turnpike party, in which he'd got by mistake. Or so everybody thought except Mr Brewer and Fowles's predecessor, William James. 'If that ruddy old Bewmont's goin' agen, I'm resignin', and that's straight', Bill James had said. 'I'll take the Blackpool lot this year and let Fowles do the Turnpikes. It'll do 'im good…'e knows French, too.' Which was true, more or less. Fowles had been in France in the war and by a few words and a lot of pantomime managed to get along. That was how he'd got drunk and got his alibi attested on the night of Dawson's death.

'Me, *'ere,* mossoo, nine hours to midnight, drinkin' avec voo. Savvy? Compris? La belle mademerselle, aussi, savvy, eh?'

And the patron of the bar, the barmaid, and six or seven customers had thoroughly understood and vociferously testified in favour of Fowles.

'Why should I wanter kill ole Dawson, even if 'e did threaten to git me the sack? Tuck objection to me havin' a glass or two of wine with me meal at Avignon. I know me way about France, see? Was 'ere in the war. Glass o' *vin rooge* never did anybody 'arm. I wasn' drunk, but that ole cow, Bewmont, took on somethin' shockin'. Dawson said he'd see Brewer give me the push when we got 'ome.'

'What did you think of that idea?'

'Tell yer the truth, Inspector, I couldn't care less. I can always get a job in my trade. I'm a mechanic as well as a driver, see? Not many o' my sort on the road. Took to driving because I got bad lungs. Orful cough in winter, see?'

'All right, Fowles. I'll grant your alibi. But did you see anything suspicious going on during the trip down?'

Fowles inserted a fag in the corner of his mouth and lit it. Then he looked round the room to see if there was anything to drink, sighed when he drew a blank, and sprayed out a jet of smoke.

'Such as wot?'

Littlejohn left it to him.

'That little perisher Marriott 'ates Dawson's guts, if you ask me. You see, I'll give it to Dawson; he knows 'is way about France. Served 'ere in the war, *and* in these parts. Got swankin' to the ladies a bit on the way. Sort o' read 'em a lecture on France and as we got down south, he got more and more lecturing, like. It got on Marriott's nerves. Kep' trying to change the conversation and every time we stopped, Marriott kep' complainin' to me about wot a bore ole Dawson was. "I could wring 'is blasted neck," he sez.'

'Perfectly natural, I suppose.'

'And then there was Gauld and that stuck-up Hannon girl.

Good-looker and no mistake, but the cold and standoffish sort. Can't stand 'em that way meself. Like 'em a bit hot, like the one in the *Bivouac Bar*, jest behind 'ere, the one who give me the alibi. Bertine's 'er name and… Oh boy…!'

He whistled shrilly through his bad teeth.

'I don't care 'ow long we're stranded 'ere, between you an' me, Inspector.'

'What about Gauld and Miss Hannon?'

'There's somethin' *going on* there. Bit of a nerve, you know, bringin' it on one of the Turnpike outin's, but then luv is luv, ain't it, Inspector? It's been goin' on quite a bit at home. My boss, Brewer, runs a taxi business as well as motor-coaches, and some of the taxi drivers could tell you a thing or two about Miss H and Gauld and the trips they make out of town. Not that the taxi boys talk. Wot goes on in the taxi line is nobody's business, see? But I'm jest tellin' *you*.'

'But how does that affect Dawson?'

''Ow does it affect Dawson! I'll tell you. There was a ruddy row between Dawson and Gauld at Lyons, where we put up the second night. The Alderman had been playin' the watch-dog over the morals of the party and Gauld got mad. Somethin' must have been said about Miss H and 'im. I'd been round the town and got in about midnight. There was nobody about in the hotel 'cept Gauld an' Dawson, goin' at it 'ammer and tongs in the hotel lounge. I didn't 'ear much except Dawson shoutin' at Gauld. "I know about your carryin's on with Miss Hannon in Bolchester and you're not bringin'em on this trip. If I'd known, I'd 'ave seen you didn't come with us. We're respectable people…" Somethin' like that. I went up to me room. Didn't want to get mixed up.'

'Is that all?'

'*All*? Isn't it enough? The rest was jest chicken-feed. The sort o' thing you see on all these 'oliday trips. Dawson bein' gallant to

Mrs Sheldon and 'er lappin' it up. Saw 'im squeezin' her hand under the dinner table at Lyons after he'd 'ad a few.'

'Was her husband there?'

'Of course. Nice fellow, but she's the boss there. Daren't say a word, daren't old Sheldon. Just puts up with it.'

'What about the Moles? Do you know exactly what kept them away?'

'She wasn't well, they said. Mole called to tell the boss that she ought to be better in a day or two and they'd fly to Lucerne and pick up the party there. Mr Mole's an accountant and very well thought of in Bolchester. And his wife keeps a gown shop. *Maison Lola*. That's 'er name, Lola. Best shop of its kind in the town. A good-looker, she is, too. Big, bonny sort. Bit 'ighly strung and given now and then to tantrums. Many's the time they've booked a taxi for some big local event or other an' Mole's had to cancel it. Another of her *does*, the taxi boys'll say. Always 'appenin' and I wouldn't be surprised if they didn't call off this trip because she'd had a *do* about somethin'. They'll turn up as if nothin' 'ad 'appened when we get to Lucerne, if we ever do. How much longer we goin' to be held up 'ere? Not that I mind with a girl like Bertine to keep me comp'ny, but you like to know, don't you?'

Littlejohn almost had to push him from the room to get rid of him.

Outside, he felt just as if, by taking a single step out of the hall at *Bagatelle*, he'd crossed the frontier from England into France. The hostel was, as Marriott had said, 'ome from 'ome, even down to the hall-stand and the drainpipe painted green which held umbrellas.

He resisted Marriott's efforts to tack himself on and walked to the Croisette to get a taxi or a bus for Juan-les-Pins. The promenade was busy and much of it was monopolised by a film company from England taking exotic shots they could very well have made at Blackpool or Bournemouth. The hot sun shone in a cloudless blue sky and it filled Littlejohn with the holiday feeling again. He crossed the soft, hot asphalt to the shade of an awning over a small café and ordered beer. With half-closed eyes he sat enjoying the heat and the coloured sights of the promenade and gardens.

Damn Dawson! The Chief Inspector and his wife ought to have been mixing with the crowds, taking walks and excursions, enjoying the views and the sun. He opened his eyes and scanned the long stretch of coast with the yachts and motorboats scuttering from point to point, and the sea alive with bathers.

Here he was, up to the neck in crime again, and no nearer. Not even a theory about who'd done it, in spite of the day's work.

'You buy carpet? Jewels? I show you postcard?'

He brushed the dusky hawker aside, paid his bill, and lazily raised his hand for a taxi.

It was dark and clear when his wife saw him off from Var Airport at ten-to-three next morning, after a good sleep. At six o'clock they touched down at London Airport in pouring rain. There had been no cricket for three days and although it was early summer, people were going about in winter overcoats.

7
BOLCHESTER

It was just a hunch. In any case, I couldn't have done any good hanging around *Bagatelle* and trying to solve the case in the holiday spirit of Cannes. I wanted to see what Bolchester was like and what they thought at home of the local members of the Turnpike party.'

Littlejohn hadn't even called at Scotland Yard. He'd just telephoned and asked Sergeant Cromwell to meet him at St Pancras with a raincoat and a few other essentials. They talked together as he waited for the train to Bolchester, where the police had been forewarned of his arrival.

As they strode on the platform, Cromwell only got a faint idea of what it was all about. William Dawson had been killed at Cannes on the Turnpike outing. His companions had been mainly the small-town shopkeeper and business types and the whole affair was confused by the fact that Dawson had been a traitor in the *maquis* during the war and it was quite likely that someone on the Riviera had killed him. To add to the muddle, a crooked barkeeper had been murdered on the same spot as Dawson.

Littlejohn didn't tell his tale very coherently. He had been travelling all night on a bumpy journey and the changes of climate and temperature had damped his enthusiasm. Still, Cromwell was like a faithful sporting dog. Provided he was hunting with Littlejohn, he was content.

By the time Littlejohn had eaten his breakfast on the train and had a snooze, it was running into Bolchester. He was met there by Inspector Scrivener, who took him to the police station in a car right away. Littlejohn smiled as he compared Scrivener with Dorange. Tall, fair, heavy-featured, with his hair cut close *en brosse,* big hands and feet, no sense of humour at all, and the slow conventional police stride. A neat regulation uniform, bright buttons, official police boots... The Chief Inspector thought of the light grey nylon suit and snakeskin shoes...and, of course, the red carnation and the innumerable Pernods...

A small, compact town squatting in a saucer-shaped valley on the fringe of the Pennines. Half a dozen main streets laid out regularly and paved in asphalt; the rest a medley of slummy, cobblestoned side alleys. Old houses in brick, many of them with black and white fronts; the remainder, a motley of modern erections, chromium-fronted shops, fake Elizabethan and Georgian. A sprawling town hall of grey stone, with a large clock tower and a lot of gothic complications on the front. Dominating the whole, the old Minster on a hill at the top of the town.

The police station was in the town hall. Beefy constables wandering here and there. A magistrates' court just ready to go in session, and lawyers bustling along corridors in gowns and cravats because it was also county court day.

'You've come at a bad time, sir. I'm prosecuting in the petty sessions this morning. We've just run in a gang of local Teddy boys and it's likely to last all morning.'

'That's all right, Inspector. Carry on. It won't inconvenience me at all to find my own way around. It isn't as if the crime had been committed in Bolchester. I'm just after a bit of local colour.'

Scrivener looked at Littlejohn as if he'd gone mad. Local colour, and Alderman Dawson lying dead in France! He didn't quite know what Scotland Yard were doing on the case at all. They had their own CID in Bolchester. Well... If that was the way they wanted it...

'Can I help in any way?'

'If you don't mind giving me a list and a rough idea of where the various parties on the trip live, it would help.'

Scrivener seized his mouth and nose with the palm of his hand in a nervous, bothered gesture.

'I'll send Haddock round with you. He's a plain clothes man and we won't need him today...'

He rang a bell.

'Send Haddock in.'

They never needed Constable Haddock on public occasions connected with the constabulary. The cases he solved were always presented to the bench and the public by others, although he often did most of the work. The present Teddy boys, for instance. He'd told the men in uniform where to lay hands on them in the act of breaking the law, but others would appear before the magistrates and take the credit for the arrests. Haddock liked it that way.

Henry Haddock came of a good local family and was near retiring age. In his early days, he'd been one of the smartest constables in the Bolchester force. Then he had arrested, single-handed, two local safe-crackers just as their charge of dynamite went off prematurely. Both the burglars had died and Haddock had been a bit queer ever after. He was a great favourite with his comrades and most of the good children of the town. At the annual police Christmas party, he dressed up as Father Christmas and was lowered down the town hall chimney.

'This is Detective-Constable Haddock...'

A tall, fat man, with a red face, heavy grey moustache, and sad, kindly blue eyes. He was dressed from head to foot in black and wore starched white linen. His boots shone like jet and were distorted in shape, for he had bunions from tramping patiently all over the place in search of news and clues. He had the entrée where many of the uniformed constabulary would find the door shut. He carried a bowler hat and a rolled umbrella and was trying to hide the fact that he was sucking a barley-sugar drop. A heavy pipe smoker off duty, he withstood the temptation to smoke with the help of sweets which he also distributed freely among the children he met on his rounds.

Haddock shook hands solemnly.

'Sit down, Haddock.'

The chair was so small and Haddock so large that he seemed to lose it in the heavy folds of his body and looked to be sitting in mid-air.

A constable entered with an armful of books, a briefcase and a map, placed them before Scrivener, and left the room after a glance at the clock which ticked with a hollow, heavy sound on the wall of the office.

'Have you found out who might have done it, yet, Chief Inspector?'

Scrivener seemed to regard Haddock as a piece of office furniture and addressed himself to Littlejohn.

'I've not been kept informed of how the case is proceeding, but I gather it's really in the hands of the French police. I believe they don't use our methods and everybody's guilty till they're proved innocent.'

He said it in a tone of contempt, as though the French force was incapable of handling the business properly. Littlejohn wondered what Scrivener would have said if he'd seen M'sieur Joliclerc, or, better still, Dorange, with his red carnation.

'I have the complete dossier with me, sir, but it's all in French. Would you like to see it?'

'I haven't time just now. I must be getting to court, but we'll have a chat afterwards if you care to call, sir. Meanwhile, I'll leave you in the capable hands of Haddock.'

The sun was breaking out and streamed through the upper halves of the office windows, which were of stained glass, and cast patches of green, purple and blue light on Scrivener's bristled head and florid face. He rose and gathered his papers, books and maps. The Teddy boys were obviously in for a gruelling time.

'I'll see you later, then, sir. If I can help in any way...'

He was gone. It was obvious that Scrivener was leaving the body and the murder of the late Alderman in the hands of the French police and Littlejohn. If Dawson allowed himself to be murdered in foreign parts remote from Bolchester, it was his own look-out.

'Sad loss to the town, Alderman Dawson.'

Haddock looked ready to burst into tears. His voice was deep and musical, like a bass-bassoon.

'He was well-liked, locally?'

'Oh, yes, sir. Very popular.'

'And yet, between ourselves, Haddock, the dossier of the case shows that most of the people on the trip to Cannes had reasons for bearing him a grudge. Funny he should be so popular.'

Constable Haddock looked hurt. He turned his sad prominent eyes on Littlejohn.

'The more you get on, the more people are jealous and resentful, aren't they?'

'I think I'd like a walk round the town, if you'll be so good as to guide me, Haddock. I'd like to see the places where the people on this trip live and work and as we go, you can tell me something about them all.'

Haddock rose, took up his umbrella, and carefully put on his bowler hat.

'With the greatest of pleasure. Where shall we begin, sir?'

'Marriott's shop.'

They left the town hall and crossed the square which was laid out in gardens in the middle and arranged round the statue of a politician, aggressively addressing the town in general with his fingers raised aloft.

'Mr Gladstone,' said Haddock laconically.

The shop was right opposite. A long, low frontage, with two shabby windows obscured by green paint to stop you seeing what was going on inside. A large dray was drawn-up in front and two burly workmen were unloading barrels and rolling them across the pavement and down a chute into the cellars. 'That's Marriott's. He did the bulk of the trade in the town, but the business is going down.'

'Is he a native?'

'He wasn't born here, sir, but his father bought the business and Mr Marriott inherited it from him.'

The sun was quite warm and the main street very pleasant, The shops were just beginning to wake up. An ironmonger on one side of Marriott's carried out a stack of buckets and put them at the side of the door and his next-door neighbour, a pleasant little man, came out of his outfitter's shop and nailed a card on the door-jamb. *Sale of Raincoats*. The three banks in the street were getting busy and clerks came and went, dealing with the morning's local clearing.

'Marriott and Dawson didn't get on?'

'I never heard much of them quarrelling, sir. They were on opposite sides politically and didn't agree about that. But who does, sir?'

Again, the sad blue eyes questioned Littlejohn's face. 'Hullo, Henry...'

One of the huge brutes hauling barrels about as if they were tin buckets, paused in his toil to greet the local detective.

'Good morning, Wilfred. How's your wife today?'

'Spent a better night, thanks.'

'Where is Dawson's coal business, Haddock?'

'Just round the back here...'

They plunged in the warren of old grimy streets. Chandlers, cheap grocers, old clothes shops, with here and there a dirty tenement between. In the end, the railway lines spanning a viaduct beneath the arches of which were huge stacks of coal protected by a surrounding paling fence with a large gate. A brick office, a public weighing-machine, and a lot of carts and lorries loading coal. Business as usual, by the look of it.

'They're carrying on the business, then?'

'Oh, yes. It's a limited company, you know. There's a manager runs it. Alderman Dawson spent most of his time on public bodies... The council, the Infirmary, the courts... Like to see the manager? Mr Lovelace, he's called.'

'We may as well.'

They entered the yard, over the entrance of which was spread a sign. *William Dawson & Co Ltd, Coal Merchants*. Through the yard and beyond the arches a canal flowed and after that were green fields.

'It's a very old, established firm, sir. It started on the canal bank, so long ago, and then when the railway came, it was handy. They bring the wagons down the ramp from the goods yard and the empties are hauled back by a winch.'

About a dozen lorries manoeuvred about the enclosure, their drivers shouting above the noises of the hoppers which mechanically loaded the coal. Overhead, trains thundered across the viaduct.

Lovelace was in his office. A stocky, bull-necked man with a large head, black moustache, and a shock of untidy black hair. A slovenly, shabbily dressed type, used to associating with the coalmen and drivers of the yard. The office was a rudimentary place, with a few plain wooden stools, a chair upholstered in leather from which the stuffing was leaking, and a roll-top desk cluttered with pieces of dirty paper and weight notes. A cheap safe and a rack holding a few ledgers.

'What's all this about the boss? Was he murdered, or what? Nobody seems to have a proper tale.'

'He was murdered right enough. Will it make much difference here?'

Littlejohn sat in the leather chair and started to fill his pipe. Haddock strolled into the yard and started talking to the man at the weighing-machine, a little fellow with a wooden leg.

Lovelace eyed Littlejohn suspiciously as though he might have come to wind-up the firm.

'It's a company, you know, and there are other shareholders, although the boss held most of the shares.'

'Who's likely to inherit Dawson's interest?'

'Miss Blair, I reckon. She's the only relative he has left.'

'Did the Alderman spend much time here?'

'Not since the war. I looked after things while he was in the forces and when he came back, he still left 'em to me. He was busy with other things...town council and the like, although he took his fair whack of the profits.'

Lovelace pulled out a short pipe and started to fill it from an oiled-silk pouch. A swarthy man, with black mats of hair on the backs of his hands. Hairs even sprouted on the tip of his broad nose.

'It's a profitable business, I reckon.'

'*Now* it is, and I might say I've had a lot to do with making it pay. The way Alderman Dawson ran it before the war, it never paid. Spent too little time here and took too much out. It's been bankrupt once.'

Lovelace had a grievance and it was manifest in every word and gesture. He thought he ought to be better paid and own a bigger block of shares than he did.

'Did anybody lose much money when the business went bust?'

'Dawson and two or three shareholders. Dawson saw what was comin' and must have tucked a bit away. The rest lost a packet. They say it killed one of them, a chap called Bewmont…'

'Beaumont. The dentist?'

'Yes; know him?'

'I met his wife. She was on the motor-coach trip with Dawson when he met his death.'

'I know that. Perhaps she did him in. They say her old man lost round ten thousand pounds when Dawson's went broke. In fact, he'd retired from his practice and it made it that he'd to set up again. Not for long, though, because he died a bit later. If he hadn't been well insured, they say his wife would have been in the cart. She'd have had to go on the stage again…'

'Was she on the stage?'

Outside the loading was going on furiously and they had to shout above the noise of the coal sliding down the hoppers. Haddock was still talking to the weighing-machine keeper, sitting on a stool in his office resting his aching feet.

'Mrs Bewmont came with a musical comedy show to the local theatre and Bewmont, who was a bachelor at the time, fell for her. When the show left, Mrs Bewmont…I forget her maiden name…stayed behind and she and Bewmont painted the town red for a bit. Quite a local scandal. Then they married and settled down. You wouldn't think to see her now that she'd been a good-looker of the Gibson Girl type in her day, now would you? I've heard she broke a few hearts before she married old Bewmont.'

'She lives alone?'

'Yes. Up town…'

Haddock, who had now returned and was standing in the doorway, intervened in a deep bassoon.

'I'll take you there, sir, when we leave here.'

Coalmen kept running in with notes from the weigh house

and Lovelace stopped to make entries in his books and initial their check-slips.

'I believe Dawson didn't draw a ticket in the ballot, but bought one from one of your men. Is the man here?'

'No. He's taken his family to Blackpool. Pity Dawson ever bought the tickets. But he seemed very keen to go. He'd served there with the French Underground in the war. Never stopped talkin' about it locally. Used to give lectures on what he did in France. You'd have thought he won the whole blasted war to 'ear him talk. I guess he wanted to go there again to swank to the rest of the party. Well…see what he got himself.'

Littlejohn eyed Lovelace dubiously.

'You don't sound very fond of your late boss, Mr Lovelace.'

The little hairy man met Littlejohn's glance with his own bilious one.

'I'd nothing against him, except…'

Except… There it was again.

'…except that he liked chuckin' his weight about and took too much out of the firm and put little in it. That's all. I suppose I'se be carryin' on for Miss Blair now.'

There didn't seem much more to do at the coal-yard and the pair went back to the high street. People greeted Haddock and stared at Littlejohn as they made their way to the car park. They passed a spick-and-span shop facing the town hall gardens. *Maison Lola. Modes.* The blinds were drawn and the door closed.

'Is that Mrs Mole's place, Haddock?'

'Yes, sir. You'll know her, won't you?'

'I've not met her, but I hear that she and her husband are waiting for the Turnpike party at Lucerne, if they ever get there.'

'Yes. Mr Mole's office is on the other side of the town hall. He's the main accountant in Bolchester. There was a bit of talk about him and his wife winning in the Turnpike ballot. Some said the whole thing was cooked, but I can't see that.'

'Is he accountant for Dawson's firm, do you know?'

'Yes, because when they went bankrupt years ago, he was put in to manage it by the Official Receiver and stayed on as auditor after. He's a very decent chap.'

'What about his wife?'

Haddock shrugged his shoulders. He was a bachelor living with an unmarried sister and he'd never had a love affair in his life.

'She's good-lookin', sir, and a good business woman, too. They've no children and I suppose she took the shop to keep her out of mischief, as you might say.'

'Mischief?'

'I believe Mr Mole's had a bit of a job keeping her in order, sir. At one time there was talk of a separation or divorce, but they must have patched it up. She's always been a bit flighty.'

Haddock said it all diffidently and as though he'd heard it all casually and in the way of rumour. Actually, his brain was like a card-index of facts he'd collected in a lifetime and all he said was authentic.

'Where do the Moles live?'

'Warwick Road, sir. That's the best part of the town. Their house is just opposite Mrs Beaumont's. We'll see it on our way.'

Haddock sighed with relief as he sat down in the driving seat of the police car and wriggled his sore feet round in his boots. They threaded their way through traffic, passed the Minster, and were in the suburbs.

Warwick Road. A long avenue planted with trees and with houses built far back behind shrubs and grass verges.

Dunnottar. Mrs Beaumont's place.

It was a new house surrounded by a large garden with flowers in full bloom and lawns well cut. Everything about it was trim and opulent. An old gardener was mowing the front lawn with a motor-mower. Haddock called to him.

'Now, Jeff!'

The old man, a little knotted creature with a grave face,

stopped in his course and slowly shuffled to the front gate. 'Mornin', Mr 'Addock. Wantin' to see me?'

He eyed Littlejohn with a mixture of curiosity and cupidity. 'House shut up, Jeff?'

The ancient pointed to the place with a dirty paw.

'Shuttered and sheeted, as you might say, Mr 'Addock. But I got a key to see that all's right an' feed the fish.'

The curtains were all drawn at the house and it looked dead in its trimness.

'I've often heard of Mrs Beaumont's fish. Interested in them myself. But I've never seen them…'

The old man paused, torn between duty to keep the place shut up and the pleasure of showing off his employer's aquarium.

'Come in for a minute, then, but don't you say I let you in, now. Else the old un'll give me what-for when she learns of it.'

He opened the gate after making sure there was nobody about in the road to see and betray him.

'*You* can come along as well. Might as well be 'anged for a sheep as a lamb.'

Littlejohn followed.

They went in at the back entrance which faced a rose bed with a kitchen garden beyond.

'A lot o' ground for one like me to be lookin' after.'

He put the key in the lock and opened the door.

'She's *near* with her money, is the old un. Won't pay for nobody else.'

The place smelled cold and a bit damp. An odour of slightly musty carpets and soot.

'Wipe yer feet, both of you, or else the old un…'

He led them through the kitchen and a corridor and into the lounge. It was a sombre room, darkened by the drawn curtains, but comfortable and elegant in a heavy way. Large armchairs, a huge sideboard, small tables, and a bookcase, half the contents of which were on dental surgery.

The old man didn't draw the curtains but went to the kitchen, fumbled with the main switches, and then returned to put on the lights. In the alcove near the window, a large illuminated aquarium in which a number of portly goldfish were slowly swimming.

'She's fond of fish. Can't see much in 'em myself. Jest swimming round and round. Can't even bark or anythin' to guard the 'ouse. Jest useless lumber.'

He took some ants' eggs from a packet and sprinkled them in the water.

Haddock, having used his wits to gain entrance, had to make a show of being interested in the fish.

'A very nice lot, Jeff. They're company, you know, and they make no noise. Restful...very restful.'

One of the fish fixed Haddock with unwinking eyes and opened its mouth like a round O.

'They're quite tame, aren't they?'

They stood looking around. Photographs in frames on the large mantelpiece. One similar to that Mrs Beaumont had shown Littlejohn; the dental surgeon swathed in mackintosh ready to ride his ancient motorcar.

'She 'as a dog and a cat, too, but they've gone boardin' to the vet's. Can't be bothered lookin' after a whole menagerie on me own.'

The gardener led the way to the door. As they passed through the hall, Littlejohn paused to glance at the large framed photographs taken years ago in family album fashion. A young, good-looking woman with the smile that wouldn't come off. Hair piled on her head and an opulent bosom decked in the standards of decency of the time. A real Gibson Girl.

'That's the old un, though you wouldn't think it, would you?

Teaches you a lesson, don't it? Lovely when they're young, is women; 'orrible when they gets old…'

All my love. Penelope.

It was scribbled in faded ink across the bottom of the photograph.

'Who'd think to see 'er now, that there was a proper queue at the stage door of the theatre for 'er. Remember it meself, time she was at the Royalty in a musical show. Look at 'er now. Well, come on an' let's get locked up. Didn't oughter let you in at all.'

'Pity about Alderman Dawson,' said Littlejohn to the old man as they parted at the gate.

'Aye. Big loss to the council, for what good they do.'

'Was he a friend of Mrs Beaumont's ?'

'Once 'e was, when the old man was alive. Old Beaumont and Dawson ran the coal-yard till it went bust. After it broke, the old man 'ad to go back to pullin' teeth agen till he popped-off not long after. Killed 'im, his investments goin' wrong like that. It wasn't for a long time that Mrs Beaumont would speak to Dawson after her old man snuffed it. But they got friends agen and he'd offen call on 'er when in these parts. After all, they needn't be enemies, I heard Dawson once say to 'er, seein' he 'imself had lost all he 'ad as well as old Beaumont…'

'Has he been here lately?'

'Matter of fact, he called the day before they went on the trip 'e got murdered on.'

'What sort of a man was the late Mr Beaumont?'

'A proper gent, sir. One of the old families of Bolchester, 'e came from. He'd money and the airs and graces, as you might say. Came as a bit of a shock to the eligible young ladies of the town when he married a girl off the stage. Still, Mrs Beaumont was a good-looker, and half the young bucks were after 'er. Trouble with Mr Beaumont was, 'e was too trustin'.'

'In what way?'

''E oughter 'ave known better than put all he'd got in a tumbledown old coal business like Dawson's, and that just because Dawson was 'is friend and said it 'ad prospects. Good job Mr Beaumont 'ad a profession to fall back on, else he'd 'ave been in queer street…on 'is uppers properly.'

Opposite stood a large red house with a conservatory at one side. The curtains were drawn and there was nobody about.

'That's the Moles' place, sir.'

Haddock started the engine of the car.

'Where now, sir?'

'Where did Dawson live?'

'Not far from his coal-yard. It's the old family place and though it's right in town, the Alderman kept it up. There's a housekeeper…Mrs White. Nice woman, too. One of the best.'

'Let's go, then…or perhaps we'd better see his lawyer about looking over it?'

'I don't think you need bother, sir. In any case, Mr Marshall, the late Alderman's solicitor, will be at court just now. Think we might risk it without?'

'Very well, Haddock. You're the boss. Drive on.'

The great clock of the Minster was striking eleven as they passed, and on a platform beneath the dial, a string of figures in armour emerged and started to tilt mechanically at one another.

8

THE HOUSE ACROSS THE CANAL

Littlejohn felt himself still on the fringe of the Dawson case. Somewhere there was a key which would unlock the whole mystery, but, so far, he'd come nowhere near it. Just a lot of small-town talk, and a crowd of holiday trippers who had already been together just too long and were beginning to be peevish with one another. Or else, starting silly little flirtations or love affairs which would probably fizzle out when the holiday ended.

The car had threaded its way through the main streets again, turned into a string of smaller side-streets, and crossed the canal by a humpbacked bridge. Littlejohn looked out and was surprised to find they were on the fringe of the town, with green fields and trees on one side and on the other, the canal, the railway, and then Dawson's dingy coal-yard.

Dawson's house was on the edge of a meadow in which a lot of goats were tethered and a horse was running around. When he saw the car halt, the horse halted, too, and neighed.

The house itself was an old-fashioned three storey affair in blackened brick, with a whitethorn hedge all round, a large wooden gate, and a neglected garden. From the upper windows there would be a full view of the coal-yard. Standing at the garden gate, you could see the cranes working and the wagons moving up and down the ramp to the goods yard beyond the viaduct. The road past the house was paved and ran straight in the direction of the town, passing over another canal bridge and past Dawson's yard. Probably he'd walked along it to work every morning.

Haddock led the way down the gravel drive to the front door, a large grained-and-varnished affair in brown with a bright brass knob. He had to ring twice before they heard footsteps approaching inside. Haddock just had time to say a word or two before the housekeeper appeared.

'Mrs White, the housekeeper, is the widow of the late pastor at the Baptist church where the Alderman attended. Her husband died whilst he was minister here. She's a very respectable woman…'

Haddock said it as though Littlejohn had doubts about her virtue or her honesty, and before the Chief Inspector could answer, there she was. She blushed and looked confused when she saw Haddock who, in turn, reddened and cleared his throat nervously.

'Good morning, Mrs White. I'm sorry we're disturbing you, but…'

'I quite understand, Mr Haddock. Come inside.'

It looked as if she had been forewarned of the visit. Littlejohn had wondered what Haddock had been doing in the gatehouse of the coal-yard earlier in the morning and he now got the idea that some surreptitious telephoning had been going on. As they passed down the lobby, he saw two telephones; one the usual affair to the exchange, the other a more antique arrangement which obviously connected the house to the business premises across the canal. There were two switches: *Office, Gatehouse*. So that was it! And Haddock was conducting a rather melancholy wooing in spite of the forthcoming funeral.

'This way.'

A stuffy, overcrowded house, with a dark hall carpeted in turkey-red which ran up the stairs as well. The room they entered was full of old commonplace furniture and was probably not used except on special occasions when callers arrived. Over the mantelpiece, a large oil portrait of Dawson in his mayoral robes and chain. The last time Littlejohn had seen him he was stretched out in death on the hospital bed, pale and in repose. The picture gave another aspect of Dawson. Ruddy, sure of himself, pompous in his robes and cocky with a sense of his high office. On the shelf below, a smaller photograph of a kindly-looking, buxom grey-haired woman, also wearing a chain of office and presumably Mrs Dawson in the year of her husband's glory.

'Please be seated.'

There were two leather armchairs facing an electric heater which the housekeeper had switched on. The two men sat in them.

'You've come about Mr Dawson?'

Mrs White must have been suffering from mixed emotions. Her lower lip quivered, but she was so obviously pleased to see Haddock that she was smiling as well.

A well-bred, good-looking, middle-aged woman with greying hair, regular features and a good figure. Haddock briefly introduced her to Littlejohn and explained what the visit was about. Once, he called her Alice, corrected himself, and they both blushed like youngsters again.

'Mrs White is an old friend of mine, sir. We both attend the same church.'

'You must excuse the state of the house, Inspector. I have been away in the Alderman's absence. The whole thing is unbelievable. Alderman Dawson, of all people. He was a man respected by everybody.'

'But was everybody *fond* of him? Would you say he was loved by everybody, Mrs White?'

There was a pause.

'Better tell the Chief Inspector everything, Alice…er…Mrs White. It will help him solve the case.'

She reddened slightly again.

'He wasn't what you would call a lovable man, sir. He wanted his own way too much and never liked to appear weak. I mean, even a show of emotion seemed to disgust him.'

It was a difficult job trying to get candid information about Dawson in the circumstances. A parson's widow, obviously cultured and kindly, and far from a woman of the world. She would soon be shocked by any straight questions about the Alderman's life and behaviour where women were concerned. And the presence of Haddock didn't improve matters.

'How long have you been Mr Dawson's housekeeper, Mrs White?'

'Three years, sir. I came almost immediately after his wife's death. Miss Blair didn't want to be responsible for him and he had to have somebody to look after the place and his needs. My husband had just passed on and the job came to me providentially.'

'You found him a good master? Kind, considerate, decent?'

'Yes. I lived my own life and had my own friends. I looked after the house and the Alderman's food and…well…the usual housekeeper's tasks.'

'Did he ever think of marrying again?'

There was a pause. She was standing, leaning one hand on the back of a chair. Haddock rose and bowed her into it.

'I don't honestly know, Chief Inspector. If he did, he never took me into his confidence. There were times when…well…I thought he got moody through lack of a wife. Knowing him, I was always prepared for a change. I mean, I knew I'd have to find a new job one day. He was the kind…the…the…the marrying sort, who…'

She paused and twisted her fingers.

'The sort who was fond of women, would you say?'

Haddock gave Littlejohn a look of sad reproach, but Mrs White didn't need any protection. She seemed to have made a resolution and had grown calm.

'You said I must tell the truth, Mr Haddock. During my years as a minister's wife, I learned something of the world. It is not all rosy. There are…er…unpleasant things. As you say, Chief Inspector, Mr Dawson was fond of the ladies. It was well-known among my own sex locally. It disgusted some and fascinated others. It was one of the reasons why Miss Blair left this house. He had grown too familiar. There were others, too. I need not name them. You will not know any of them.'

'I might.'

'I expect you would like to look over the house?'

Littlejohn didn't try to bring her back to the subject she had skated over. Instead, he rose and indicated that he would follow her. Haddock brought up the rear.

Up the red-carpeted stairs, with the bathroom facing, and the door open. Hanging from the middle window-frame a large magnifying shaving-mirror before which Dawson must have performed every morning.

'This was the Alderman's room…'

It looked aldermanic! A huge double four-poster bed from which the bedding had been removed. A heavy mahogany wardrobe and a chest of drawers with an old-fashioned toilet mirror on the top. Photographs on the walls showing Dawson as mayor in several groups of officials, the chain of office ever preponderant. In one Littlejohn made out little Marriott.

'That's Mr Marriott, isn't it?'

'Yes. And that's Mrs Beaumont.'

She pointed to a group with an inscription at the foot. *Justices of the Peace*. 1950.

'Alderman Dawson was a great friend of Mrs Beaumont?'

'Yes. They met on the bench and at many public functions. He was friendly with her husband when he was alive, I believe. I wasn't here then, of course.'

She smiled at her own thoughts.

'There were rumours that the Alderman fancied Mrs Beaumont as the second Mrs Dawson, at one time. They were of about the same age and knew each other well. It was even rumoured that Mrs Beaumont wasn't averse to the idea. However, it died out.'

'Were you surprised?'

'No. I think he would have fancied a younger, better-looking woman.'

She turned almost coyly on Haddock and addressed him. 'You said I was to tell the truth, didn't you, Henry?' Torn between joy and sorrow, the detective-constable twisted his poor feet in his shoes until the leather squeaked loudly.

Littlejohn looked round the room. Thick Indian carpet, an alabaster reading-lamp with an expensive shade at the bedside, an electric razor on the chest of drawers, an elaborate gas-fire in the fireplace. Every modern comfort.

'Would you say Mr Dawson was wealthy?'

Mrs White hesitated.

'He *was*. This room was fitted when he was better off. My own, at the end of the corridor, was Miss Blair's and is quite nicely furnished, too, but of late the money hasn't been so free.'

Haddock looked her suddenly in the face.

'But I thought… The way he spent his money…'

'Yes. So did a lot of other people. But the woman who balances the domestic budget knows better. If he spent as usual outside, he tried to cut down expenses here. He even complained about the cost of food and repairs to the place and asked me to help him economise.'

'The business wasn't doing so well, then?'

'I believe it went bankrupt once and after that, Mr Dawson worked hard and set it on its feet again. There was money to spend. Then, after the war, times were better, too, but nationalisation took a lot of the profits. Of late...well...I don't think the money came so easily.'

Haddock drank it all in and nodded appreciatively. Littlejohn's eyes sparkled as he watched him and he felt it was time to be going before his smile widened into a grin.

'Would you like to see the other rooms?'

'No, I think not, thanks. What is in the wardrobe and the chest of drawers? Clothes? Books? Personal letters or diaries? I only ask in case there is anything...'

'Clothes in the wardrobe, of course, and his linen and the like spread among the rest. Would you like to see them?'

'I think not, unless you think...'

She paused, a smile on her lips.

'There's one thing arising out of your comments on Mrs Beaumont.'

She opened the top drawer of the chest and took out a photograph in a silver frame.

Ever yours sincerely, Penelope.

A smaller replica of the photograph they'd seen earlier at the Beaumonts' home, with a much milder superscription. 'What is this about, Mrs White?'

'I think he must have had it when his wife was alive and kept it in his drawer. Then, after her death, he had it put in this frame and whenever Mrs Beaumont came to tea, he put it in a place of honour on the dining room mantelpiece.'

The Gibson Girl again! Littlejohn's eyes danced.

'Whatever for? Was that when he was contemplating making her the second Mrs Dawson?'

'I don't think so, specially, although he might have wanted to give her that impression. I think he used it to flatter her when he borrowed money from her.'

Haddock breathed heavily.

'Borrow? He did that?'

'Yes, Mr Haddock, I think he did, though I couldn't be sure. She came to dinner twice and each time he came from the dining room into his study for his cheque-book. They both used the same bank and she might not have had hers with her.'

'But may he not have been giving *her* a cheque for something?'

She hesitated and grew a bit red.

'I know it was wrong of me, but I looked at the blotting-paper on the desk afterwards. Each time it bore the signature of Mrs Beaumont.'

Haddock looked at Littlejohn, then at Mrs White, and then at the photograph of Mrs Beaumont, which had been erected on the chest. He smoothed his hair and gave a very faint but gratified smile, followed by a look of intense admiration for Mrs White. What a woman! What a detective's wife! You could almost hear him thinking it.

'What do you think of Mrs Beaumont, Mrs White?'

'She's a good woman, I think. Presides over all the ladies' charities, a big worker at the Minster, a leader of the intellectual life of the town…I mean the lecture society and the luncheon club. You wouldn't think she was once an actress.'

'Why?'

'She seems…well…so staid and so cultured.'

Littlejohn didn't say that he knew a lot of staid and cultured actresses. It was just her small-town way of thinking and doubtless she had old-fashioned ideas on the subject. A minister's widow.

'A good woman, you said. Did she ever strike you as being a bit bitter and...what shall I say...bossy?'

'They say she took her husband's death rather badly. It seems it was a love-match and he was responsible for much of the high esteem in which she was eventually held in this town. He gave her the touch of culture and refinement she lacked before. Perhaps she found things hard after he passed on. I know... I have suffered the same thing.'

Her lower lip trembled again. Poor Haddock looked down at the pattern on the carpet. When he glanced up again, he found her smiling at him through two big tears. Littlejohn felt *de trop*.

'We'd better go, I think. There's still a lot to do. Haddock is invaluable and I mustn't waste his time.'

He felt he owed a bit of a testimonial to the modest minor detective. Something to ginger up his wooing and settle Mrs White for life now that Dawson was out of the way.

Littlejohn's huge bulk seemed to fill the narrow staircase on the way down.

'This is a strange house for Dawson to live in, isn't it, Mrs White? I'm sure you find it a bit hard to run.'

They were at the door again, ready to go.

'Yes. It goes with the coal-yard, of course, and is very handy for it. Mr Dawson's father built it more than sixty years ago. The Alderman often talked of moving up-town, but never did. Whenever he thought of moving, the money factor arose. I suppose it will be sold now and not easily, I'm afraid. It's not a house people will fancy.'

The clock in the car was on noon.

'Will Lovelace still be at the yard, Haddock?'

'Yes. They close for lunch at half-past.'

'Let's call on him, then.'

Lovelace was still in his office, busy scribbling on grubby slips and writing in his shabby books. Cranes rattled and trains passed across the great viaduct and coal slid down the long chutes into waiting carts and lorries. A coating of coal-dust hung over everything.

'Hullo. 'Ere again. What can I do for you now?'

'Earlier this morning, you told me that this was a profitable business, Mr Lovelace. Is that true? Now, I want a proper answer, because it might affect the case seriously.'

Lovelace clenched his powerful hairy hands and the colour of his bull-neck turned purple.

'What the 'ell's it got to do with you? I'd like to know 'ow the blazes it'll 'elp you solve this case, because I don't...'

'Wait a minute, Lovelace. I'm just giving you the chance to put yourself right, to correct the erroneous statement you made this morning. It's dangerous to lie to the police, even if your pride *is* at stake. You know this business isn't paying. You know that of late years it's been going on the rocks. Dawson has taken too much out and put too little in. In spite of all your efforts, Dawson's looks like going broke again.'

'And who the 'ell's told *you*? Is it that Mrs Bewmont? Because...'

And then the whole gross, hairy mass of Mr Lovelace seemed to deflate itself like a pricked balloon. He sagged as he stood, groped for a chair, sat down, and remained slumped in his seat.

'What's the use. What the 'ell's the use. The firm *is* broke. Damn well broke, in spite of all I've done. Dawson did it. Mr Clever Dawson. Mr High-and-Mighty Dawson. Too proud to work, that's what he was.'

'How long has this been going on, Mr Lovelace?'

'Three years or more.'

Now that the truth was out and he needn't bluff himself any more, Lovelace was a pathetic sight. His eyes, dark rimmed with coal-dust, looked tired and bloodshot and his stiff, stocky figure of a minute ago was flabby and shrunken.

'Weight-note wanted.'

A coalman, with rolling eyes and white gleaming teeth, thrust in his eager face.

'Go to hell! Take your coal-note to blazes! Every ton makes a loss. Might as well leave the stuff in the yard.'

A flare-up of spirit, and Lovelace relapsed again in his brooding.

They could hear the coalman shouting above the din of the loading-gear. 'Old Lovelace 'as gone barmy. Clean off 'is ruddy nut.'

'Who's been helping Dawson through over the past few years? Who's been staving off the evil day, Mr Lovelace?'

'I did, at first. All my ruddy savings gone. I've kept on in the 'ope of better things. And I intend to keep on now that Dawson's kicked the bucket. I'll buy this place cheap from the exors once the accountant's been through it and valued it. I'll soon pull it together. You'll see…'

The reminder that Dawson was dead suddenly suffused Lovelace like a tonic. He rushed to the door and called the coalman back.

''Ere. Bring that ruddy note in the office. Tryin' to get out without it bein' booked, are you?'

The astonished man returned, his clear eyes goggling in their surround of coal-dust.

'Well, I'll be damned! But then we might 'ave expected this, Mr Lovelace. Old Dawson havin' croaked must 'ave been a blow to you…'

Littlejohn waited until the process ended and then:

'Who else put money in this concern?'

'I see you know all about things, guv'nor. Go on, then, I'll bite. It was Mrs Bewmont.'

'I thought so. She was a friend of Dawson's, wasn't she? And he somehow persuaded her to put money in the business. How did he do it?'

'He said it was to tide 'im over the nationalisation change.

First she lent him a thousand. You could have blown me down when I saw the cheque come in. You could have blown me down again when I saw that Dawson had drawn the bulk of it for his own uses. I told 'im it was plain swindlin', but he told me to mind my business; he knew what he was doin'.'

'And the second cheque?'

The bloodshot eyes opened wide.

'Who's been talkin' to you? The second cheque was for two thousand *and* it didn't go through the books. I saw it when he pulled it out with some papers from his pocket. He whipped it back damn quick, I can tell you, but I knew he'd been talking soft and sweet to Mrs B again.'

'When was that?'

'About twelve months ago. Then, last week, I saw Dawson draw a cheque for three hundred in favour of Mrs Bewmont. I thought 'e was, maybe, payin' somethin' back and then, it dawned on me. Three hundred was ten per cent of the three thousand he'd borrowed. He was pretendin' it had earned ten per cent, and payin' a dividend.'

'When was this?'

'A couple of days before Dawson left for France.'

'He must have taken it in person to Mrs Beaumont's home. He was there on a visit about then.'

Lovelace went on as though he hadn't heard.

'It didn't strike me what he was doin' till after the party had left. Even then, he *might* have been payin' her back some capital. But it was unlikely. There was no capital to pay back. It had all been spent by Dawson. When it dawned on me, I didn't know what to do. I thought it out, and then I decided I'd write to Mrs B and warn 'er and tell 'er to ask Dawson was the money dividend or repaid capital, because if he said it was dividend, he was a damn liar, the firm had made big losses for three years. Felt I ought to tell 'er. Her husband was a toff to me when he was a director here. And after the dirty trick Dawson did to him…'

'You wrote to France?'

'Yes. Dawson had left me his address in case any business needed writing about. I knew Mrs Bewmont was at the same place. So I wrote to her.'

'Get any reply?'

'Nope. Didn't expect one.'

'Well, thanks very much, Mr Lovelace. I hope you pull things round. You certainly deserve to.'

'I appreciate that, guv'nor.'

Full of new life, Lovelace thereupon bustled into the coal-yard and started bullying the carters.

'Get them ruddy lorries out o' there and get crackin'. We've work to do and you're gummin' up the yard... Get weavin', now.'

The klaxon on top of the office began to grind and thereupon the tallymen and labourers downed tools in the middle of their jobs and scuttered like ants to the brewing-shed.

'Time for lunch for us, too, Haddock. We've had a busy morning. Shall we eat?'

'Yes, sir. I'll be honoured.'

As they passed the police station, the constable obviously looking out for them on the steps waved his hand. Haddock pulled up.

'The police have been on from Cannes, sir. Scotland Yard must have told them you were here. We'd a terrible job findin' somebody who knew French to speak to them. It seems they don't speak English in the French force.'

He looked disgusted.

'Do *you* speak French in the Bolchester force?'

'No, sir.'

'Well, then... What was it all about?'

The constable was going to tell his own tale in his own time.

'We eventually fetched Mr Lampriere, one of the barristers in court. He's a Channel Islands man and speaks it like a native.'

'What did Cannes want?'

'They said to tell you there'd been another murder and would you ring them back as soon as possible.'

Littlejohn smiled grimly as he thought of the Cannes Parquet getting to work once more. They could manage very well for an hour or so.

'Right, constable. But Mr Haddock and I are very hungry. Cannes can wait until we've eaten. Drive on, Haddock. To the *Station and Victoria,* or whatever you say it's called.'

'Well, for ruddy-well cryin' out loud!' said the bobby on the steps to the square in general. 'If Scotland Yard don't take the biscuit for cool cheek! That'll just teach the French police not to try to shove us around. Speakin' French indeed!'

9
ELIMINATION

It was obvious that Haddock wasn't used to drinking much. They'd had a glass of sherry apiece before the meal and two half-pints of beer with the roast beef and two veg, and here was Haddock with his face flushed and anxious to do all the talking.

'There are a lot of things I could tell you, sir, about one and another in this case.'

The Station Hotel was old-fashioned but the food was good. Gilt mirrors and red plush and a head waiter with a bottle nose who kept buzzing round asking if everything was to their liking. Most of the business men in the town seemed to be there for their midday meal and Littlejohn's table was the centre of interest.

'I'll bet they're all dying to know what's going on, sir.' Haddock was glowing under his new-found notoriety. 'Two coffees, please. Black.'

Littlejohn handed Haddock a cigar and lit one himself. Marriott had given them to him the day before. 'Take a couple of cigars, Chief Inspector. They're good ones…'

'First of all, Haddock, what do you know about Dawson and his French escapades during the war?'

Haddock gave a short laugh.

'Everybody in the town knows about them, sir. He wrote a book on it. Published locally. And as for lectures: Every Rotary and lunch club for miles round has had Dawson and his *maquis*...'

'How did he get in the French Underground to start with?' Haddock pulled on his cigar opulently and then removed it.

'I'll try to get you a copy of his book, sir, just as a matter of interest, but I can tell you most of what went on. Dawson spoke French well. He was in the first war and seemed to get taken up with the language then. He studied it as a hobby at the local evening schools and joined the local French Circle. He held a commission in the artillery in the first war and fancied himself a bit of an authority on gunnery. I don't know whether you heard of the Mullett gun, sir, but Mullett, the inventor, was a Bolchester man. The Mullett Engineering Co, who made the guns in the war, has its works just outside Bolchester and Ernest Mullett was a personal friend of Dawson. Supplies of the gun were dropped over France for the Underground and news came through that something or other was wrong with them. Mullett took it so badly that nothing would do but he must go and be dropped himself to investigate. As it turned out, the gun was all right but a bit difficult to assemble. It was a sort of modified Sten, and Mullett soon had it okay when he got there.'

'What about Dawson?'

'Mullett took Dawson with him as a sort of interpreter. I don't know what he wanted with a chap like William Dawson, when there were so many good young men who would have done better. But Dawson seemed to push himself, and with being Mr Mullett's friend... When they got there, somebody shot at Dawson as he was in his parachute, wounded him in the shoulder, and he was laid up in the French Underground for weeks. He had a secret name, Vallouris, or something such, and Mullett was called La Colle. Never heard the last of it when

Dawson got back. He made two or three trips all told, all about the Mullett gun.'

'Was he married, then?'

'Oh, yes. His wife died about three years ago.'

Probably Dawson's subsequent trips were to the girl he'd left behind him in the *maquis*. The girl to whom he'd betrayed his comrades.

'Was he a ladies' man?'

Haddock smiled, puffed his cigar, leaned back in his seat, and put the thumb of his spare hand in the armhole of his waistcoat.

'On the QT, yes, sir. He kept his amours very dark, but the police see and learn a lot that's not expected, don't they, sir?'

'Yes. And what did they learn about Dawson?'

'There must have been somethin' about the man that *upset* the ladies, sir. Married women with good husbands seemed eager to betray them on account of him.'

He made patterns in the air with his cigar.

'Such as… ?'

'Well, sir, there's a number of ladies you wouldn't know, but I can tell you this. Some of the matrimonial trouble of the Moles was due to Dawson. At one time, he seemed he couldn't leave Lola Mole alone. Then it fizzled out. I think Mole must have stepped in and threatened what he'd do if it didn't stop. Dawson behaved himself for a time after that. His wife had died in the meantime, sir, and it got round that Mrs Beaumont was to be the next. Several local ladies were disappointed at hearin' that news, sir, and must have been relieved when Mrs Beaumont denied it. She was a good friend of Dawson's, but not to that extent. A cut above him, too, if you ask me.'

'Anybody else I'd know?'

'Well, yes. Perhaps you met on the Turnpike tour a lady called Mrs Sheldon. Irene Sheldon. Now, I've got to be careful, here, so you'll keep this dark, sir. I did hear from reliable sources that before his wife died, Dawson and Mrs Sheldon was more than friends. She was a widow, then. Mrs Briggs. Her first husband was a major and killed in the war. It was said that Mrs Briggs and Dawson was carryin' on before Mrs Dawson's death. When Dawson's wife died, I suppose Mrs Briggs had hopes. Which was dashed when the rumour spread about Mrs Beaumont, you see. So, to show she didn't care, or out of spite, who does Mrs Briggs go and marry, but a chap called Sheldon who'd gone from these parts to India tea-plantin' years ago and had lost his wife out there. It seems he'd always been keen on her from boyhood, as you might say, and 'ad wanted her when Major Briggs beat him to it. She married Sheldon, then, and has since, from all accounts, led the poor chap a dog's life. Furthermore…'

Haddock paused for effect, flicked the ash from his cigar, and leaned confidentially across the table.

'Furthermore… It's rumoured that she and Dawson were a bit too friendly after she married. Makin' a mug of Sheldon behind his back, you see. But poor old Sheldon worships the ground his wife treads on. A perfect gentleman, is Sheldon, and *honi soit qui mal y pense,* as you might say. He wouldn't believe a wrong thing of his wife, I'm sure. Now that Dawson's out of the way, perhaps Sheldon's life'll be a bit easier.'

Haddock paused, pondered, and a profound thought seemed to strike him.

''Ere… I hope you don't suspect, sir, that Mr Sheldon did Dawson in on account of his wife. Mr Sheldon's the last man alive to do such a thing.'

Lunch was over, the head waiter was unctuously handing out the bills, and the local business men were leaving. Some of them greeted Haddock and stared hard at Littlejohn.

'What do we do next, sir?'

'I've to get back to the police station to ring up Cannes. I wonder who's been killed this time.'

Littlejohn realised that this tepid interest in the case was not like the usual zest. Even now, he felt like sitting back and taking a good snooze. The sudden change of air and temperature, coming on top of a sleepless night, had sapped his energy completely.

'Was Dawson keen on Mrs Beaumont in her young days, do you know? Or was she friendly with him through her late husband? She seems to be a woman of strong character who could perhaps tell me a lot more than she's already done. Do you know anything about her background and the history of her friendship with Dawson?'

'Can't say I do, sir. But I think I know who would. Miss Liddell, the borough librarian, is a great friend of hers…'as been for a long time. She might know. Like me to try while you telephone? The library's only just behind the town hall.'

'Yes, do, please. Then we might just have another look round town before I go. I must get the night plane back. The Turnpike party will be clamouring for me, and I don't want them to know I've been here and got information about some of them.'

They put on their hats and parted.

It turned out that Dorange had telephoned and had asked Littlejohn to ring back to the Commissariat of Police at Nice. It didn't take long to get through.

'Hullo, Dorange…'

'Allo, Littlezhon. *Comment-ca-va?*'

There had been another murder with a vengeance, this time. No complications of the Underground or low life of Cannes. Henri, the son of the concierge at *Bagatelle,* had been killed. His body had been found in some bushes on La Californie just behind *Bagatelle*. He had been throttled, choked with someone's tie or scarf.

'A nasty little boy,' added Dorange. 'The sort who might have proved troublesome to us when he grew up. However, that doesn't say he should have been murdered. When are you coming back?'

'By plane tonight, Dorange.'

'See you soon, then, old man.'

So, young Henri had seen or heard something and had either said too much or tried to cash in on his information. This new development seemed to focus the inquiry more than ever on *Bagatelle*. Now that the *maquis* motive had been eliminated, Littlejohn could imagine with what fervour M'sieur Joliclerc would press his inquiry. Somebody at *Bagatelle* would be going through it!

They were still fully occupied with the Teddy boys at the local police station and, until Haddock returned, Littlejohn felt like a fish out of water. Haddock wasn't long. The librarian was out at lunch for an hour.

'I ought to have thought of it, sir.'

'Let's take a run round to the Hannons' house and see where the Sheldons live. And, by the way, do you know much about Humphries, the schoolmaster who's the conductor of the Turnpike tour?'

'A very decent young fellow, sir. Well-liked at the school. Nothing much wrong with him, I can assure you. He's keen on Dawson's niece, Miss Blair, and Dawson was dead against it. Said she was too good for Humphries, who was after her money. Miss Blair comes into quite a nice bit from her parents' estates, I know. They were prominent drapers in the town and did well. Dawson was her mother's brother and her guardian till she came of age, and one of her trustees till she came into her capital on marriage. Dawson used to boast about it. Said with him being the trustee, any young man who wished to marry her would have to ask his consent. "*And* the bank's, because the bank's the other trustee," he'd say. Sort of evergreen joke. Lucky the bank's in it, too. It stopped Dawson fiddling with the funds…'

They got in the car.

'Two nice young women, the Hannons. Miss Lizzie's a bit on the tittering side. Their father drank himself to death. He was borough treasurer at one time and very steady. Then his wife died. He never got over it. Booze, booze, booze. It was pathetic to see it, sir.'

The large sad eyes fell on Littlejohn, the car swerved, and Haddock hastily turned his thoughts to the road again.

'Do you know the Curries, Haddock?'

'Yes. Sober, sensible, churchgoing people. Couldn't wish for nicer. He's manager of the local building society. If Mr Currie had had any grudge against Dawson, we'd have known in the police, sir. I think you might cross 'im off.'

That's all *you* know! thought Littlejohn.

'Wasn't Dawson a director of the building society?'

'Oh, yes. All prominent local men. But in a concern of that size and sort, Dawson couldn't have done Currie any harm. Did you meet that young red-head, Gauld, on the trip, sir? A bit of a bolshie, if you ask me. Prominent in local politics. And there's rumours he doesn't hit it with his wife and 'as been seen around with Miss Mary Hannon. Pity those two young women 'aven't got an elder brother, sir, to give Gauld a proper thrashin'. Miss Hannon must have sort of got infatuated with him. But he's not the kind to kill Dawson, believe me. For all his wrong principles, as you might call 'em, he's no killer. On the contrary. He's all for non-aggression, peace campaigns, and the sort. Non-violence, if you get me, sir. And yet, sir, there's nothing queerer than people, is there? I bring to mind that Gauld was brought up before the magistrates once for assault. Found a man beating a dog, got mad…typical red-head…and knocked the man down. Fined ten bob, I believe, and then the cruelty to animals people took up the man who was knocked down for cruelty to the dog, and he got five pounds and costs. Funny things do 'appen, don't they?'

Haddock roared with laughter at the queerness of folks. 'No, sir. No. I'd cross Gauld off as a murderer if I was you.'

At this rate, Haddock would soon solve the case by process of elimination, if he'd anybody left to pin it on when he'd done! His sad eyes scanned the road until he saw what he was seeking.

'That's the Hannons' place.'

An old semi-detached house with a front garden surrounded by gloomy old trees. A large family house, which, now that the money and most of its former occupants had gone, was slowly decaying from disuse and lack of care. A coach-house and stables on one side looked just as they might have done, only more dilapidated, in the days when the former borough treasurer had gone to his office in a carriage and pair. The structure had not even been converted into a garage.

The front door of the house was open and Haddock's surprise at this vanished when he saw four painters sitting in the hall drinking tea.

'Afternoon, Mr 'Addock.'

One of them greeted him. They all remained squatting, holding their teacups in a kind of solemn Passover from which nobody must disturb them.

'The young ladies having the place decorated whilst they're away?'

Haddock spoke more slowly than usual, careful of each word, on the look-out for his aitches. It was the patriarchal tone he used to the lower orders, or before the magistrates on the rare occasions when he appeared in petty sessions.

'Four rooms, that's all. Outside ud do with doin', too, Mr 'Addock, but money's probably a bit tight.'

Haddock looked along the line of celebrants of the ritual tea.

'No wonder.'

He strolled in with Littlejohn, apparently inspecting the art of the white-smocked men, whose tackle was all over the place.

Old-fashioned furniture, frayed carpets, an atmosphere of

stuffiness and dust, promoted by the long plush curtains and the chairs with threadbare tapestry. In prosperous days, doubtless a fine well-kept house. Now, neglected and dying on its feet. Probably a hard place to sell, even if its owners wanted to move to something more modern elsewhere. The sort of house a spirited girl would do her best to get away from, even if it meant kicking over the traces a bit. And as for a girl without much spirit; she tittered and twittered and hoped for the best.

'You couldn't say, sir, could you, that either of the two Misses Hannons was likely to 'ave done for the late Alderman? Though livin' here, day in day out, as you might say, must have made them both a bit queer. Livin' in the past, eh?'

He pointed to a large framed photograph of an elderly gentleman glaring through his glasses from above the fireplace at all in the room. A tyrant of an old man, with a great square chin, the bulbous nose and horse-nostrils he'd passed on to his daughters, and just a twinkle of spite in his eyes. A hard, firm man, and yet he'd folded up and died when he lost his wife. Her picture, a dumpy, timid-looking woman with a faint smile, hung on the wall opposite her husband's.

One of those obscure places where tragedy had been played out to the full with no audience to watch it.

'No, I wouldn't think either of the Misses Hannons...'

Haddock was still eliminating. He wore his hat and carried his umbrella at the slope. You might have mistaken him for a bum, arrived to value and sell the place to satisfy a writ.

'Neither would I, Haddock. Let's go.'

It was sheer intrusion and better ended. The workmen gave them a cheery goodbye.

'Bit of a tumbledown warren, eh, Mr 'Addock?' one of them shouted after him. He lived in a council house with a nice wife and two kids, and tragedy of the kind written large in the place he was decorating did not strike him at all. He was only twenty-five.

'What about the Sheldons', sir?'

'Is it far from here?'

'Five minutes.'

The car was soon there. *Darjeeling,* The Close. It was a modernised cottage under the large wall which surrounded the Minster. A well-kept little garden, small tightly-mown lawns, an old stone house with all the curtains drawn. And it was here that Dawson had called on the Sheldons and, thinking her husband wasn't looking, had smiled a knowing smile at Mrs Sheldon behind his back. And Sheldon had spotted it and made light of it…or pretended to.

The whole neighbourhood had a sedate, ecclesiastical air. A parson in gaiters crossed the close, two old ladies descended from a taxi and rang the bell of another neat cottage, presumably on their way to tea and muffins, a gardener mowing the grass among the graves alongside the church sharpened his scythe musically, and the clock in the great tower chimed and struck four.

Dawson, who'd spent his life in this place and in the town below, had gone off to Cannes and been stabbed in the back on a rubbish heap. And the crime had arisen from passions roused here in the close or down in the quiet town. Littlejohn thought of the stiff body in the clinic of *Les Petites Sœurs de la Miséricorde*. It was fantastic.

'Doesn't look as if we'll get in, sir. We've been lucky so far, but our luck ends here. It's locked up and blinds down. All the same Mr Sheldon was too much of a gentleman to kill anybody. Why, he's one of the council of the Friends of Bolchester Minster, who collect funds to keep up the fabric of this old place. I'm a nonconformist myself, but I'd hate to see this old church fall into disrepair, sir. It's a public jewel, in a matter of speakin'.'

Somebody started to play the organ in the church and the great swell of sound filled the close through the open main doors. A woman in an apron and an old hat emerged and started to sweep away the confetti from an earlier wedding. The man in gaiters returned holding a small dog on a lead and talking tenderly to it.

'That's Bishop Driver, sir. He's retired now. You wouldn't think, to look at 'im, that he's only sixty. Somewhere in the East, he was, and refused to leave his people when the enemy came in. Every time anybody broke rules in the camp, they took it out of the bishop. He's a great friend of Mr Sheldon.'

Haddock said it as though giving Sheldon a testimonial, an exemption from the murder of Dawson. The bishop passed them, greeted them, and then turned back his kindly glance to the dog, whose good brown eyes helped him to forget the past and the wickedness of men.

'I'm sure Mr Sheldon...'

Haddock, the advocate, seemed to be pleading the cause of all his fellow townsfolk.

'That only leaves Marriott, then, according to your mathematics, Haddock.'

Littlejohn smiled, took out his pipe, and started to fill it. Haddock did the same; an old pouch, a little briar with a curved stem, and a bowl thick with carbon.

'You might go farther and fare worse than Marriott, sir.' Littlejohn paused.

'Why?'

'He hated Dawson. Once he said he thought he'd have to kill him to get any peace. He was drunk, of course. It was just after the town plannin' committee, of which Dawson was chairman, and by that I mean he more or less ran the show. Marriott's shop is right on the development line and is to be compulsorily purchased. It's to be set back a good twenty yards. It's not doin' too well and Marriott says if it's shut up for a time or made less, it'll ruin him. Dawson pressed it on vindictively.'

'And got his way?'

'Oh, yes. As usual. The night the committee decided, Marriott went to the local gentlemen's club and got properly tight. He swore he'd get even with Dawson. All his life, he said, Dawson had thwarted him. He'd even, when they were boys, won a scholarship that would otherwise have gone to Marriott. The result was, accordin' to Marriott, that Dawson was educated, whereas Marriott, to use his own words, was a bloody illiterate. He was drunk, as I said. But you see, he'd a deep hate for Dawson, who also opposed him and threw him off the council at the elections. If that hadn't happened, Marriott would have been where Dawson was and saved his shop and his fortune.'

Haddock slowly lit his pipe.

Littlejohn did the same and, as the flame of the match rose and fell, he remembered. Marriott had been the one who'd dragged the Vallouris red-herring across the trail. He only had said Dawson's last words had referred to his *maquis* pseudonym. Marriott, who'd known all about Dawson's escapades in the French Underground, and probably of his betrayal of his friends there as well.

'All the same…Marriott's got no guts. He couldn't murder a rice pudding, as the saying goes.'

'So, nobody on the Turnpike trip put paid to Dawson, Haddock, according to your deductions?'

'It couldn't have been suicide, sir?'

Haddock's sad eyes almost pleaded for it.

'No. Dawson would have needed to be a contortionist to stab himself in the back that way.'

Haddock sighed deeply.

'I'm not much of a detective, sir.'

'You've been very useful to me and I'm grateful.'

They left the close behind and coasted downhill to the town again. Littlejohn sat in the car whilst Haddock hurried in the library to consult Miss Liddell. He wasn't long away.

'There's not much to tell about Mrs Beaumont, sir. She just came on tour with a company that played here nearly a month in the old theatre. She never went on with the company when they left. She got engaged to Mr Beaumont and they were married soon after. They say she was a beauty and that Dawson was an admirer, too, in those days. Her baptismal name was Penelope Clarke, but she went under another one on the stage. Valerie Nelson...'

'Valerie? Was she known by that among friends after her marriage?'

'Yes. I think a lot of them still called her Valerie as a sort of pet name, though when she became what you might call a respectable Mrs Beaumont, she used her own name. Miss Liddell says a lot of her old friends, particularly the men, call her Valerie still...a sort of tribute or remembrance of her heyday as you might say.'

'Well, well. Valerie isn't far from Vallouris, is it, if you pronounce it French fashion?'

'No, it isn't, sir. Why?'

'Because, according to Marriott, Dawson's last word was Valerie or Vallouris. Take your choice.'

'Good heavens! It can't be. She'd never...'

'Now, now, Haddock. No more eliminations, please. By the way, what do you know of Alf Fowles, the driver of the motor coach?'

'Fowles? Let me see. Lives in a row of houses down by the river. Married, with a family. A bit addicted to drink and has been up a time or two for drunk and disorderly. But never in connection with his driving. His licence is quite clear. Is he a suspect, too, sir?'

'Like the rest, but he has an alibi. Drunk all the time the crime was being committed, with French pals to prove it.'

'He's not likely to have...'

Haddock paused and smiled sadly.

'I'm too unsuspecting ever to be a good detective. I'll make inquiries, sir, and if I find any link between Fowles and the Alderman, I'll let you know.'

'That should do.'

Littlejohn's train left at 5.30 and after thanking Scrivener for the help he hadn't given and for the use of Haddock, the Chief Inspector left for the station. Scrivener was still immersed in his Teddy boys case.

A bit of gossip, a bit of local colour, squabbles, loves, hates, and Mrs Beaumont on the stage as Valerie. That was all Littlejohn had got from his trip to Bolchester.

'I'll keep in touch with you, Haddock, and many thanks for your help. Let me know how things develop.'

'You mean, sir…'

'In the house across the canal.'

The Chief Inspector's eyes twinkled and Haddock blushed.

The last thing Littlejohn saw of his honest friend as the train gathered speed was a slowly waving umbrella and a bowler hat held at arm's length.

Six months later Haddock married Mrs White!

10

DEATH OF A NAUGHTY BOY

Cromwell met his chief again at St Pancras. They had time to dine together before Littlejohn caught the 22.25 plane back to Nice. Cromwell had, in the course of the day, eliminated the Moles from the case.

'I had a word with Zurich, sir, and the police there got in touch with Lucerne. They did a good, quick job of work. It seems that the Moles arrived there from London on the night that Dawson was murdered. Since then, they've behaved perfectly normally. The hotel manager, who was questioned, said they'd been in for every meal, which puts quite out of the question any flying visit to Cannes...'

'I wanted it checking, Cromwell, just in case Mole had been up to some jiggery-pokery. He'd reason to dislike Dawson, who caused trouble between him and his wife.'

Cromwell took out his large black notebook, removed the elastic band, and consulted it.

'They seem to have checked-in at a hotel pending the arrival of the party at the Lucerne *Bagatelle*, where, I guess, they proposed to join them. Mrs Mole wasn't very well, the hotel people said, and stayed in bed late every morning. The police at Zurich checked the flights. Both of them joined the plane at London at 11.30, Swiss Airways, to Basle. Got there 2.15. They arrived at the Lucerne hotel about 5 o'clock, which means they got a train straight away from Basle to Lucerne. I think we can write them off. By the way, they're on their way back, too. They were checked out of Basle back to London at 3.50.'

'They must have had enough. I don't blame them. Pity I just missed them in Bolchester. They might have thrown a bit more light on Dawson and his affairs…'

It was half-past one in the morning when Littlejohn arrived back at Var Airport. Dorange was waiting for him on the runway, looking as fresh as paint, with a new carnation sprouting from his buttonhole. Littlejohn touched the flower and admired it.

'My father grows them at his farm above Nice. Thousands of them there. Sometimes I wish I'd been a flower-grower, too, old man. Much happier and more profitable than police work… Your wife is waiting in the car.'

Dorange insisted on returning to Nice without discussing the case.

'You need a good sleep first. I'll see you in the morning.'

At ten, Dorange was waiting for Littlejohn at *La Reserve* and talked to him over breakfast.

'This murder of Henri. The brutal killing of a child of thirteen is detestable at any time, but I must say I'd feel harder about it if Henri had been a nice little boy. As it is, he's been a great trouble to his parents and, sooner or later, would have been in our hands. A big, precocious boy, always stealing and lying to his father and mother.'

'The Curries must feel a bit put out about letting their boy, Peter, associate with him at all.'

'I haven't told them Henri's character. He could be very ingratiating and had a suave sort of charm. They might have found no wrong in him, although what Peter told them has shocked them, I admit.'

'What happened there?'

Littlejohn stretched himself voluptuously in his chair. It had been pouring with rain when he left London. Here the skies were blue and the sun hot, and he'd gone back into his light suit and underclothes. The gay throng was hurrying down to the beach, most of them clad in next-to-nothing, the sea was like glass, and the panorama of the coast clear and magnificent. The African and his camel passed on their way for another day of sweet nothing to do.

'The Curries allowed their little boy to go about with Henri, hoping it would improve Peter's French. You will remember, Peter returned home sick the other night after a day with Henri. After Henri's murder, M'sieur Joliclerc asked them to question their son about what they did.'

Dorange paused for effect and took a drink of his coffee.

'It was not a happy tale. Henri had a pocketful of money and paid for everything. He certainly added to Peter's experience of France. They not only ate their fill of ice-cream, but drank a number of apéritifs. Henri told Peter that Italian Vermouth was a fruit drink! Peter drank four Martinis. No wonder he was sick! Furthermore, Henri said he knew where he could get plenty of money. His parents deny giving him any. On the contrary, they hoped the Curries would pay for the boys' outings. They have missed no money of their own at *Bagatelle*...'

'When did it happen?'

'Henri was found early in the morning after you left. He had been murdered the night before, about eight o'clock. I have the dossier of the English people at *Bagatelle* here with me. It is just the same as before. They were all indoors at the time.'

'Wasn't Henri missed after eight on the night in question?'

'No. He told his parents goodnight just after seven and went to his room. They are busy with the affairs of the guests until late. He sleeps in one of the attics and they didn't go up to see him again. Next morning a motorist on La Californie saw a hand projecting from a bush just off the road and stopped to investigate. It was Henri…'

'Had he been up there, then, the night before and been killed?'

'Your guess is as good as mine, Littlejohn. This case is becoming more difficult, because we can't pursue the usual routine without causing a fuss. Had those involved been French we could have…'

'A *passage á tabac*?'

Dorange did not smile.

'Exactly. As it is, we must rely on you to use your own methods. Did you find anything helpful in England…in what is the place?'

'Bolchester? No. Nothing much except atmosphere and a lot of gossip. It may help.'

It helped a lot, though.

Littlejohn found when he got to *Bagatelle*, that it had made a lot of difference to his outlook on the case. He was able to set Mrs Beaumont in her correct perspective as a well-respected woman of the town and one who'd helped, almost befriended Dawson. Marriott in his shabby little shop. The Hannon sisters in their dismal old-fashioned home, dominated by the shade of their father. Gauld, a rebel at home, hating Dawson and his sort, and finding some kind of recompense in Mary Hannon's company and in carrying on an affair with her. It was the same with them all. Littlejohn realised that after his visit to Bolchester, the characters in the Dawson case had altered. They would never be the same again to him. It was like changing spectacles on the physical plane.

Dorange had left him to it and gone to join M'sieur Joliclerc at his office.

'Well! And where the 'ell have you been? Don't you know

we've been all over the place for you? Your wife wouldn't say where you were and there's been another murder.'

Marriott greeted Littlejohn on the doorstep and looked ready to burst into a torrent of abuse.

'I've been to Bolchester.'

No use beating about the bush any longer. Marriott turned sickly pale.

'What for?'

'That's my business. I want a word with you first, sir.' Marriott stood aside and let Littlejohn in.

'The French police said you'd be here at eleven. So I stayed in. The rest have gone to Grasse for a change. They'll be back to lunch. They can't stop in all the time. It's not good enough. At this rate, we'll all soon be barmy. The French police won't say when we can go 'ome and we've had another of those gruellin' inquiries. They gave us 'ell again. And it wasn't as if any of us had killed the boy. It's just some dirty local swine who's done it. And you away just at the time we needed you most.'

Littlejohn let him go on. Marriott was completely demoralised. All his cheek and swagger had given way to a dejected kind of hysteria. His complexion was yellow and there were dark circles under his eyes. He'd been helping himself with alcohol in some form or other...probably whisky.

'Well?'

Marriott was almost in tears. He didn't wait for Littlejohn's answer. Instead, he continued his hysterical chatter.

'You don't know what it's been like here since the third murder. Police everywhere. And they questioned us for half an hour a time...each one of us...half an hour without stop. And they tried to tie us up and get us to betray one another and say one or the other of us was out at the time of the murder and had done it. It's not right. We ought to have a lawyer. And we had Madeleine and Joe, the caretaker and his wife here...we had them going crackers because of their son. He's been taken to the mortuary and she's gone to 'er mother's. Joe took it better, although he's like one stunned. I don't blame 'im, but it's rotten for us. We got a new cook and waitress this mornin', but yesterday the ladies of the party 'ad to make the beds and Mrs Bewmont did the cookin'... Joe stayed and did the buyin' and sweepin' out and such, but what'll 'appen next, I don't know. And they won't give us permission to go back to England. I've tried to get the consul 'ere, but he's on holiday and his deputy's French and he's not much 'elp. *If only they'd let us go 'ome...'*

He stopped out of sheer exhaustion, tears running down his cheeks and off his chin to be dried up in his tie. He'd been drinking and was at the end of his tether.

Littlejohn looked through the window until Marriott could control himself. The villa stood on rising ground and below he could see the sea, with all the diversions of holiday-making going on. Yachts, bathing, clusters of striped sunshades, streams of cars running along the Croisette. Immediately beneath, the main road to Nice from Aix-en-Provence, with a string of ever-moving cars hurling itself past the end of the avenue which ran straight down from the door of *Bagatelle* to the sea. Down the avenue, across the main road, and turn left; then straight on for a bit. Then you'd be right at the spot where Dawson and Sammy had been found.

'What did you want me for?'

Marriott was sniffing and mopping his face with his handkerchief.

'You'll excuse me. We're all at our wits' end. I sent 'em all out to Grasse to get 'em out of here. There's a curse on the place. It's been 'ell lately. I don't know what we'd 'ave done without Mrs Bewmont. I take back all I've said about that woman. She's kept up the morale of the party. We'd all 'ave gone crackers if she 'adn't been 'ere. I've got to 'and it to her.'

Littlejohn hardly heard. He was watching the man outside.

'Who's this?'

'It's Joe…Joseph Bernard's his full name. Him and his wife 'ave been caretakers 'ere for several years. A good couple and it's a pity about their son. He was a rotten little beggar, but they don't deserve what's come to 'em.'

Still Littlejohn hardly heard.

Bernard had arrived mounted on a strange vehicle, familiar in France, but never seen at home. A motor bicycle behind and, in front, a kind of low cart, like a small hand-cart, which the bike pushed along before it, with the rider steering the whole contraption from the back. Bernard had been to market and the cart was loaded with a basket of vegetables, bottles of wine and Vichy water in a crate, three chickens flung on the bare boards…

Bernard started to unload his cargo, slowly carrying one bundle after another through to the kitchen behind. He seemed in a dream, automatically doing what had to be done, shuffling with tired feet to and fro, a picture of grief and hopelessness. Then, the vehicle unloaded, he started the engine again with the kick-starter and guided it into a wooden shed in the garden at the side. Littlejohn listened.

'Be quiet a minute!'

Marriott almost jumped out of his skin, but stopped his whining tale.

No sound of the engine.

'Is this window glazed with plate-glass, do you know?'

'Yes. It's all plate-glass. I believe Mr Turnpike couldn't stand noise and after he bought this 'ouse, he found he got annoyed by the traffic on the road and the sounds of the town. So, he had plate-glass put in and that made it better.'

Littlejohn left the astonished wine merchant and went out by the front door to where Joe was putting away his cart. He spoke to the man in French.

'Sorry, Joe, about what I hear. My wife and I offer you both our sympathy.'

The glazed eyes turned to his own.

'Thank you, sir. Why did they do it? What had my boy done to them? If I could get these hands on whoever…' He did it all mechanically.

'Do you always lock the doors of this shed?'

'No, sir. Why should we? Nobody would want to steal this poor affair. It is only good for bringing stuff from the market.'

'It is easy to start, Joe?'

'Certainly. I keep it in good order. If it goes wrong, I have to walk to town and bring back the load. It always starts well. See…'

He'd forgotten his grief momentarily, turned on the petrol, and gave the starter a kick. The engine purred into life.

'Could anyone take it out and use it without your knowing?'

'Why not? The windows don't let in much noise and there is always something going on inside the villa. Do you wish to borrow it, sir?'

'Later, perhaps.'

Joe was so bemused that he didn't even show astonishment. Instead, he stopped the engine, closed the doors and slowly slouched to the kitchen.

Marriott was on the doorstep watching it all.

'I thought you wanted to ask me somethin'.'

'I do. You knew that Dawson's name in the *maquis* was Vallouris?'

'Everybody did. He did enough spouting about it back home.'

'You also knew that Mrs Beaumont's name when she was on the stage was Valerie?'

Marriott's mouth dropped, his eyes popped, and his yellow complexion turned an even dirtier hue…like putty.

'Why…I…'

'Answer me, Marriott! This business has gone on long enough. Why did you start the Vallouris red-herring when you knew Dawson was speaking of Mrs Beaumont? He was half delirious and spoke the pet name her friends called her long ago.'

Marriott licked his lips.

'I thought Humphries had heard Dawson say it, too. He said since he didn't, but how was I to know at the time? Dawson might 'ave said Valerie. It's likely. I said Vallouris so that the French wouldn't pick on Mrs Beaumont. After all, she's one of us. I didn't want to get 'er in trouble. She's English, isn't she? We've got to 'ang together, 'aven't we?'

'You've said it, Marriott. Hang together. That's just what you will do if you don't show some sense. *Did you think Dawson meant Valerie?*'

Marriott hung his head.

'Yes. I was only...'

'I don't want to know why you started this red-herring. All I'm concerned about is finding out who killed Dawson and getting these poor, unhappy people home to Bolchester.'

The charabanc was pulling up at the gate. The only cheerful-looking member of the party was Alf Fowles, his lips pursed in a soundless whistle, his cap perched askew on the side of his head. The rest looked to be coming from a funeral.

'They've still got Alderman Dawson in the mortuary.' Marriott whined it *a propos* of nothing. Perhaps the mournful new arrivals reminded him of it.

The tourists had formed a ragged, rather bewildered group round the door of the coach; Sheldon was handing down his wife. Their visit to Grasse didn't seem to have relieved the tension. They formed a procession and sauntered to the front door of *Bagatelle*. Some of the women were carrying packets and parcels of scent and soap, obviously bought from the factories they had visited.

'I'll be back in a few minutes...'

Littlejohn left Marriott and made for the kitchens. The new cook, shapeless, dumpy and voluble, and the new maid, dark, passionate-looking and spoiled by a squint, were busy with the lunch. Joe Bernard was gathering things together and making a parcel of them.

'Could I see Henri's room, Joe? Are you leaving?'

The caretaker turned his glazed, grieved eyes on Littlejohn. A cigarette hung from the corner of his mouth, but he'd forgotten to light it.

'Yes, sir. I can't stay here any longer. I'm going now that these ladies have come to look after things.'

He nodded in the direction of the cook and the girl with a squint.

'They have always been decent to me and my family, but now…'

He looked at the two women and jerked his head in the direction of the stairs. Littlejohn joined him and together they mounted to the attics, two small, low-roofed rooms in the eaves. One of them was Henri's. An iron bed, a rough chest of drawers, and a curtain across one corner where the boy's spare suit had hung. The place had been tidied; it looked as if his mother had gathered together Henri's belongings before she left.

Joe was intent on finishing his tale.

'I didn't want to say it in front of the two strange women, but I can't stay here with a murderer in the house.'

'What do you mean?'

Bernard's eyes had a trace of panic in them and he started to sweat and gesticulate.

'One of my wife's knives is missing; the one she used for cleaning rabbits. She hadn't seen it since the night Monsieur Dawson was killed, when she used it for the rabbit she put in the chicken casserole. She remembered she left it on the table. Then, when she needed it again, she found it missing. We hunted everywhere. We were going to tell the police when… when they called and told us that our little Henri… After that we forgot until now.'

'Was Henri likely to be about the kitchens when the knife was stolen?'

'You mean, he saw whoever stole it…so…?'

'It may be so.'

Littlejohn didn't go into any more details. Henri, on his way to becoming a bad lot, wouldn't be averse to a little blackmail. In fact, his being flush with money and splashing it about to win the admiration of young Peter, seemed to point that way. Only Henri hadn't measured the danger. Neither, it appeared, had Sammy.

'Have you been through Henri's drawers and pockets; Joe?'

'Yes, sir. Nothing in the drawers particularly. The usual boyish things.'

But then Joe hadn't been the first to search. The police, who did it right away, found a few strange objects. A sheath-knife, a revolver without a trigger, odds and ends of jewellery, some good handkerchiefs, far too good for Henri, a murderous-looking piece of bicycle chain, and a frog left to suffocate in a box. And then five thousand francs in large notes.

'In his pockets the usual things, too, but too much money. Seventy-five francs, sir. I cannot understand it.'

Then he broke down and sobbed on the chest of drawers. Littlejohn put an arm round the heaving shoulders.

'Let's go.'

They descended the narrow staircase from the loft and reached the second floor. A long corridor with five rooms, and a bathroom and adjacent lavatory. Two of the rooms overlooked the front and two the back.

'Who occupies these?'

Joe explained with quick gesticulations. Himself and his wife, and Gauld, the two back rooms; the Curries the large front room with the adjacent small, one-time dressing room for Peter; and the two Miss Hannons in the remaining double room. Alf Fowles used the attic opposite Henri's. They could hear some of the occupants of the rooms who had come up to take off their outdoor things, talking behind the closed doors.

Another staircase and they were on the first floor. A more sumptuous affair, with a wide passage and a plaster goddess holding an electric lamp in an alcove at the end of it. Again, voices behind closed doors.

'Mrs Beaumont...'

Joe indicated room Number 1, as might be expected.

'It has its own bathroom. Also Number 3, Mr and Mrs Sheldon, has its own bathroom.'

Each private bathroom had a door giving on the corridor.

'Miss Blair in Number 2, once a dressing room for Number 1. Mr Humphries, Number 5, once a box room, and Mr Marriott in Number 6.'

As if to confirm this, Marriott emerged and solemnly entered the bathroom without speaking to either of them.

'Monsieur Dawson occupied Number 4, and there is a bedroom for the staff in the basement.'

Behind the closed door of Number 3, they could hear the Sheldons going at it *sotto voce*. They couldn't make out what was said, but it sounded like someone reciting a litany and receiving impassioned responses.

The bathroom on this floor was built over the kitchens and jutted out from the main building; at right angles to the bathroom along the corridor stood a French window. Littlejohn crossed and looked out. It overlooked the garden and the shed where Joe kept his motor-cart. There was a landing outside the window from which an iron staircase descended to ground level.

'I believe Mr Turnpike was afraid of fire. They say he had that put there for emergencies.'

Littlejohn turned the knob and opened the window.

'It's used, then?'

'My wife and I carry down the mattresses that way to air

them. It saves going down the main stairs and along the bottom corridor, sir. Will that be all?'

The man was obviously uneasy and eager to get to his wife.

'Yes, thanks.'

They went down together. Mrs Beaumont must have heard them talking and emerged from the lounge to meet them. 'Good morning, Inspector.'

There was acid reproach in the tone of it. Littlejohn didn't feel he needed to explain anything. After all, his time was his own.

'Good morning, Mrs Beaumont.'

'So you've been to Bolchester, I hear. I'm sure that would do a lot of good.'

She snapped her lips as she said it and her earrings and bangles trembled with her repressed annoyance.

'I'd like a word with you in private, if I may, Mrs Beaumont.'

She made a gesture that the lounge would do as well as anywhere else.

Littlejohn couldn't help admiring her. Three murders and the rest of the Turnpike crowd in a panic, and here she was keeping the flag flying, irritable, aggressive, claiming her rights to deference and proper attention.

'And what did you find out in Bolchester, Inspector, that you needed to leave us during such a crisis? Have you not heard that that young boy has now been foully murdered, as well? One wonders where it will all end and what the police, our own English force included, are doing about it. I've written to the Lord Lieutenant and our Member of Parliament. As far as I can see, we're going to be held here for the rest of our lives, if somebody doesn't make a stand. I have no intention of dying in Cannes...'

She paused to gulp in more air.

'First of all, Mrs Beaumont, I'm doing my best. I'm supposed to be on holiday, but that has, of course, taken second place. I'm not complaining, but I expect a reasonable amount of cooperation and good manners from all of you here.'

Partly because a catch of breath deprived her of the necessary air, and then again because she wasn't used to being rebuked in such fashion, Mrs Beaumont found herself speechless.

'Have you any idea how young Henri came to be involved in this business? It looks to me as if he were blackmailing someone in a small way and proved dangerous.'

Mrs Beaumont, now that she was asked to cooperate, changed her tack and became business-like.

'Of course, the boy must have seen or overheard something. A nasty little boy, who didn't wash his neck and picked his nose. I couldn't bear him near me. Precocious, too. You should have seen him eye the good-looking ladies up and down. Miss Blair and the Hannon girls... Disgusting! My father would have taken a stick to him and beaten the wickedness out of him. He got himself murdered because he was doing something nasty, you can be sure.'

'Did he spend much time in the guests' quarters of the house?'

'Of course he did. You couldn't keep a little sneak like him away. He had to pass the rooms on his way to his attic. I made a point of keeping mine locked on that account. I've no doubt he went in the bedrooms and went through the things. And he was always about the corridors and hall. You'd find him sneaking about at all hours and places. I'd made a note to take it up at the next meeting of trustees. I like the Bernard couple, but unless they did something about that boy, I was going to recommend a change. Now... It has solved itself, but most unsatisfactorily. It is horrible.'

Her mouth began to tremble violently and Littlejohn understood what a nervous effort she must be making to keep her head and set an example to the rest.

Steps on the stairs and the party began to appear, foregathering ready for lunch.

'Will you stay for lunch, Inspector?'

'No thanks, Mrs Beaumont. But I'd like another word with you before I go. I'll be back this afternoon.'

They were all crowding round him like distressed travellers in a storm. Marriott, his mouth moving, half-drunk already; the Hannon girls, with Mary hanging behind to be near Gauld and Elizabeth tittering nervously and asking Littlejohn wherever he'd been and when they could go home. There was a sob in her voice. Sheldon was paler and worried, but greeted Littlejohn with hearty relief. His wife, who looked at him as though she blamed him for the whole ruined holiday, was pale and strained and, in her smart black costume and expensive blouse and shoes looked attractive, if it hadn't been for her look of selfish eagerness for any news Littlejohn might have about their release.

Mrs Beaumont was quick to free the Inspector from questions and greetings. It was quite a business getting away. They all wanted to shake hands with him, and were eager to take his advice and do just what he said.

Mrs Beaumont led the way to the little office Littlejohn had used before for his interviews.

'Now, Inspector. What is it?'

'It's about Dawson. I want a long talk with you about him and his goings-on in Bolchester. But first there's the matter of his dying words…'

She looked calmly at him.

'Yes. About the *maquis* or something, wasn't it? Marriott told me. He breathed the name of someone in the Resistance, didn't he? According to Marriott, the French police regarded it as a clue about who might have murdered him. I think…'

She was talking for talking's sake now. And the more she said, the faster she said it, trying to avoid the crucial question. It was obvious to Littlejohn that Marriott had already told her what he was going to ask her.

Mrs Beaumont paused, her eyes sought Littlejohn's, and there was a pleading look in them. She laid her hand across her breast as though to hold in the beating of her heart.

'Mrs Beaumont, the name Dawson uttered was taken down by Marriott. He said it was Vallouris, Dawson's nickname in the *maquis*. Actually, it was Valerie, and Marriott drew a red-herring across the trail to shield someone. Isn't it true?'

She drew in her breath with a sob.

'Isn't it true that your stage name was Valerie, and that your old friends, including Dawson, called you by it? Dawson was either wanting you or incriminating you.'

The interview there was cut short, for Mrs Beaumont, with a long low wail, subsided like a pack of cards and collapsed on the floor.

11

THE LAST OF SAMMY

Littlejohn called Mrs Currie without more ado. She seemed to be the only reliable one of the party capable of dealing with the prostrate Mrs Beaumont. Between them they gave her alternate doses of brandy and smelling salts and when Mrs Beaumont first opened her eyes and saw Littlejohn, she looked like passing out again. Her face was ashen, her lips blue, and she seemed ten years older. Although she had obviously something of great importance to tell the Chief Inspector, there was nothing for it but to put her to bed and let her be quiet. Mrs Currie saw to this and Littlejohn, to avoid the rest of the anxious guests, took himself off by the side door and went to the town hall.

Dorange and Joliclerc were in the latter's office and they both greeted Littlejohn with enthusiasm. He found it difficult to explain to them what he had done at Bolchester and they looked nonplussed at the thought that he had drawn a blank there. As far as the Chief Inspector was concerned, it amounted to nothing but filling in a kind of backcloth for the drama now playing itself out in Cannes, and although it was a part of his usual technique, he found it hard to describe and justify.

'At least, it looks as if the focus of the crime is at *Bagatelle*,' said Dorange at length. 'Unless something develops very quickly, we shall have to employ rigorous measures to find the culprit.'

Littlejohn knew what that meant. Ceaseless and ruthless grilling to the point of torture until somebody broke down. He wanted to avoid that.

M'sieur Joliclerc had another large dossier before him. Presumably *Dossier Henri,* this time. He flipped it with his forefinger.

'Forty pages and little light on the affair. They all seem to have had alibis again. We're relying on you, Chief Inspector. They can't stay in Cannes for ever. Dawson is to be buried in the English section of Cannes cemetery tomorrow. Miss Blair, his nearest relative, has agreed to this. Sammy's funeral is today…'

'I'm going to suggest to you, sir, that the crimes didn't happen where the bodies were found, but in or near *Bagatelle*. Then they were conveyed elsewhere to draw us off the scent.'

There was a hush as the thought penetrated the minds of the two Frenchmen and then they both sat bolt upright and fixed Littlejohn with their dark astonished eyes.

'In a shed adjoining the villa there is a small cart propelled by a motorcycle. If the crimes were, as I say, committed within the precincts of *Bagatelle* and then the bodies moved elsewhere, the whole matter of alibis falls down. A brief knife-thrust, the body is hidden, say in the shed, and then, at the killer's leisure, carried away on the cart. There are two entrances as well as the front door. One at the back and the other through a French window at the side. Also a staircase leading from the first floor into the garden. The late owner of *Bagatelle* couldn't bear noise, so he had thick glass put in the windows. The whole operation would have been soundless.'

Dorange and Joliclerc received it with relief and excitement.

They rose to their feet and the examining magistrate even started to clap his hands.

'The very thing. We must see the truck right away. As you say, the alibis are worthless. We'll go at once.'

And M'sieur Joliclerc put on his panama hat.

'Wait a minute. What's the hurry?'

Dorange poured himself a glass of iced water and slowly sipped it.

'We have another line of approach, too. The bank notes found in Henri's belongings and presumably part of his spoils as blackmail. Two of them were new. We hope to trace them. Our men are on the job and we expect their reports soon.'

The air was stuffy in spite of the open windows and the fan on M'sieur Joliclerc's desk, and there was hardly room to whip a cat round in the office. Law books and records filled one side, there was a large scale map of Cannes facing them, and on the third wall a huge chart of the whole of the Alpes-Maritimes. An armchair, three plain wooden ones, and then a small desk for M'sieur Joliclerc's clerk, pretending to be busy writing, but taking everything in.

It was lunch time and the streets were empty. From where he stood at the window, Littlejohn could see the Rue d'Antibes drenched in hot sunshine. The only signs of activity were in the flower market, where now and then one of the stall-holders would shout at a passerby.

The café opposite was full of diners, inside and on the little terrace which spilled over the pavement. In the bar next door a dozen or so lazy drinkers were festooned round the counter.

Then, as though it had waited until all was quiet, a hearse appeared from the thick maze of streets in the old town. A large, sombre box of a thing in black wood, quite out of place in the coloured life of the square below.

'As a rule, we hold the funerals early in the morning, but

we've too many bodies on our hands at present. We're getting rid of Sammy right away. This funeral's been a snorter…'

Dorange bared his bright even teeth in a gloomy smile and patted his carnation affectionately; then he stretched out his snakeskin shoes and regarded them with great satisfaction.

'Sammy's left all he had to Georgette, who doesn't seem to mind at all what happens to the corpse of her benefactor and late protector. With characteristic thrift, she has re-opened the bar. Sammy's mother arrived from Marseilles yesterday. We had to leave a policeman there to stop the pair of them fighting. There was a right royal row.'

The hearse had halted at the morgue under the town hall and, as though eager to get rid of it, four men hustled out an ornate oak coffin with silver handles and ornaments and large enough to accommodate three Sammies, and shoved it unceremoniously in the hearse. Passersby doffed their headgear, if they had any, or crossed themselves. Those dining within sight of the depressing scene applied themselves more vigorously to their food and pretended they didn't see it.

'It's to be a second-class funeral and it seems Sammy's father, whose identity has suddenly been established, although all his life Sammy thought he was a bastard and had none, was buried in Antibes. So they're taking Sammy to join him there. It will be on a grand scale, with a priest and everything. Whatever he missed in life, Sammy's to make his exit like a proper Christian.'

'I wanted a word with Georgette,' said Littlejohn. The other two looked surprised and then Dorange grinned.

'We'll have to hurry, then, and race the hearse. Let's go.'

They left M'sieur Joliclerc, who couldn't contain his desire to see the petrol-cart at *Bagatelle,* and Dorange drove like a madman along the Croisette, hooting everybody out of his track, to Palm Beach.

Palm Beach looked like an ant-heap. The casino was closed and so were all the cafés in the square, presumably out of respect for Sammy. Somebody had draped the doorway of *Chez Sammy* with incongruous black curtains fringed with silver, and a dusty laurel wreath had been nailed where they met at the top. The square itself was full to capacity with taxis and private cars of all shapes and sizes.

The sun beat down on the scene and everything there seemed to shimmer and frizzle with the heat. When Dorange's little car snaked its way through the rest, it created quite a stir. Half the underworld of Marseilles had turned up judging from some of the faces in the vehicles, and the unexpected arrival of the most famous and most feared detective on the Riviera caused some uneasiness and bad feeling.

'It's in damned bad taste and he ought at least to have kept off till we got rid of Sammy,' said a dope-dealer in a large Cadillac. Sammy's mother was sitting beside him holding a big wreath in one hand and a sopping handkerchief in the other.

You'd have thought it was the funeral of a public benefactor. Instead of which, everybody had to be on the look-out for pick-pockets, who, though friends of the deceased, couldn't resist doing a bit of business on the side.

Georgette was nowhere about, so Dorange had to pull up at the door of *Chez Sammy* and tell the gendarme, who was there to see that rival gangs behaved themselves, to find her. When she appeared, there was a sensation.

The mistress of the late Sammy was on the arm of Bertie, owner of *Auberge Bertie* round the corner. She was draped in deep mourning with a crêpe veil almost dragging on the floor. Bertie was in black, as well. The hand of the dope-king sitting with Sammy's mother, also hidden in a mass of crepe and black satin, flew to his chest-holster, but he decided to settle with Bertie after they'd buried Sammy.

Dorange made no bones about dealing with Georgette. He drew her into one corner of the café where the rest couldn't see them and told her to lift her veil. She had dark rings under her eyes and they suited her swarthy beauty. She treated Dorange with hostile reserve, but gave Littlejohn a lazy smile.

'Well? Must it be now?'

'Yes, Georgette, and get it over quickly before the hearse arrives. My colleague, Chief Inspector Littlejohn, wants a word with you.'

Dorange put his hand on the chest of Bertie, who was starting to protest, and, with a quick shove, propelled him halfway down the room.

Outside, a deep silence fell on the square. They were all hoping, especially Sammy's mother, that they were going to haul off Georgette and accuse her of murder.

Georgette indicated that she was prepared to listen to Littlejohn. She even flashed her fine eyes at him.

'On the night Alderman Dawson was murdered…you remember it?'

Georgette nodded.

'Did Sammy go out? It was said in evidence that he stood at the door. Do you remember whether or not he went farther than that?'

'No.'

'Where were you? In the back room or in bed with somebody?'

Dorange was more to the point than Littlejohn.

'I was eating supper at the time.'

'How do you remember that? What *was* the time?'

'Eleven. I always eat about then.'

'And when Sammy was killed… You were indoors then?'

'Yes.'

'Did you hear any noise going on…the sound of a motor or a motorbike?'

'No.'

Bertie thereupon interrupted, waving his arms and thrusting his face in.

'The hearse! The hearse! It's here.'

Dorange turned and almost spat on him.

'Shut up and get out.'

Littlejohn persisted and Georgette didn't seem to mind. In fact, if she held up the funeral all day to the discomfiture of the lot from Marseilles, she didn't care.

'Was there anybody in the bar when it happened...say at eleven on both nights?'

'Yes. I came in the bar for a bottle of lemonade, and both nights Dr Molinard was here. He often calls. He takes a stroll along the Croisette as far as here, has a couple of *Picons,* and then walks back.'

Dorange intervened again with his customary realism.

'It's not a constitutional for his health. He's a pal of Georgette's.'

Shouts and scuffling from outside told that the hearse was actually entering the square.

More taxis, more posh cars, more flowers, and more crooks began to line up in readiness. Sammy's mother and the dope pedlar were trying to edge the Cadillac first behind the hearse, but a gang of Bertie's tough-looking pals from the Cannes underworld beat them to it and one of them, a thin sallow-faced youth like a slug, entered the bar pugnaciously but lost all his stuffing when he saw Dorange.

'What are you after, Bubu?'

'We're ready.'

'Well, we're not. Go and wait outside.'

A crowd of strangers, many of them unsavoury and a few of them seeking sensation, had gathered in the square and added to the congestion. A reporter was questioning Sammy's mother through the window of the car.

'What's the order of the service? Will there be music?'

The scent of funeral flowers, human perfumes and sweat, and garlic on the breath of the onlookers rose in the hot air. A page-boy arrived with a huge bunch of roses in one hand and another of white lilies in the other, but it turned out they were for the casino and not Sammy.

'Is that all?'

'Yes.'

Georgette lowered her veil, took Bertie's arm, and stepped into the square. Noises of sympathy, rage, and disgust rose as she appeared. The man in the next café, who was having a shave, thrust his head through an upper window to see what was going on, smiled through the lather, and then shut himself in with a bang. The vehicles began to jockey for position; two more gendarmes started to direct the traffic.

A coffin fit for a king, followed by a motley collection of vehicles filled with riff-raff eager to assert their claims and their friendships. One by one they disappeared round the corner and made for the main road to Antibes.

'Want to join them?'

'No, thanks, Dorange.'

'Well, just excuse me a minute. I'd better telephone Antibes and let them know what's hitting them. There might be a few gang scuffles in church or at the graveside.'

The square was almost empty. The neighbouring cafés were pulling down their shutters and the spectators were disappearing inside for drinks. Bassino, the stoker who'd found Dawson's body, was standing almost on the exact spot where Sammy had been stabbed. He wore a blue shirt and blue canvas trousers and kept an eye on Sammy's bar lest Dorange appeared. He'd had enough of Dorange.

Littlejohn made a sign to Bassino that he wanted him. The man hesitated and then came halfway to meet the Chief Inspector.

'On the night you found Dawson's body did you hear any sound like that of a motorbike or a small car?'

'Can't say I did.'

'Where's the head waiter?'

'At home. He's got to sleep in the day. They keep him up nearly till dawn.'

The worried eyes searched Littlejohn's face. Bassino hoped they weren't going to haul him in again.

'Did he ever tell you why Sammy told him to keep his mouth shut about events on the night you found Dawson? Now hurry, before Inspector Dorange comes and *makes* you talk.'

'I've got to get back to my job. All I know is, and I can say it now that Sammy's kicked the bucket, all I can say is, Sammy seemed to know who did it. He must have got a look or something at the man who stabbed whatsisname. Don't say I said so, but I think Sammy was putting the squeeze on when he got croaked. And now I've got to go. I'll get the sack.'

He almost ran as he heard footsteps in the café. Dorange only saw his heels vanishing round the corner of the casino gardens.

'Bassino?'

'Yes.'

'What was he after?'

'I was asking him about Sammy and if he heard if Sammy saw who stabbed Dawson.'

'I could have told you that. The head waiter there told us when we questioned him. With Sammy being dead, he'd nothing to fear. I let Antibes know. They're standing by with a squad of men. There's already been a bit of bother there. It seems that three of Sammy's pals called to see that all was right and proper. The sexton at the church was out fishing and they couldn't get anybody who'd toll the bell. One of them tried to do it himself and got a broken head. Entangled himself in the rope and it pulled him up to the beam.'

'What's all the fuss about, though? You'd think Sammy was a public benefactor.'

'It's his mother who's done it. She used to be a Madame in

Marseilles till they made it illegal. Now she's in the dope trade. When she heard Georgette had inherited or helped herself to all Sammy's possessions, she turned up in force, just to show she's not to be trifled with. So Bertie, who's taken over Sammy's interest in Georgette, whistled-up his own supporters. It's ended up in a grand funeral, but what'll happen afterwards is anybody's guess. There may be a few hospital or even mortuary cases if we don't watch them.'

DR MOLINARD. GENERAL MEDICINE.
ACCOUCHEMENTS.
CONSULTATIONS BY APPOINTMENT.

The consulting rooms were on the second floor of a block in the Rue d'Antibes. Dorange accompanied Littlejohn.

'I'll leave it to you,' he said. 'But if I'm there, there won't be any nonsense.'

Molinard was evidently one of the better-class doctors. The waiting room was comfortably furnished, with a thick carpet on the floor and modern pictures of the local school of artists on the walls. There was a nurse in uniform to attend to callers.

'Have you an appointment?'

'No. Tell him it's the police and we're in a hurry.'

The nurse, a good-looking young brunette, hastily looked at the only other occupant of the room, a middle-aged woman who would have liked to look younger and was probably a psychopathic case, to make sure she hadn't overheard.

'Will you sit down? Dr Molinard is engaged at present.' Dorange remained standing.

'Tell him at once that we're here and to hurry.'

It didn't take long, and then the nurse showed out a puffy-faced, middle-aged man with a black eye.

'How d'y'do, Gustave… Lily slugged you again?' Dorange said it with a chuckle to the emerging patient, who then seemed in a bigger hurry than ever to get out of sight. 'He's too fond of the young ones and his wife doesn't like it,' he explained to Littlejohn.

'Dr Molinard will see you now.'

A large, bright consulting room, with leather upholstery, a fine antique desk, a thick carpet, half a side filled with books. Cabinets of instruments, an inspection couch, a wash basin. More modern pictures on the walls.

The doctor was standing with his back to the empty fire grate, straightening his pearl-grey tie. He wore formal clothes; black jacket, grey trousers, and shiny, patent leather shoes.

A tall slim man, with the look of an Italian. Aquiline features and sallow face. Long, tapering, restless fingers and a habit of rocking on his feet. The first thing you noticed was the livid scar from the corner of his left eye to the edge of his nose. The disfigurement was a legacy from the Gestapo, who'd done it in his own consulting room after questioning him about some allied airmen they thought he knew about.

'Good day, Dorange.'

A suave bedside voice, fruity, and well-lubricated. Obviously, Molinard was a great favourite with his women patients. He watched the nurse clear up the files on his desk and take away the soiled towel from the washbowl with an inquisitive smile, and as she left the room, his hooded dark eyes caressed her shapely figure and slim ankles.

Dorange introduced Littlejohn and told the doctor what they wanted.

'You were a regular customer at *Chez Sammy*, doctor?'

As he said it, Littlejohn could well imagine the doctor's roving eye searching the place for Georgette's attractive arrival and eyeing all the girls who hung round the casino and called at Sammy's for a drink because it was cheaper there.

'I used to take a walk along the Croisette most evenings and call there for an apéritif on the way home. I spend a lot of time indoors, as you doubtless can guess, and that is my favourite walk. Sammy's is a kind of halfway house for me. I often take the dog.'

Molinard was uneasy. There wasn't much to show it, for he had himself well under control. But the pulse which throbbed in the wound near his eye was beating too fast.

'You were there, I believe, about eleven on the night the Englishman, Dawson, was stabbed near the casino…and again when Sammy himself was killed.'

'Yes. Do sit down. Perhaps you'll take a drink with me?' They all sat down, but the police officers wouldn't drink. 'Mind if I do? I've had a busy day and an emergency even over lunch.'

He poured himself a glass of whisky and started to sip it neat. He was trying to make up his mind what his visitors were after and what risk he ran.

'You weren't called on to give medical attention at the time, then?'

'No. I wondered why, in the case of the Englishman, because I must have been in Sammy's when the body was discovered. Instead, they rang up the hospital from the casino. I had, of course, left when Sammy's body was found.'

Dorange intervened.

'Probably Sammy didn't want you to start asking questions about Dawson. He knew quite a lot about it, but didn't want asking…'

'But surely, Sammy didn't…?'

'No. But he knew who'd done it.'

'You amaze me, Dorange.'

'Tell me, doctor,' said Littlejohn, 'was Sammy at the door at eleven on the night Dawson was killed?'

'It was a hot night, I remember. He was at the door for a while. Then he took a stroll along the pavement. I heard him greeting somebody…'

'What time would that be?'

'Eleven, or thereabouts. I know, because, as a rule, I'm regular in my stroll and usually leave Sammy's at eleven. The night the Englishman was stabbed, I looked for Sammy to wish him goodnight but he wasn't at the door. He was somewhere outside, not far away.'

'What about the night Sammy died?'

'He wasn't in when I arrived and I spent some time talking with Georgette. His manageress, you know.'

Dorange smiled and didn't trouble to hide it. Molinard hastily turned a feline glance upon him and as hastily removed it.

'Now, doctor, I want you to think carefully about the next question.'

The pulse on Molinard's wound had been slackening in speed. Now, Littlejohn watched it accelerate. The doctor took a handkerchief from his sleeve, wiped his lips, and in an effort to make it look automatic, also gently mopped his brow. 'Yes?'

'You say the front door was open?'

'It was a hot night and the air was heavy. Besides, it's rarely closed.'

'You were at the counter?'

'Yes.'

'Did you by any chance hear the sound of a vehicle pulling up or driving away whilst you were there?'

'Let me think.'

The tension in the brows died away and the beat of the pulse slowed down. Molinard was obviously relieved.

'What kind of a vehicle would it be?'

'I'd rather not put a leading question. Think.'

'The night Sammy died, I can't think of it. You see, I was talking with Georgette until I left. But the Englishman...yes...I think I did hear something. It wasn't a car, because there are so many passing there. I think it was the start of a motorcycle. That's right. Throwing my mind back, I've a vague idea I noticed it. I thought casually about it. You see, there are plenty of them about in the day. They come that road and round by the sea to the main highway again; it's a pleasant run. But at night, it leads nowhere and the type of people who go to the casino at Palm Beach then don't go on motorbikes. It's a rather unusual noise in that part so late.'

He gripped his chin in his fingers and then nodded.

'Yes; it was a motorcycle I heard.'

'And that's all you can remember of the two evenings in question? You just heard a motorbike…'

Dorange had butted in with asperity.

'What else am I expected to say?'

'Do you remember anybody else drinking with you at Sammy's, or hanging around or calling in?'

'There were one or two people there, but I didn't know them.'

'No more regular customers like yourself?'

'No.'

'Are they very busy at that time of night?'

'Not around eleven. The casuals have gone and there's only an odd one or two or a caller from over at the casino.'

The pulse was hard at it again. Molinard wondered what was coming next from Dorange.

'You say you were talking with Georgette at eleven on the night Sammy was murdered?'

'Yes. Do you doubt my word, Dorange?'

'Not at all, doctor. *Where* were you talking to her?'

'At the bar.'

'Think again.'

Instead of growing angry, Molinard looked afraid. He mopped his brow again and drank the remainder of his whisky in a gulp.

'When they came to break the news about Sammy's death to

Georgette, she was in bed. And someone, presumably a man, climbed out of the window of her bedroom and beat it.'

Dorange paused for effect and the doctor said nothing.

'I'm not saying that your being in bed with Georgette at the time Sammy's murder was discovered in any way incriminates you, Dr Molinard, but I advise you to be on the level with the police and tell the truth. *Did you hear a motorbike on the night Dawson was stabbed*? Answer me! The truth!'

Molinard licked his lips.

'Yes. I heard it.'

'And?'

'I saw it. That's what you want to know, isn't it?'

'That's better. Were you out on the pavement with Sammy?'

'Yes. We saw the motorcycle with a sort of cart attached, without lights, coming away from the car park on the sea side of the casino. That's all. Except that Sammy said, "I know that vehicle and what's it doing here at this time of night?"'

'You didn't see who was mounted on the motorbike then?'

'No. It was just on the edge of the range of the lights of the square and I couldn't make out much. But I think Sammy knew. I think that's why he was killed. He must have interfered.'

'You mean blackmailed.'

'Have it that way if you wish.'

Dorange stood before the tall doctor like a ruffled gamecock. 'Why didn't you tell us all this before? Why didn't you call at the police station and help us?'

Molinard licked his dry lips again.

'I didn't wish to be involved. I have my position to think of. I can't afford to be mixed up with police and murder. My patients...'

'I'm very annoyed about this, doctor. You've caused my English colleague and me a lot of trouble and waste of time.'

'I'm sorry.'

'So you ought to be. Good day.'

And with that, Dorange gathered up Littlejohn and they left the doctor to think it over.

On their way back to the car park, Littlejohn called at the town hall with Dorange. There was news about the banknotes found in Henri's drawer at *Bagatelle*.

The local squad had been round the banks and luckily one of the offices had identified the numbers of the two notes.

They had been paid out to the cashier of the Palm Beach casino the day after Dawson died.

12

THE MAN WHO ASKED FOR HIS MONEY BACK

The cashier hadn't arrived on duty at the casino when the two detectives got there. He worked half the night and his comings and goings were erratic during the day.

'He'll be here around six.'

'Let's just have a further word with Georgette then,' said Littlejohn.

Sammy's funeral was over and the motley crowd of mourners had dispersed. Even Sammy's mother and her bodyguard of waterfront hoodlums had gone back to Marseilles. The police had advised her to get going and to keep her presence out of Cannes. She had sworn to return. Meanwhile, Georgette had opened *Chez Sammy*. It was already full. A real gala night to celebrate new management.

Georgette was at the counter doing the honours. She had put aside her weeds and was dressed in a sky-blue blouse, with slacks and shoes to match, and nothing else. Her breasts showed between the slit in the blouse which she hadn't zipped-up, but nobody seemed to mind.

'Come here,' said Dorange unceremoniously, and Georgette followed like a lamb into the back room. She had evidently been doing a bit of private entertaining there, too. There was a bottle of cognac on the table and four glasses. Somebody's health had been drunk.

'The Chief Inspector has some questions to ask you, Georgette. Answer him quickly and see you tell the truth.' Georgette rolled her eyes.

'How could I do anything else for you, M'sieur Dorange?'

'No cheek, my girl.'

Littlejohn got to business before the other two got to blows.

'We know that Sammy guessed who killed Dawson. Did he say anything to you about it, Georgette?'

'No, sir. He was a secretive type. How do you know...?'

'Let me ask the questions. The day after Dawson was stabbed outside here, were you in the bar all day?'

'Yes.'

'What was Sammy doing?'

'He went out.'

'What time was this?'

Outside in the café it was like a jubilee. Voices raised, health being drunk. They even toasted Sammy, spoke well of him, and asked that he might rest in peace as they downed their apéritifs.

'What time? It was early. He used to stay in bed late in the mornings, but that day, he got up about nine, ate his breakfast, and went off before I got up.'

'How did he seem?'

'*Pardon...*'

'Was he pleased with himself, jovial...or thoughtful?'

'Ah! He was very occupied, but in a good humour. He always was when he'd profitable business to attend to.'

'And he didn't say what it was. Did you ask him?'

'No.'

'What time did he leave here?'

'About ten.'

'Do you know what direction he took?'

'Yes. He turned the corner and went along the edge of the shore towards the Nice road. He walked, too, which was most unusual.'

'I thought you were in bed.'

She turned on Dorange.

'I could get up to see which way he went, couldn't I? I looked through the window.'

'And when he returned?'

'He was very pleased with himself. He had money.'

'How do you know?'

'I saw him put it in the box in the desk drawer. They aren't there now.'

'I'll bet they're not!' said Dorange bitterly, and left it at that.

'How much would there be about?'

'I don't know. Not very much. Perhaps ten one-thousand notes.'

'Did he go out again?'

Georgette thought a bit. Dorange was quick to take her up.

'You were in bed when we found you after Sammy's murder. I'm not asking any questions about you personally or who was with you, but was Sammy out the night he died and for how long?'

'He went out about seven and I never saw him again.'

'Did he come back at all?'

'I wasn't in the bar.'

'We know all about that, but who was serving drinks while Sammy was away?'

'Odette. She's left. She went when Sammy died. We didn't get on.'

'I'm sure you didn't! Did Odette say anything about seeing Sammy after seven o'clock?'

'Yes. She told M'sieur Joliclerc he'd been away since seven. I'm surprised you didn't know.'

'No cheek, my girl. You'd better get off and see to your

customers. Otherwise you'll have no takings. They seem to be having drinks on the house.'

Georgette, swinging her hips, accompanied them to the door.

The cashier had arrived at the casino and they found him arranging his desk and setting out his racks of *jetons*. A small fair man with a little moustache smeared across his upper lip, and buck teeth. He looked half asleep.

The manager of the casino introduced Littlejohn; the cashier knew Dorange already and treated him with great respect. The casino detective was leaning against the desk; a tall, thin, cadaverous man, with a long nose and a poker face.

Dorange took the lead.

'You've heard of the death of the little boy at *Bagatelle*?' The cashier made noises of concern.

'Shocking!'

'Uhu,' said the house-detective without moving a muscle.

'He had in his possession two new thousand-franc notes which we find you drew from the bank on the day after Alderman Dawson died. You've heard of Alderman Dawson?'

'Certainly. A shocking business.'

'Uhu.'

'Now I know this is going to be difficult, because you've so many people changing notes for chips and back again. But do you remember handing out any new notes to English people, say last Tuesday at any time?'

Littlejohn intervened.

'It would probably be during the day. As far as we know, they didn't come here at night.'

The cashier looked completely blank and shook his head.

'We have so many… No… I couldn't remember particularly. So many come and I'm too busy seeing I get the right money and pay out correctly.'

The casino detective made noises showing that he was thinking and getting ready to talk.

'Uhu. Did you keep the admission card that was cancelled?'

The cashier still looked blank.

'The card that was returned. The row between the man and the woman. She wouldn't let him play and we gave him back his subscription.'

The cashier was desolated, but didn't seem to remember anything about it. But the manager did.

'Of course. It was referred to me. I agreed to refund the money. The English have so little to spare these days. It was the least we could do.'

Dorange was getting fed-up.

'We don't want to know about your private sentiments. What's all this about?'

The manager almost ran to his office and returned with a small card.

'The card of admission to the gaming tables. Here it is.'

'But how is this connected with banknotes given out by your cashier?'

The manager gesticulated and was voluble.

'To enter the gaming rooms one must have a membership ticket; weekly, monthly, or yearly. The Englishman who took out that ticket must have wished to gamble for a month. He seemed embarrassed when he found that the cost was two thousand francs. He was more embarrassed when his wife came to him and asked him what he had paid for it. They quarrelled and he then asked if we would take back the ticket and return his money. I agreed, of course. With the present currency allowance, it is difficult. But, I must say, his wife need not have made such a fool of him before everybody. She called his attention to what he could buy for her with what he had paid for the ticket, said he was a fool, and that as they were only in Cannes for a little over a week, it was like his stupidity to take a ticket for a month.'

The cashier had just remembered and showed an inclination to join in but the casino detective silenced him with a gesture from his long, cigarette-stained fingers.

'While all this was going on, money was passing, so, of course, we didn't return the actual notes the Englishman had paid; he received others.'

'And those,' said Dorange, 'you had drawn from the bank that day?'

'Yes.'

Littlejohn hardly heard what was going on. It was the name on the ticket which staggered him.

J Sheldon.

He handed it over to Dorange.

'We must interview Monsieur Sheldon again. This time at the police station...'

Littlejohn didn't like the idea at all.

'Will you give me another day to investigate further, Dorange, and, if I'm no nearer a solution, we can take and question Sheldon at your office then. I feel that any precipitate move now, might upset everything. After all, it's not proof positive that Sheldon killed Henri. The notes might have been given out to someone else by the cashier here...'

'No, sir,' said the detective at the desk. 'We have the sequence numbers of the notes. Those were the ones refunded to the Englishman, Sheldon. It was done in the afternoon, not, as is usual, in the evening, and the numbers you give tally with those at the top of the bundle we got from the bank. We also know the day, because it is the last of the shift on which M'sieur Ducreaux...'

He indicated the buck-teethed cashier.

'The last of the early shift. One week M'sieur Ducreaux works afternoons; the next nights.'

Ducreaux nodded to show that, at least, this was clear to him.

'Thank you.'

As the detectives left the place, Dorange looked worried. 'I shall be happy to leave Sheldon to you, Littlejohn, but if he...'

'If he bolts or shoots himself? I'll be responsible.'

'Very well, my friend.'

They shook hands and left each other. They were always shaking hands, as though it were the first or last time.

Littlejohn walked back to *Bagatelle*. The sun was setting and there was a chill in the air. People on the quiet beach between the casino and the main Nice road were gathering together their things and departing. It was the hour of the apéritif again. It suddenly struck Littlejohn that in the excitement and worry of the new revelation about the banknotes, he and Dorange had forgotten their usual evening Pernod.

Littlejohn let himself in through the fine wrought-iron gates of *Bagatelle*. The garden was at its best. The sight of the tropical trees and exotic flowers and the scent on the air... You wouldn't have thought it was a centre of tragedy and confused passions. Here and there the frogs were starting their evening symphony, croaking and quacking in the pools of the villas and hotels.

As Littlejohn approached the front door, Marriott appeared round the corner from the side garden. He had shed more clothes and was now wearing a nautical-looking singlet with blue stripes on a white ground. White canvas trousers, white shoes, and the same white cap. Marriott was the type who felt undressed if his head was uncovered.

'Evenin', Inspector. Any news? No? Dawson's funeral's tomorrow.'

He was smoking a cigar.

'I've lost me pipe somewhere and I'm reduced to smokin'

these things in the afternoon. Not bad…and cheap. You comin' to the funeral?'

'I don't know yet, Mr Marriott.'

'Trouble here is, you don't know what to wear. Hot as hell in the day and chilly in the evenin's. I'se be gettin' cold if I don't get indoors and put some warmer things on. Then there's the funeral. It's awkward. None of us has mournin' clothes and we've certainly not got the money to buy any. Why Marie Ann wanted Dawson buryin' here for, I can't think. It's not right. A man like him ought to have a public funeral in his own town. I gather it'll be expensive to get him 'ome and I believe he has a friend or two buried in the cemetery here. So it isn't as if…'

'No, it isn't.'

'Eleven in the mornin', it'll be. The Mayor and Town Clerk of Bolchester are flyin' over and should be here early. They'll 'ave to take us as they find us…in our holiday clothes at the funeral.'

Indoors, Mrs Currie greeted Littlejohn with the news that Mrs Beaumont was better and taking things quietly in her room.

'She said she wants to see you when you arrive. Would you care to go up?'

Mrs Beaumont was sitting in a chaise longue. She looked better and most of her vigour had returned. She was surrounded by the offerings of her Turnpike friends: chocolates, grapes, candies, flowers. She might have been a permanent invalid. Largest of all, a huge bowl of red roses, presumably grown in Nice and bought wholesale. Mrs Beaumont noticing Littlejohn's admiring look at them, smiled and said they were a gift from Marriott.

Things were looking up! Marriott, only a few days ago, had been blackguarding Mrs Beaumont for all he was worth.

'I'm sorry I behaved so stupidly last time we met, Chief Inspector. I've had rather a lot to put up with since we arrived here, you'll admit, and as a trustee, the responsibility has been very heavy.'

'Was that all, Mrs Beaumont? Now, I don't wish to distress you, and I can wait with my questions, but I'm sorry to say, time is running out and if I don't discover who's at the bottom of these crimes, the French police will take a firmer hand. You know what that means.'

She nodded anxiously.

'Indeed, I do. My dear late husband was once in a French prison arising out of a motoring accident. He was ultimately absolved from blame, but the few days he spent being questioned left their mark on him all his life. So much so, that when they invited him to become a JP in Bolchester, he felt he couldn't face it and refused. I do indeed understand...'

She paused for breath.

'First of all, then, Mrs Beaumont, I understand Lovelace, the late Alderman's manager at the coal-yard, wrote to you here. He mentioned, I think, that the business was not paying, owing to Dawson's way of life and the amount he drew from the company. Lovelace warned you not to put more money in.'

Mrs Beaumont's mouth opened and she looked annoyed. 'Who told you that?'

'It's my business to find out these things, madam. I've been to Bolchester recently, you know. Please understand me; I am not asking questions unconnected with this case.'

'Of course not. You've been very kind. Excuse my attitude. What do you wish to know, Inspector?'

'What did you do when you got the letter?'

'It was waiting here when we arrived, with the rest of the English mail. I opened it, read it, and then at once spoke to Alderman Dawson. He had recently given me a cheque in dividend. I asked him how he could pay a dividend if the company was almost bankrupt. I'm afraid he tried to bluff me and I got angry. I told him some home truths.'

'What exactly did you say, Mrs Beaumont? This is most important.'

'I accused him of using the funds I had invested in his business for his own extravagant purposes. I am rather hot-tempered when roused, Inspector, and I'm afraid I said things which would better have been left unsaid…'

'Such as?'

She paused, and then seemed to make up her mind.

'I told him I'd see him punished for the way in which he'd spent the money of myself and his other creditors. It wasn't so much loss to me as to poorer local people who looked like never getting their money back. My husband didn't leave me very well-off, but somehow, I seem to have a flair for the stock-exchange and I've made quite a lot of money from investments.'

She smiled and nodded almost coyly at Littlejohn.

'I fear I even went further than that. I accused him of throwing away money on good living he couldn't afford and spending it on certain women he liked to impress and with whom his relations were talked about in Bolchester. That was too bad of me, because, after that, he confessed such a lot to me and how he was trying to put things right, that I forgave him.'

Suddenly she halted, put her face in her hands, and started to weep bitterly.

And as she raised her grief-stricken face, streaming with tears, Littlejohn knew the truth.

'Did he ask you to marry him, Mrs Beaumont?'

It took her some time to collect herself. She mopped her face and drank some of the Vichy water from the carafe at her elbow.

'Yes. It wasn't the first time.'

Littlejohn could hardly hear her say it.

'He had asked you before and you had refused?'

'Yes. Twice, at home. In those days, he seemed to expect me to jump at the offer. He was presumptuous. On the night of his death, however, he was so contrite and humble. He spoke of his loneliness, of the prospect of a solitary existence, and a lonely end. I know it sounds silly and sentimental. Perhaps the place and the holiday had something to do with creating an atmosphere. I don't know. He said I was the same. Lonely and with nobody to look after me. We were old friends and knew the best and worst of each other. He said he had had stupid affairs with other women, but that he never respected any of them enough to ask them to marry him and share his life.'

It sounded like passages from Ouida, but Mrs Beaumont was moved and sincere and it was her own way of putting things.

'I denied that I was lonely and helpless, but now, I must admit his appeal stirred me deeply. I had half an idea that my money counted largely in the matter, but Alderman Dawson was a new man to me that night. I felt I could look very favourably on his proposal.'

'You told him so?'

'I did more. I was carried away by his appeal. Nobody has spoken to me so kindly and considerately since my late husband…'

More tears. It was embarrassing. The proud Mrs Beaumont had suddenly, in a gush, taken Littlejohn into her confidence and disclosed a holiday romance more in keeping with teenagers than elderly and staid dignitaries of a strait-laced town like Bolchester. And yet, why shouldn't they?

'I told him I'd marry him, but he must keep it secret until I said it could be made public. There were things to be arranged…friends to be prepared. We were not young people. It had to be announced and done with dignity…'

'Yes.'

'After our talk and its results, I must confess, Inspector, I enjoyed my dinner. A little excitement is the spice of life. Then, Alderman Dawson suggested a short stroll afterwards. I felt it would only cause the rest to talk and cast insinuations, so I declined. He said he'd go for a walk himself. He went to his death. That is why I take it so badly. If only I had gone with him... All this...'

Tears again.

'Is that all, Inspector?'

She looked at him with puffy eyes and face, thinking she'd said enough.

'Where did this important conversation occur, Mrs Beaumont?'

'In the little morning room where you held your interviews. You remember?'

'Yes. It lies at the foot of the stairs and people passing might overhear?'

'I agree. They might have done. The first part was so exciting and upsetting, that I may have raised my voice. In fact, I did, and I went to the door and closed it. I remember that.'

'Did you mention, by name, any of the women who were linked, perhaps in unsavoury fashion, with Dawson at home?'

She looked upset again.

'I fear I did in my rage. I threw in his teeth certain suspicions.'

'Such as the one that he had taken this trip to be near Mrs Sheldon?'

'How do you know that? I have never mentioned it to a soul since.'

'I heard things in Bolchester..."

'I did say that. I thought that was why he came. He said, quite humbly, that he had come to be near me and ask me again to marry him. I had already accused him of an affair with Mrs Sheldon, of spending the money from his business on her, and of being with the Turnpike excursion to be with her and make a fool of poor Sheldon behind his back.'

'I see. And when you closed the door... Did you see anyone about?'

She didn't want to answer. Her eyes fell and she started to wring her damp handkerchief.

'Well?'

'Yes. I saw poor Mr Sheldon going upstairs. He was carrying a heavy suitcase. I expect his wife couldn't wait for the porter to take it up. She must have sent him down for it.'

'And he overheard your references to his wife?'

'I'm so ashamed about it, Inspector. I wouldn't hurt that dear good man for the world. He has so much to bear from his wife and leads such a patient, exemplary life at home. And he does love her and puts up with so much. He did not see me as I closed the door after looking if anyone was about. He must have overheard the conversation, though. It was the way he carried the bag…as though all his strength had left him.'

Things were piling up for Sheldon with a vengeance! The banknotes, and now his overhearing the part of the Beaumont-Dawson dialogue, in which Dawson's connections with Mrs Sheldon had been very plainly stated.

'It does not seem to have made any difference to his gentlemanly way of treating his wife. She does not deserve it.'

Littlejohn nodded, then: 'Did Alderman Dawson always call you Valerie, Mrs Beaumont?'

'Yes. Many of my men friends did. The ones who knew me when I was on the stage years ago.'

'You know, of course, that Dawson's last word was `Valerie'? Marriott, who was there with Humphries, thought he was saying something connected with his spell in the *maquis*. He mistook it for Vallouris. It rather put us off the track for a start.'

Her lips quivered again.

'I like to think that William's last thought was of me and that, if he called for me by the pet name he knew me by, he perhaps wished them to bring me to his bedside. I was annoyed when I heard of Marriott's stupid behaviour. It prevented my going there. Not that it mattered, for he had died soon after. But

Marriott knew that I was known as Valerie by friends in Bolchester. He was one of the circle in the old days, though rather on the fringe, I must admit. It is rather like him to make a silly mistake like that. To put it simply, Marriott is not very bright. His father left him a fine business and he's let it run down out of sheer lack of enterprise and common intelligence. All the same, I bear him no ill-will.'

'And Alderman Dawson's movements on the day he met his death; can you give me some fuller details?'

She paused and thought.

'We arrived here from Lyons late in the afternoon. We'd stayed at Avignon and looked round there after lunch. We did some shopping and then came on here.'

'When you got to *Bagatelle* it would be tea-time, Mrs Beaumont?'

'Yes.'

'Then, you went to your rooms and changed and unpacked?'

'We hadn't very much luggage with coming by coach. We took up our light bags and left the larger ones down for the porter. I read my mail after I'd washed and I must admit I was eager to see William Dawson on account of what Lovelace had said. I came down at once and found the rest hadn't appeared, but William was here. It was then we had our talk.'

'And after that?'

'The heavier cases went up to our rooms, we unpacked, and then assembled for dinner. After dinner...well...I think you know the rest.'

'Dawson was in all the time until he took his walk after dinner?'

'Yes, as far as I'm aware.'

'Since Dawson's death, have you seen anyone hanging round the place; anyone suspicious?'

'There have been plenty, especially the police. After the Alderman died, they kept us under their eye lest one or another of us decided to flee, I expect. We have a gendarme in uniform always with us when we make our trips. Before him, I saw a man in a beret hanging round. I expect he was a plain clothes man…'

'When was this?'

'Almost from the very morning William Dawson died. About eleven o'clock, I looked out and saw a man watching the place from over the road. He wore a beret and a navy blue shirt and canvas slacks to match. He disappeared in the course of the day.'

'Can you give a closer description?'

'I'm afraid not. He was too far away. I know that he was medium built, rather stout, Italian-looking. In fact, a bit queer for a policeman. But then they've all kinds in the police here. Look at that little man, Dorange. You'd never find a detective like him in our British force. And the policeman who accompanies us on our trips; he wears a light canvas uniform and even takes off his coat and smokes cigarettes whilst on duty. Most inappropriate.'

'The man who was watching. When did he disappear?'

'After lunch. He watched everybody coming and going and then when I went out after lunch, he'd gone.'

'About Henri…'

'That dreadful boy!'

'Yes. Did you see him in conversation with anyone after the death of the Alderman?'

'He was in conversation with everybody. Irrepressible and cheeky. One never knew where one would find him next.'

'Did you ever see him in, shall we say, *tête-á-tête* with anyone?'

'I don't think so. He and Fowles used to lark about a bit; they slept in the attics. Also Peter Currie and Henri were together until Peter's mother didn't like the way Henri was leading Peter into mischief. I saw him talking to Mr Gauld once, and he did an errand or two for Mr Marriott…tobacco, I think. Oh…yes…

Once I came across Mr Sheldon talking with Henri. He was giving him some money. Another errand, no doubt. The money that boy earned…'

Sheldon again. This time, handing money to Henri. And that confirmed the casino account of the affair.

Another day to go and, if Littlejohn hadn't cleared up the case, the French police would arrest Sheldon and sweat it out of him at the police station.

'You know, of course, that the Alderman is to be buried in Cannes tomorrow morning?'

Littlejohn has forgotten Mrs Beaumont!

'He was very fond of France and when Marie Ann asked me about the interment here, I said it would be a good idea and avoid a lot of embarrassment taking back the coffin and making all the arrangements there. Will you and Mrs Littlejohn be coming? I do hope so. The Alderman would so much have appreciated what you have done on his behalf.'

Littlejohn wondered.

13

THE END OF AN ALDERMAN

It was dark when Littlejohn left *Bagatelle* after his talk with Mrs Beaumont. He felt he wanted a quiet night with his wife and he refused to stay for dinner.

All the lights of Cannes were on and in the bay a visiting American destroyer was illuminated. As he walked down to the nearest rank to get a taxi, Littlejohn met several American sailors dressed in white, cycling back from their afternoon's leave.

When he got to *La Reserve* his wife was waiting with a message from Dorange. He apologised for forgetting to make a rendezvous to bring the Chief Inspector back to Juan by car; he had rung up *Bagatelle,* but someone had said Littlejohn wasn't there. So on his way home he'd left a parcel for his colleague. It contained *Dossier Henri.*

'A bit of light reading for after dinner,' said Littlejohn. But he took his wife to the casino instead and didn't get to M'sieur Joliclerc's file until after midnight. With coffee and his pipe, he settled down and his wife read a library book to keep him company. Outside, the *mistral* had started to blow and they could hear the waves dashing on the beach and the trees groaning in the wind.

M'sieur Joliclerc had put all the inhabitants of *Bagatelle* on the grille again about the death of Henri. In some cases, he'd turned them over and over and could be said to have cooked them well on both sides. Especially Alf Fowles, *né* Alfred, whom the examining magistrate didn't seem to like at all.

Question: *You slept on the same floor as the deceased?*
Answer: *Yes. I've told you that about a dozen times already.*

Question: *Was his behaviour whilst you were there in any way strange?*
Answer: *It was always strange. He was a nasty bit of work.*

Question: *Give me any examples of his strange behaviour.*
Answer: *What's all this about? I didn't kill him.*

So it went on and on, monotonous, devoid of humour, patient, detailed and exhausting. In the end, Alf Fowles had defeated the examining magistrate. He'd passed on to someone else to recover his equanimity. *Procès-verbal d'Alf Fowles* (*né Alfred*) *terminé*). Alf Fowles's statement finished. It was scrawled in ink, like a dying message, across the foot of the paper.

As far as Littlejohn could make out, his own theory about the use of the motor-truck at *Bagatelle* had blown the question of alibis sky high.

Suppose it was Sheldon…

He'd been suspicious about his wife's carrying on with Dawson even back in Bolchester. Almost as soon as they arrive at *Bagatelle* he hears Mrs Beaumont having a row with Dawson and flinging in his teeth an accusation of spending her money on Mrs Sheldon and having an affair with her behind her husband's back.

After dinner, Dawson, elated by his success with Mrs Beaumont, goes for a stroll. Sheldon, mad with rage, hunting for some means of paying accounts with Dawson, sees the rabbit knife on the kitchen table. He takes it, follows Dawson into the garden of *Bagatelle,* and stabs him. It is all the work of five minutes to knife the Alderman, hide his body, and return indoors and join his wife with the rest.

As the night passes, Sheldon is urgently faced with the hiding of the body. He has seen the motor-cart in the shed. He and his wife retire about eleven. Whilst he's supposed to be in the bathroom, Sheldon has gone down the outside staircase from the first floor, taken the body on the truck, and dumped it on the shore.

Henri has seen Sheldon take the knife or making off with the motor-cart. And as Sheldon leaves Palm Beach after disposing of the body, Sammy spots him and recognises him. Sheldon has now two blackmailers to deal with.

Sammy arrives early next day at *Bagatelle* and watches the place. He knows the motor-truck belongs there; he also knows that Dawson is a guest there. He waits till he recognises the one he'd dimly seen the night before. Then, he approaches him and starts to put on the screw. They arrange to meet. It is the same technique as the Dawson affair, except that Sammy dies straight away.

When Henri starts to hint, Sheldon at first pays him to allay his suspicions and then, coming upon him alone, chokes him. Again the motor-cart at a convenient opportunity, and this time the body is taken to *La Californie,* just in case the police are keeping watch at Palm Beach.

The swift thrust of the knife or the twist of the scarf, and the rest by instalments at the murderer's early convenience. Littlejohn even remembered on the very night he and his wife had gone to dine at *Bagatelle* — the night Sammy died — Sheldon had been absent for ten minutes, changing his tie by order of his wife.

It seemed all right on paper. Motive; opportunity; and a man who though gentle in the presence of the woman who'd provoked this mad storm of passion and murder, had spent much of his life abroad in circumstances demanding ruthlessness and quick powers of action.

Yet, you could drive a carriage and pair through it all. How did Sammy recognise Sheldon, a perfect stranger, in the half-light?

How did Sheldon know of Palm Beach as a dumping ground near where he killed his victims? Had he been at Cannes before?

In the short time they'd been at *Bagatelle,* how did he know about the motor-cart and how to manipulate it?

And lastly, he didn't seem the killer type, although that wasn't much to go by. Littlejohn had known men too soft hearted to wring the neck of a chicken in their poultry-run or put their foot on a mouse from behind the skirting board, who, under passionate provocation, had committed the foulest crimes.

It was after one o'clock when his wife wakened Littlejohn. He'd fallen asleep over M'sieur Joliclerc's mass of questions and answers, his coffee was stone cold, and his pipe had fallen from his hand and singed the carpet.

The *mistral* was still whistling along the promenade and overhead a night plane from Nice was droning its way across the Alps behind...

Next morning Dorange called to pick up Littlejohn at nearly ten o'clock.

'The funeral of Alderman Dawson?' he said raising his eyebrows in question. In the boot of his car, Dorange had brought bunches of roses and carnations from his father's gardens.

'From you and me to our best customer,' he said as he

showed them to Littlejohn, who appreciated the gesture, but thought the comment a bit out of place.

Dorange made no reference to the time limit imposed on Littlejohn for the solution of the crimes in his own way, but the Chief Inspector had no doubt about the expiry of the ultimatum.

The wind had dropped and the sun was baking everything again. Holiday-makers already in crowds on the beaches at Juan-les-Pins and Golfe-Juan, all the little cafés busy, people sporting in the sea, frisky old gentlemen taking their morning promenades and eyeing the best-looking women and the most audacious bathing wear. The whole coast as far as you could see was bathed in sunshine, white hot and glowing under it.

...And Dawson had come here for his holiday and today they were attending his funeral.

Marie Ann Blair, assisted by Humphries, had spent a lot of time trying to find a suitable vehicle to replace the lugubrious continental hearse and Dawson's body went to the cemetery in a black motor-van, followed by the mourning excursionists from *Bagatelle*. Littlejohn and Dorange joined them at the graveside, after a service at the English church in the town. The Mayor of Bolchester, in his chain of office, the Town Clerk, the Mayor's valet, and another Alderman and a Councillor from Dawson's colleagues were also present. To mark this unofficial visit, the Mayor of Cannes, in his sash, was also present with many dignitaries.

It was the kind of finish Dawson would have liked. Sunshine, officials, brief graveside tributes, and great masses of local roses to speed him on his way.

The mourners from *Bagatelle,* unable to equip themselves in black, wore what they could. Quite in keeping with the sunshine and flowers which marked the occasion.

The Mayor of Bolchester, introduced to Littlejohn before the procession formed, wrung the Chief Inspector by the hand.

'Thanks for what you're doing, Chief Inspector. Bolchester is grateful. Get the swine who did this to Dawson!'

He didn't seem concerned with Sammy or Henri!

Humphries was dancing attendance on Marie Ann Blair, and Marriott was several inches too small, so, by universal request, Littlejohn joined Sheldon, Gauld and Currie in carrying the coffin to the grave.

Littlejohn and Sheldon stood together at the front of the cortege and the Chief Inspector wondered what were the thoughts of his partner. Solemn, upright, with a guileless look on his face, Sheldon kept casting his eyes in his wife's direction, as though to reassure her. She was dressed in white with a small black hat — the only *chic* member there — busy whispering to the Mayor. She had found some black earrings somewhere.

Marriott wore his tweed suit, a black tie, and carried his white cap. Littlejohn's eye caught the cap and he looked puzzled.

The English chaplain began to intone the burial service. Dawson's funeral seemed simple beside that of a neighbouring one, with a priest, an acolyte, the aspergillum, and the sonorous Latin of the committal. The deep black of the nearby mourners, too, contrasted sharply with those of the English party.

The ropes creaked as Dawson descended to his earth. A few handfuls of soil on the coffin by those gathered round; it seemed out of place to call them mourners. They looked too wrapped up in their own sorry plight with the police to grieve much. The only one who appeared in any way moved was Mrs Beaumont, who remained behind for a minute after the rest had gone and was seen detaching a rose from one of the large bunches and dropping it into the open grave which the diggers were already itching to fill in.

The civic party from Bolchester were eager to depart. The Mayor was to be the guest of the Mayor of Cannes at the restaurant at Var airport and, after a brief round of handshakes and farewells, the corporation officers divided themselves from the Turnpike excursionists and made for their cars. The Mayor, in departing, promised to communicate with the MP for Bolchester as soon as he got home and see that what he called 'the unjust detention of British subjects' should be dealt with.

'Get whoever is responsible for this, Chief Inspector, as soon as possible. It's appalling!'

The Mayor wrung Littlejohn's hand warmly, shook hands all round again, and was gone.

Sheldon tacked himself on to Littlejohn as they made their way back to the coach from *Bagatelle.*

'Are we likely to be allowed to make our way home very soon, Chief Inspector? This suspense and the upset of recent events are tellin' badly on my wife's nerves. She'll have a breakdown if it lasts much longer.'

He was as red as a turkey-cock from exposure to the sun, and the top of his bald head was beginning to shrivel and skin from the heat.

'Mind if we walk back to *Bagatelle,* sir?' asked Littlejohn. 'It isn't far and I'd like to talk with you.'

'Certainly. I'll tell Fowles we're not joinin' the party.'

Sheldon hurried to the coach and spoke to the driver and his wife. She seemed annoyed and looked back at Littlejohn with a scowl. She was never happy unless her husband was near, dancing attendance.

'My wife seems a bit put out. She depends a lot on me, Littlejohn. I told her we'll be back almost as soon as they are.'

The motor coach started and all the occupants looked anxiously at the two men left behind, as though Littlejohn were detaining Sheldon and they might never see him again.

Still difficult to concentrate on the case. The pair of them might have been taking a stroll; just a couple of companions thrown together on a holiday. There was even a spirit of comradeship between them. Sheldon took out his pouch, offered it to Littlejohn, and then filled and lit his own pipe.

'It's an English mixture I managed to get at a shop on the Croisette. You'll like it, I think.'

Trim villas ablaze with flowers, the hot sun, parties of holiday-makers passing in cars, and beyond, the sea alive with bathers, little boats, and the white sails of trim yachts taking part in a race.

'Do you know Cannes, Sheldon? Ever been here before?'

Sheldon nodded. He didn't seem to suspect that he was being questioned with a purpose, paused to look at the distant blue water and the long stretch of splendid coast, and breathed deeply in appreciation.

'Yes. I like it. Spent my honeymoon here. Been married twice. First wife came with me. Lost her years ago in India. Always wanted to see the place again. Can't say I'd have chosen these circumstances, though.'

He stopped to admire one of the gardens they passed.

'Wish we could raise flowers at home like they do here. I'm a bit of a gardener myself. Fond of exotic stuff. Colourful, eh?'

'The place changed much since you came years ago?'

'Can't say it has. Stayed at the Carlton in the old days. Can't do it now on the allowance and I must confess I'm not so flush with cash as I was then. Retired pay, you know.'

'Talking of cash, did you give any money to young Henri before he died?'

Littlejohn almost held his breath. But if he expected their relations to change through the question, he was mistaken.

Sheldon removed his pipe, tapped out the ash in the palm of his hand, and flung it away.

'Can't say I did. Why?'

'Think again, sir. You were seen handing over some notes to the boy. Were you sending him on an errand, or giving him a tip, or what?'

'I really don't understand quite what you're gettin' at, Littlejohn, but if you're suggestin' I had anythin' to do with that boy or his unhappy end, you're barkin' up the wrong tree. It's hardly fair of you to suggest...'

Littlejohn halted in his stride and faced Sheldon.

'Look, sir. You and I haven't had a talk since the murders occurred. I've got to question you all until I get the truth about everything that's happened at *Bagatelle* since you arrived. Unless I do and find out something very quickly, the French police will intervene with more ruthlessness than I've shown.'

'But you're not insinuatin' that I...?'

'I may as well tell you the truth, sir. Unless you've a very good tale to tell me, you will soon find yourself at the police station undergoing a typical French grilling. Are you aware that the local police found, hidden among Henri's possessions, some banknotes which have been traced to you?'

A funny thing about Sheldon; he looked hot-blooded and peppery, and yet he never seemed to lose his temper or his self-possession. He was either very stupid, very cunning, or else a man of strong and invulnerable character. Littlejohn was beginning to think it was the latter. Instead of losing his nerve at the news, Sheldon stood there, filling his pipe again, looking puzzled.

'What is all this about, Chief Inspector? You're not tellin' me that the police suspect me of all these crimes. As for the banknotes, how do I come in there?'

'You went to the casino the other day, sir?'

'Yes. I intended havin' a little flutter at roulette. Had to pay a sort of entrance fee to the gamin' tables, so bought a ticket which certainly cost me more than I intended. Felt a bit of a fool when they told me the price, but paid it. Then, Mrs Sheldon came up and made me see how silly it was payin' through the nose with currency so short. Saw her point. Explained matters to the man in charge. Refunded the money. Must say it was very decent of them.'

'And the thousand-franc notes you got back were found among Henri's belongings, sir. So you see...'

Sheldon gave one of his rare laughs, but it was a troubled one.

'I can explain that. My wife wanted some money and I'd nothin' but thousand-franc notes. Bit awkward, you'll admit, although they're only worth a pound a time. All the same, a woman wants some small change. Was goin' downstairs to see if anybody could change me a couple of large notes for smaller ones. Met young Henri on the stairs and asked him if his father could do it, or if he could get them changed. Young blighter said he could do it himself. Pulled out a fistful of small change and handed me the equivalent. Must have been those two notes the police found.'

'Have you spent all the small change Henri gave you?'

'No. Gave my wife the cleanest and kept the rest in my pocket-book. Want to see what are left? I paid for tobacco and some odds and ends, but I think I've about five hundred in hundreds or fifties here.'

He paused again. They were by this time nearing *Bagatelle* and to finish the talk before they got there, Littlejohn drew Sheldon to a wayside seat and they sat and examined the money which Sheldon produced.

'Here it is. Bit dirty. Somebody seems to have scraped the bottom of the barrel to produce a lot like this. Can't think where the boy got 'em.'

They were a soiled lot and one of them had been frayed at the edge and repaired with a strip of gummed-paper. There was the faint impression of a rubber stamp on the adhesive strip. Littlejohn held it up and could just make out the words.

FOWLERS BAN...

'Looks like Fowlers Bank, Littlejohn. Must have been brought over by someone from the old country, what?'

'Have they a branch in Bolchester, sir?'

'Yes. Don't use 'em myself, but it's the biggest bank in the town. Use the North and South bank, myself. Looks as if one of our party brought it over and gave young Henri a *pourboire,* as they call 'em over here. What?'

'It does. If what you say is true, sir, I'm very relieved. You see, I suspect Henri knew something about Dawson's death, or Sammy's, and was perhaps being paid to keep his mouth shut. If your explanation of the money which passed between you is right, it should prevent more awkward questions for you. Who of the party uses Fowlers Bank in Bolchester?'

Sheldon thought a moment.

'Can't help you, Chief Inspector. I'm not familiar with the party except as a fellow-traveller on the Turnpike excursion. Must confess that but for my wife, I wouldn't be here. She likes parties and people. I'd rather be just the pair of us together on a holiday. Perhaps you think I'm a queer cuss. Made that way, though.'

Sheldon seemed completely to have missed the implications of Henri's possessing a banknote given him by one of the party, and it was perhaps as well. He looked very relieved. In fact, his step was more springy and his shoulders well set back, like a man who's shed a burden.

'There are just one or two other questions before we turn in, sir. The night Dawson was stabbed. The statement shows you and your wife retired to bed at eleven. You left the party after being with them all the time since dinner.'

'Quite correct, Littlejohn. Why?'

'Did you turn in right away?'

'Absolutely. Sleep in the same room as my wife. She'll tell you I did. Felt tired after the trip. Wanted a bath badly, but this blasted French plumbin'... Somebody'd used all the hot water.

The tap was runnin' stone cold. Cold bath at bedtime not in my line. Left it till mornin'. Washed and turned in.'

'Did you hear anything going on after you reached your room? For example, did you hear noises of cars or motorbikes near *Bagatelle*?'

'There seemed to be plenty on the road goin' past. The windows are thick glass and soundproof, but can't bear sleepin' with 'em closed. Heard quite a lot of traffic. Bit of a nuisance havin' to sleep with the windows wide here, though. Mosquitoes, you know. Hell of a pest.'

'No sound of anyone driving up and putting away a car or anything at *Bagatelle*?'

'No. Why?'

Littlejohn didn't answer the question.

'Did you know the fellow Sammy, who was murdered? He keeps a bar near Palm Beach.'

'I've seen the place. Had a drink there, I think. A woman served us. Wouldn't know Sammy from Adam.'

'On your way to bed the night Dawson was attacked, did you see anyone on the stairs or landings?'

Sheldon thought again, smoking his pipe in hasty little puffs.

'Think we saw that lad Henri goin' up the stairs to the upper floor. Understand he slept there. Yes, I remember remarkin' to the wife that he was late up.'

'Did he see you?'

'No. He was dawdlin' along, apparently lost in his own thoughts.'

They were within sight of *Bagatelle* and they could make out Marriott standing by the charabanc, which Fowles was polishing at the gate, ready for garaging it.

'Bit of a nuisance, that little fellah Marriott. Common little chap. Wine merchant in Bolchester. Can't stand that white cap he wears. We've all got hats with us and we abandoned 'em when we got over here. One or two bought panamas for the sun, but this fellah got a linen cap a shade too big for him. Awful thing. Lets the side down, you know.'

'Has Marriott been in these parts before?'

'Says not. Says he was in France in the 1914-18 war and knows a bit o' French, but I've yet to find him make himself understood. As I said before, prefer not to be with parties. Never know what you're gettin', do you?'

Marriott spotted them in the distance and waved to them. Then he set out to meet them.

'Hello, you two. Solved the mystery on the way? Time the thing was settled, Inspector. You know we can't stay here for the rest of our lives, nice as it is. Give me 'ome sweet 'ome after this. Any nearer the solution?'

'No, sir. I'm doing my best, but three murders is rather a tall order.'

'Are you comin' to join us for a bit o' food? The new cook's not so bad, but I'll be glad when I'm sittin' down with me knees under me own table back 'ome in Bolchester and a nice steak and chips on me plate. I've 'ad enough.'

A hoot on a car-horn and Dorange drew up.

'I've safely seen your Mayor of Bolchester to the airport, and left them all enjoying an excellent meal. Can I give you a lift anywhere, old man, or are you staying at *Bagatelle*?'

Littlejohn had noticed Dorange leaving the cemetery with the official party and guessed the French inspector was giving him a further chance to pursue his inquiries. He knew now that the answer was expected which would either free Sheldon from suspicion, or else call for his arrest and questioning by the local police.

'I'll come with you to the town hall if you're going there.' It was a relief to get away from *Bagatelle* and the Turnpikers for a bit.

'Well? Anything new to report, Littlejohn?'

They were cruising along the Croisette again. Dorange seemed always intent on combining business with pleasure.

'Yes. Sheldon changed the large notes he got from the casino for smaller ones. Henri did it for him from a wad he had in his pocket. Sheldon seemed quite surprised.'

Dorange shrugged his shoulders.

'Without Henri here to confirm that, we can't rely on the statement much. Anybody might say that, when driven in a corner…'

He skimmed across the roundabout near the town casino, the constable on duty there saluted smartly, and they drew up at the police station.

The atmosphere between the two men was getting strained. No more suggestions about lunch or an apéritif now. Dorange was nursing the impression that Littlejohn was shielding his compatriots just because they were English.

'That's not all, Dorange. Among the small notes which Sheldon got from Henri, there is a frayed one bearing on the adhesive tape used to repair it, the stamp of a bank in Bolchester.'

Still the shrug of the shoulders.

'Who's to say that Sheldon wasn't showing you small notes which have no connection with the event, just to prove his case?'

'The note has passed through the hands of one or the other of Sheldon's fellow-trippers. He doesn't bank with the firm whose name appears on the note.'

'What's the next move, then? I think I ought to warn you, Littlejohn, that the Prefect has been speaking with Paris, who, in turn, have contacted the British Embassy. He has complained that the discretion asked by your Embassy is hampering the investigations of the local police.'

Dorange handed Littlejohn one of his cheroots, just to show he was still friendly, and lit both of them.

'This is not my doing. The head of the *Sûreté* at Nice keeps asking me for results. I tell him word has gone forth that the affair must be treated with discretion. He has lost patience. My instructions now are to bring in and interview every suspect. Sheldon is the first. I have complained about pressure of today's business. The time limit is ten tomorrow morning. Sheldon is to appear at the police station then.'

'So that gives me just tonight?'

'I wouldn't put it that way. We aren't antagonists, you know. Both of us want to bring the guilty man to justice. You can be present at the interview.'

'The *passage á tabac*?'

Dorange smiled sadly and shrugged again.

'I'm sorry. We both have our own ways of doing our duty.'

'May I telephone?'

'Certainly.'

Littlejohn put an urgent call through to Bolchester and asked for Haddock. The humble detective was soon speaking back, with what sounded like a plum in his mouth, for his agitation at the importance of a long-distance call from his famous new friend had almost bereft him of speech.

Littlejohn asked him to find out from Fowlers Bank, if he could, who had been issued with the damaged note and, failing that, to find out which of the Turnpike trippers was a client of Fowlers.

Dorange, who had been listening, again shrugged his shoulders.

'It doesn't seem much to go on, old fellow, but I hope it works. After all your trouble and a spoiled holiday, you've earned success. And a good lunch. Let's go the *Champs Elysées* and drink to your success.'

They left the police station arm in arm.

14
A LADY VANISHES

The lunch wasn't very successful. They ate a spread of hors d'oeuvres, omelettes, cheese, and then went on to coffee and more of Dorange's cheroots. Both men tried to be sociable, but each had his own problem. The French detective was the more serious of the two. He was obviously worried, wondering if his confidence in Littlejohn was going to be misplaced.

Littlejohn's glance wandered round the café. A youth and a girl eating ices on the next table, but more interested in each other than in their food. He kept caressing her, kissing her bare arms and neck, and then taking another mouthful of ice-cream. On the pavement a father was trying to take a snapshot of his family of three with a Kodak. The youngest boy, a child of about five, wouldn't keep still and his father eventually boxed his ears in a rage.

'If you don't think Sheldon committed the crimes, who did?'

Dorange had left the subject of contention until the lunch was over. Now they were back again. Who killed William Dawson?

'I don't know…'

'Then why… ?'

'But I think I'll know before morning.'

Dorange slowly flicked the ash from his cheroot. He looked tired and his face was drawn and anxious. The head of the *Sûreté* at Nice had given him the rounds of the kitchen that morning. In fact, he'd told Dorange that his confidence in Littlejohn had been foolish and that the English detective was working against the French police to get his fellow-countrymen out of a jam.

'Can't you tell me whom you suspect, Littlejohn?'

'If I tell you, it adds to your responsibility; if I keep my own counsel for a few more hours, I can give you a proper tale, I think.'

Suddenly a gendarme from the police office appeared round the corner, anxiously peering in the cafés on the waterfront. When his eyes fell on Dorange he almost broke into a run. The two Inspectors were on their feet in a minute and hurried to meet him.

Mrs Beaumont had vanished from *Bagatelle*!

The man on duty, watching the excursionists at *Bagatelle*, had been taken completely off his guard. The party had lunched without Mrs Beaumont, who'd had a tray taken to her room. She'd said she was too upset by the funeral.

After lunch the motor coach had drawn up at the front gate. They were having a drive to Nice to take their minds off things and to do some shopping. Mrs Beaumont had said she didn't want to stay in alone and had agreed to join them after resting a little.

The party had been sitting waiting in the coach for five minutes, when somebody had suggested that Mrs Beaumont was perhaps asleep or had forgotten the arrangement. Marie Ann Blair had gone to her room to remind her. The place was empty and Mrs Beaumont nowhere to be seen. Not only that, her luggage had gone as well.

Dorange gave Littlejohn a disappointed look as they both set out for the town hall. The police had already got busy. All round

Cannes gendarmes were combing the roads, stopping all cars, watching all stations and the airport.

And in the midst of it all, the telephone rang and Haddock came on with his report for Littlejohn. It all seemed irrelevant and unimportant amid the present unpleasantness.

Mrs Beaumont, Dawson and Marriott used Fowlers Bank; Sheldon, the North and South; the Curries and the Hannons, the Building Society which did bank work; and Gauld banked with the Home Counties, which Miss Blair used as well. Humphries didn't seem to have a bank account, at least in Bolchester.

Haddock patiently ploughed his way through it all, whilst Dorange paced impatiently to and fro in the small office. He was anxious to get to *Bagatelle* as soon as possible.

'And I might add, sir, that the sooner Mr Marriott gets back the better. His creditors have been round to the police station, asking if he's absconded or something. We've had to explain and reassure them, but they say he's kept them waiting long enough and it can't go on much longer.'

Marriott had already told Littlejohn all about wanting to get back in view of his business. Everything seemed to be happening at once.

'Did you manage to find out who got the torn note from Fowlers?'

'No, sir. They paid out so much about that time and, of course, didn't take the numbers of small soiled notes.'

'Thank you very much, Haddock…'

M'sieur Joliclerc wasn't in his office. On hearing the news of Mrs Beaumont's flight, he'd stormed out, leaving a nasty message for Dorange. There had been another murder in a bistro at Mandelieu, and the *Parquet* had therefore transferred itself to something a bit easier than the Dawson affair, and on which it could practise its usual technique.

All the way to *Bagatelle*, police were stopping astonished

holiday-makers and others and examining their cars and papers. There seemed to be police everywhere. There were two detectives at the gate of the villa when the Inspectors got there.

All the English trippers were indoors and another detective was trying to keep them in order until his superiors arrived. This was difficult, because his English was halting and queer. The first thing Littlejohn noticed was Alf Fowles, sitting between two gendarmes, looking like a condemned man. He rose as the Chief Inspector entered, but the policemen seized him and sat him down hard in his seat again.

Fowles had lost none of his effrontery. He was smoking a cigarette.

'How come?' he shouted at Littlejohn. 'These Frenchies don't unnerstand a word of wot I'm sayin'. Marriott's told 'em in their own lingo that it was me got the taxi for Mrs Bewmont. Wot's wrong in that? I didn't do no conjurin' tricks with 'er and vanish 'er. She done that herself…'

Marriott was scuttering here and there and clutched Littlejohn by the arm.

'This is a damn nightmare, Chief Inspector. They're goin' to drive us all stark, starin' mad. Mrs Bewmont's the first to go off her rocker, and she'll not be the last, if this goes on.'

Littlejohn calmed him and eventually got a proper tale.

During lunch, it seemed, Mrs Beaumont had caught Fowles coming from his room and asked him to get her a taxi at the back door. Fowles, thinking nothing was amiss, had telephoned the garage he used and where they spoke English and the cab had arrived ten minutes later. After seeing it arrive, Fowles had gone for his own lunch in the kitchen. And that was all.

Nobody had seen Mrs Beaumont leave. Presumably she'd used the stairs from the first floor; the flight which went down the outer wall and ended in the garden. Thence, it was easy to the back entrance.

'She's bin a bit queer of late, and Miss Blair, who occupies the next room, tells us she 'eard her pacin' up and down her bedroom in the night. The whole business 'as got on top of her. And she won't be the only one at this rate.'

Marriott was working himself up almost into a fit of hysterics. The rest were standing helplessly around like a lot of trapped animals.

'Oughtn't we to get a lawyer, or something? The way things are, we'll be here till kingdom come,' said Currie, and the rest muttered agreement.

Dorange went from one to the other, asking the same questions.

Had anyone seen Mrs Beaumont go? Had she left any message, made any threats, dropped any hints? The answer was always the same: no.

There was nothing for it but to wait for the police to pick up the fugitive.

'Meanwhile, nobody will leave this house. You will all remain indoors, and two of my men will see that you obey these instructions. Call it house-arrest, if you like. It will remain so until we find the murderer of William Dawson, Sammy, and Henri.'

'But we can't stay penned up here. We'll all go off our heads.'

Marriott was acting as spokesman again and shrill in his complaints.

Dorange shrugged his shoulders, made no reply, and left the room, seizing Littlejohn by the arm and taking him along with him.

'Was the person you suspected Mrs Beaumont?'

'No. She didn't do it. Can you see her quietly killing three people and driving them off on a motor-cart and hiding them?'

'I don't know her well enough. In my experience there seem to be no limits to what a furious woman will do.'

'There are mechanical limits. I'm sure she doesn't know a thing about motorbikes.'

'Assuming the petrol-cart was used.'

'I'm sure it was. But I'm also sure of another thing. Mrs Beaumont has either guessed or stumbled upon the murderer, and she's scared to death thinking she'll be the next. She's been under the weather, nervously, of late and this flight is simply a sort of reaction to a form of claustrophobia.'

'Whatever it is, she'll get into trouble for it. I can't leave this to you, Littlejohn. I'm sorry, but this has gone far enough. I take over from here. You can be with me, of course, but the whole case is now my responsibility. By order of the Prefect.'

It was four o'clock and the heat of the day was almost unbearable. Outside, the roads were still alive with police watching all the cars, stopping them, asking questions. Otherwise, life was going on as usual. Bathers coming and going, a squad of workmen building a villa opposite, and the distant sea alive with people trying to keep cool and enjoy themselves.

'Are you coming back with me, Littlejohn?'

'No. I think I'll get back to Juan-les-Pins. I haven't seen my wife all day. She'll wonder what's happened.'

'I'll ring you if we find Mrs Beaumont and send a car to bring you to the police station. She will, of course, be detained for questioning.'

The Chief Inspector had only time to take a cup of tea with his wife and tell her of the day's events when Dorange was on the line.

Mrs Beaumont had been run to earth at Var airport. She was trying to book a ticket home to London. She hadn't been in any way contrite about her behaviour. In fact, she'd pitched into the police hot and strong for detaining her and the rest of the party for so long. After all, she'd said, it wasn't as if they were criminals on the run. The police would know where to find them if they wanted them at any time later. In Bolchester, of course. Where did the police think they were going? Somewhere else in France, after the way they'd been treated?

Dorange had had it all from the officers at Var, and reeled it off to Littlejohn. He even laughed at Mrs Beaumont's fighting spirit. He sounded relieved and more like his old self. Littlejohn wondered if they were going to charge Mrs Beaumont with the crimes, after all, and then call it a day and let the rest go home.

'I'll send the car, as promised, Littlejohn. You'll be here almost as soon as the lady, who has just left Nice, under escort, of course.'

They were bringing Mrs Beaumont into the police station when Littlejohn arrived there. There had been some delay, due to formalities at the airport. She looked very self-possessed. Sitting upright, dignified and calm, just as though she were on a sightseeing tour or an educational visit to the town hall.

Littlejohn gave her a reproachful glance as they entered the Inspector's room together; she smiled back at him.

'You may sit down.'

'Thank you, M'sieur Dorange.'

Dorange sat in the swivel-chair behind the desk and Littlejohn and Mrs Beaumont faced him on the other side, like a couple of allies.

A rectangle of bright sunshine shone through the window and lit up the scene like a limelight. It fell fully on Mrs Beaumont's face and Littlejohn couldn't help admiring the calmness there. It was as if she were being brought to account for some minor prank, instead of running away from a murder case.

She wore a tweed costume and a green felt hat of a good style. Dressed as she was, instead of the usual billowing frocks in which the Chief Inspector had always seen her before, she looked younger and slimmer. She wore nylon stockings and brown brogue shoes with flat heels. Her legs and ankles were substantially middle-aged.

Under the costume coat, a plain green finely knitted jumper, and in the lapel, an old cameo brooch. She had a gold bracelet on her wrist, and on her fingers two fine diamond rings as well as her wedding ring.

The secretary was sitting at his little table, all ready to start another file. This time *Dossier Beaumont*.

'Well, madam?'

It seemed as if they had all been waiting for someone to start the ball rolling. Now Dorange began with an almost smiling question, such as one asks to a child who hasn't misbehaved too badly.

'What do you mean, Inspector? Am I supposed to give a full account of my present plight and escapades?'

'It will be better if you make a statement first. Then we can question you later.'

Mrs Beaumont took it quite casually, placed her large leather handbag on the floor beside her, and cleared her throat.

'Please don't think I was running away because I am guilty.'

She paused.

'Do you and that young man…?'

She indicated the secretary, now busy taking down her words in shorthand.

'Do you and that young man understand English properly?' Dorange smiled pleasantly.

'Yes, I think we do. M'sieur Monnet, the secretary, is, as you have already learned by experience, a trained interpreter. We get so many English people here. As for myself, I get along, madam. I can follow you. In any case, if we have difficulty, Chief Inspector Littlejohn will help us.'

'That is all right, then. I was saying, I wasn't running away at all. I was simply going back to London to hire, or whatever you call it, some lawyer, acquainted with your strange French ways of doing things, and bring him back with me.'

'I wish you had told us. We may not have such men here on the Riviera, but there are plenty in Paris. We could have got you one without all this fuss. Are you sure that is the only reason?'

Mrs Beaumont bridled.

'What other could there be?'

'Could it be that you have a guilty conscience, madam? Could it be that you held a grudge against your compatriot, Dawson, and in rage vented your spleen against him with a knife? And then…please don't interrupt…and then, having been seen in your crime, you had to save yourself by more crimes?'

Mrs Beaumont drew in a loud rush of air, almost like an angry sob.

'I never heard anything so stupid in my life! Why should *I* want to murder Dawson? I'd nothing against him.'

'Not even some affair at home, some insult, some injury which, when you were brought closely together on a trip, such as you are now enjoying, was intensified so much?'

'I wish to hear no more silly theories. If this is the way you carry on an investigation, it's no wonder we all look like remaining here for ever!'

One felt somehow, that Mrs Beaumont was used to facing the police. She was quite at ease, with a touch of contempt in her expression.

'You have caused us a lot of trouble. We have had police out on all roads and stations, searching for you. And all because of a whim, an impatience which you could not control.'

'I have told you, the way you have conducted this investigation is very trying to one's nerves.'

Dorange took it all in very good humour.

'Then, may I ask, madam, how you would have conducted it yourself?'

'I am not a policeman.'

'I can quite see that. Hitherto, we have hardly conducted the case at all. We have asked very polite questions, given you and your fellow travellers every consideration, and even allowed your English Chief Inspector here to do most of the work, in spite of the fact that he is on a holiday. From now on, madam, we are taking a firm hand ourselves. I can assure you that all but the guilty one will soon be on the way home. So don't try to leave *Bagatelle* again without my personal permission.'

'You mean to say...?'

'You are at liberty to go back to *Bagatelle,* madam.'

Dorange rose and bowed to her.

'I must say this is very generous of you and doesn't go unappreciated. I must agree I behaved impulsively, but believe me, I thought it in the best interests.'

'Please leave us to judge in future which are the best interests. By the way, do you drive a car, madam?'

'No, I do not. My late husband was very interested in motorcars during his lifetime, but I have never wished to drive them myself. When I need a car, I hire one with a chauffeur.'

'You have never driven a motorcycle?'

Mrs Beaumont's eyes opened wide and her jaw dropped.

'Good gracious! One of those awful things! You must think me mad, young man. Certainly not!'

She drew on her gloves and gathered up her bag.

'Please tell me before you leave us, have you any views of your own about these crimes? Do you suspect anyone?'

'No. I cannot say that I do.'

'You were not leaving France to get away from anyone? I mean, you were not fleeing in fear of your own life from the one who has already murdered three people?'

There was a pause. Then she shook her head.

'No.'

'Are you sure?'

'Of course, I am. Don't you believe me?'

'Yes. But the pause you took before you replied: It suggested doubt.'

'Well, there's no doubt, Inspector. May I go now? I am very tired.'

'The car will take you back to *Bagatelle. Bon jour, Madame.*'

'Bon jour, M'sieur le Commissaire.'

Littlejohn, alter seeing Mrs Beaumont to her car, returned to Dorange.

'Well?'

'Well, Dorange?'

'What do you think?'

'I still think she's quite innocent of any crime, but I'm sure she knows more than she's told us.'

'I agree. That is why I've let her go home. Now the ball is with you, to use your own idiom. You must find out what she is concealing.'

'I'll do my best.'

'Has what has happened altered your views, changed the theory you have in mind?'

'No. I can't say it has. In fact, it's strengthened it. I think Mrs Beaumont is afraid of someone and was bolting, not out of guilt, but in fear of her life. If she's right, we'd better keep a close eye on her. We don't want another murder on our hands.'

Dorange threw up his arms.

'God forbid! It would certainly be the end of me, and I should then join my father, growing roses and carnations.'

It reminded him of the flower in his own coat, which he examined, straightened, patted affectionately, as if it were a pet of some kind.

'I'll drop off at *Bagatelle* again on my way to Juan...'

'The car is at your disposal. Till ten o'clock in the morning then, *mon ami.*'

'I'd like to make it noon, Dorange, and you and I join the excursionists for lunch at *Bagatelle.*'

'If you've solved the case by then, there won't be many with an appetite.'

'Meanwhile, will you see that someone keeps an eye on Mrs Beaumont...one of your plain clothes men? He might even be stationed inside *Bagatelle.*'

'That is already done. We aren't going to have any more of that party bolting and giving us trouble. There will always be a man there until they leave Cannes for good.'

'Splendid! And now I'll be off.'

At the villa there was quite a festive atmosphere. Mrs Beaumont had explained to the Turnpikers why she had tried to get back to England in their interest, and they had expressed their gratitude and allowed her to go and lie down in her room for a rest.

'She wants to see you, Chief Inspector, as soon as you get here. She said you were sure to call,' said Mrs Currie, who was again in charge of Mrs Beaumont, whom she treated as a semi-invalid.

'She seems worried.'

The same kind of interview as before. The chaise longue, with Mrs Beaumont resting on it, the table with the grapes, the peaches and the pears, and a large vase filled with local roses. She was fast becoming the heroine, the darling of the party.

Littlejohn, remembering the aggressive woman he'd met when he arrived, reminded himself that first impressions aren't always the best.

'I was sure you'd want to see me, Chief Inspector. I can talk to you. You seem to understand me. The French police have a strange effect on me. I become a kind of oyster, instinctively. I can't help myself. I just can't open up to them.'

She paused for breath and gulped in air.

Littlejohn sat on the chair beside the chaise longue.

'You *were* afraid, weren't you, Mrs Beaumont?'

She hesitated.

'Yes. I simply couldn't tell the French Inspector. One feels, in a foreign country, that one ought not to betray one's fellow English. We must stick together. It would be wrong…'

'This is murder…threefold murder, Mrs Beaumont, and

Inspector Dorange is a very decent fellow. I would be the last to try to impede him in a case like this.'

'I'm not suggesting that we don't do our best to discover who…'

She passed her hand across her brow in a troubled gesture. 'If only it had happened at home. One thinks of the French police, the law courts here and…and do they still guillotine murderers? If only it had happened in Bolchester instead of here.'

The window was open and the heat of the day seemed to enter in gusts, almost as scorching as those of a furnace. Outside, someone was mowing a lawn and they could hear the swish of a hosepipe.

Littlejohn didn't tell Mrs Beaumont that murder and its results were the same wherever they occurred. So was the punishment. Men died violently and their killers paid the price and it didn't make much difference where…

'You were afraid. Why?'

'I have had a growing presentiment that I am somehow in danger.'

'Get rid of it, Mrs Beaumont. We're attending to that. From now on, you'll be safe. I'll see to that.'

She didn't quite know how to reply, but her face grew calmer and she gave him a look of gratitude, stretched out her hand, and laid it for a moment on the back of Littlejohn's own.

'You have been *such* a help, Chief Inspector, and I do thank you for all you have done. Last night seemed to confirm my fears. I was so afraid after what happened, that I stayed awake till morning and then started to pack my bags. I was seized with a mad desire to get away to the safety of home. I couldn't go before William's funeral, but when it was over I…I'm sorry I caused so much trouble. I ought to have told you.'

'But you decided to go without telling us what had

happened. You were shielding someone because you didn't wish the French police to take him?'

'I didn't wish to be responsible for his arrest. I told nobody, but just took matters into my own hands and fled.'

'Who was it?'

She hesitated, and then spoke with a great effort.

'Jeremy Sheldon.'

Again! It always seemed to come round to Sheldon!

'Why?'

'I couldn't sleep last night. I was upset by today's funeral, and you know how much I blame myself for William Dawson's death. You know how one gets. I heard it strike midnight, and then one. I could hear the bell on St Honorat ringing for the offices. People passing late. And, as one does, I said to myself, if I'm not asleep in a quarter of an hour, I'll get up and take a tablet. But I was too cosy to do it.'

Outside, on the landing, they could hear footsteps ascending and then voices.

'It's so stupid of you. Why must you always show me up in front of people?'

'But, my dear, I thought it best…'

'Best! You never think of me. It's always the same.'

A door slammed. The Sheldons again.

Mrs Beaumont paused and listened. It was as though the near presence of the man who had scared her, gave her a pang of further fear.

'I must have dozed off after hearing it strike two. Then, suddenly, I was awake. Someone was outside the door. I could *feel* him there. I heard the knob slowly turn with a slight grating noise. I put on the light and rushed to the door, impulsively. Whoever was there had tiptoed away, but I saw the Sheldons' door, which is opposite, as you know, gently closing, as though someone were sneaking back.'

She gulped for air and put her hand over her heart.

'He must have been trying to get in and...'

'But why? Surely you have no evidence which would incriminate him?'

'I did tell you that when William and I had our quarrel, the name of Mrs Sheldon was mentioned and that I thought her husband overheard. In the course of the investigation, if that came out, it might be damning. On the other hand, the very fact that I was, in a way, blackening his wife's good name might have affected him. He dotes on her so much that maybe the strain and the things we said about her have unhinged him. He may have become mad and homicidal. I am terribly afraid, Inspector.'

Littlejohn rose.

'We'll settle this, here and now.'

Hastily he crossed the landing and tapped on the Sheldons' door.

Their wrangling voices ceased and there was a pause as they listened silently and wondered who was knocking.

Sheldon appeared at length.

'Hullo, Inspector! What can I do for you?'

'Will you kindly accompany me to Mrs Beaumont's room?'

'What's the matter?'

His wife's head appeared round the door frame.

'What has happened?'

The pair of them followed Littlejohn with slow puzzled steps.

Mrs Beaumont rose and out of emotion didn't answer when they greeted her and asked her how she was.

They stood in a group.

'You were up in the night, about two o'clock, Mr Sheldon?'

Husband and wife exchanged glances.

'I told you what it would be. You would interfere. Trouble, trouble, trouble.'

She was starting a fresh row, her eyes blazing and her disgust apparent.

'I thought I heard someone prowling round on the landin'. My wife didn't want me to interfere, but after all, with things goin' on as they have done in this place, I didn't feel I could let it pass. I got up and went to see. It was just somebody goin' to the bathroom.'

'You didn't see who it was?'

'No. But it could only have been Marriott, if it wasn't Miss Blair. The other floors have their own bathrooms. I spoke to Miss Blair this mornin'. Apologised if I'd disturbed her. You see, she told us that Mrs Beaumont sounded unsettled in the night. Walkin' about, she said. So I said I hoped it wasn't through me. I'd tried to be quiet.'

His wife snorted with disgust again.

'She…Miss Blair, I mean, said she was asleep well before two…and didn't wake for the first time till four, when she heard Mrs Beaumont movin' about.'

Littlejohn turned to Mrs Sheldon.

'You confirm that?'

'Of course. My husband only went briefly in and out.'

'Very well. Please don't mention this to the others. It's very disturbing and there's been enough disturbance here already. Thank you.'

The Sheldons left without another word, very serious, almost crestfallen.

As the door closed, they could hear Mrs Sheldon start rebuking her husband again.

'Please don't mention all this downstairs, Mrs Beaumont. In fact, don't say a word about your fears or last night's episode. Keep up the tale that you were trying to get to London for legal help for the rest of your friends here.'

'I see. But when will it all end?'

Littlejohn patted her hand comfortingly, like a doctor reassuring a patient.

'Not long, now. Stay in your room today…*all the time*. There's a detective keeping an eye on you. You'll be safe. I'll call to see you again before dinner. Remember, keep to your room.'

'I promise, Chief Inspector.'

'You haven't something else to tell me? Something you're reticent about. Something a kindly woman like yourself wouldn't mention?'

She looked surprised at first, and then nodded.

'Yes.'

It was said in a whisper.

'Marriott also asked you to marry him, didn't he?'

'Yes. Twice…in Bolchester. I refused emphatically. I was sure it was my money. He is reputed to be very badly-off…almost bankrupt.'

'Did he ask you on this trip?'

'No. But I think he was getting ready to do so. In fact, that might have been the reason for his coming. He was behaving as if ready for another try. I hate to say all this. It hardly seems fair.'

Two ageing men, courting a comfortable, plain elderly woman, and perhaps her money, as well. Two elderly rivals. And now one was in the cemetery at Cannes. And the other…

On the way down, Littlejohn again tapped on the Sheldons' door.

'Again, Inspector?'

'Just another word with you, sir. On the night of Dawson's death, you overheard him having high words in the morning room with Mrs Beaumont?'

Sheldon flushed angrily. He closed the door between himself and his wife.

'My wife's name was mentioned. I resented it, sir. Most disturbin', and a lie, as well.'

'You were taking a bag upstairs?'

'Yes. How do you know?'

'Was there anyone else about as you got the bag?'

'Yes. That fellah Marriott. He was in the corridor which goes past the door of the mornin' room to the kitchen.'

'Thank you. Please keep this to yourself.'

'I must say I resented very strongly the lyin' remarks about my wife. If Dawson hadn't died and caused all this fuss, I'd have made him answer to me for it. I could have killed the fellah.'

He suddenly realised what he had said, and he covered his mouth with his hand.

15
A FAREWELL PARTY

'Excuse me! My name's Landru of the *Journal de Nice*...'
Landru! What a name! It made Littlejohn shudder.

A small, thick-set man, with grey hair and a skin wrinkled in fine lines. Hooded eyes under bushy brows and a beret askew on his head.

'Have you any statement to make to the press? I take it you're one of the guests at *Bagatelle*...'

The reporter had evidently been watching the place and had popped out from behind a huge eucalyptus as soon as Littlejohn appeared outside.

Passersby looked hard at the pair of them and a nursemaid, strolling along with a magnificent pram containing a dark-skinned baby which looked like the offspring of some Eastern potentate, rolled her eyes at Landru.

'So far, the French police have kept us off with promises. It's time we got a proper tale. May I have your name, sir, please?'

Littlejohn smiled and removed his pipe.

'Chief Inspector Littlejohn, of Scotland Yard...'

The reporter's eyes grew wide and greedy and he prepared for a scoop.

'Yes. I'm resuming my holiday with my wife and the French police are taking over the case entirely. That's all. Good afternoon.'

The man called Landru could hardly get to the nearest telephone fast enough.

It was almost six o'clock and the silence of before dinner was falling over Cannes again. Lights were appearing in the villas along the road and down the long straight stretch which led from *Bagatelle* to Palm Beach. Somewhere a gramophone was churning out jazz and a few doors away a quartet of addicts were indulging in a jam-session. The rival noises mingled, one set out blaring the other and then itself being out blared...

Beyond everything, the sea, calm and darkening with approaching night. A luxury yacht was making for the harbour and the last motorboat was hurrying to port from the Lérins. In the far distance, the mountains of the Esterel etched against a sky of pink and green.

When the party in the lounge at *Bagatelle* had asked Littlejohn to dinner, he had accepted but excused his wife. He didn't want her involved in any emotional scenes and there looked like being plenty.

'This will be a farewell party. I'm finishing on the case tonight. The French police are taking over.'

The Turnpikers were flabbergasted and dismayed. They all began to talk at once and ask why he was deserting them. Even the phlegmatic Curries and the bored Mary Hannon seemed put out.

'You see, I'm not getting anywhere. Those of you who could help me, won't. We're no nearer a solution of the case than when we started.'

Marriott had begun to get excited, but this time Gauld pushed him aside.

'What do you mean, we won't help? If we don't know

anything, you can't expect us to make up a tale. Why this sudden decision to throw up the sponge?'

Littlejohn patiently puffed his pipe.

'I'm not in charge of the case, you know. It's by courtesy of the French police that I've had any standing at all. And that because the diplomatic powers-that-be in Paris asked that I be allowed to handle the preliminary inquiry and keep things discreet. It doesn't seem to have worked, and now orders are that the local police are to have it their own way.'

'And what does that mean?'

Marriott's voice grew reedy with an emotion which sounded like fear.

'It simply means that all suspects will be questioned and questioned again, until one or another cracks and tells a whole tale. So far, nobody has cooperated with me. Not even Mrs Beaumont, who knows quite a lot she won't tell. Now, the cooperation is going to end. From the English aspect of all being innocent till you're proved otherwise, you will all be guilty, French fashion, until you're proved innocent.'

'But you aren't going to leave us in the lurch like this, Chief Inspector?'

Marie Ann Blair was at last showing some interest and Humphries was looking as furious as he could to back her up.

'It's not good enough. We ought to have been home long ago.'

Littlejohn rose and made ready to go.

'You seem to have a funny idea of what is and what isn't good enough, Humphries. There have been three deaths here since the party arrived. I've tried to find out who committed these crimes so that you could all go home without being grilled in an undignified manner by the local police. And not one of you has helped me. All you've told me or the French police has been dragged out of you. You seem to have the idea that because you're all English and one of you is a murderer on French soil, you ought to hang together and get away by hook or by crook, irrespective of the crimes. Who really feels Dawson ought to be avenged? Not one of you. You all want to go home.'

They all started to shout at once, but the Inspector opened the door.

'I shall be back about eight. Think it over and if any of you have information for me, that will be your last chance. *Au revoir*.'

And when the reporter caught him on the doorstep, he gave him the news for the evening edition, just to underline his decision.

No wonder the dinner at *Bagatelle* that evening was a strange affair. The party there was suffering from conflicting emotions. They were grateful for what Littlejohn had done, angry at his decision to leave them, afraid of what would happen when Dorange and Joliclerc had them completely at their mercy, and eager to appease Littlejohn so that he would change his mind. There had evidently been a meeting before the Inspector arrived.

'Don't come to a hasty decision, Chief Inspector. Let's enjoy our dinner first and then talk it over...'

Marriott, fortified by a whisky or two, met Littlejohn on the mat and almost fawned on him in his anxiety to please. 'Let's have a drink or two before we start.'

He rang a bell and the cross-eyed waitress arrived.

'Just bring in the Inspector's favourite drink, Fonsine. Oh, I forgot; you no compry...*Emportay lu Pernod. Savvy?*'

'How is Mrs Beaumont, Marriott?'

'Better, I think. She's comin' down to dinner. I 'aven't seen her myself, but Mrs Currie says she's bucked up this afternoon.'

'I promised I'd have a word with her before dinner. Could I?'

'I suppose so.'

Marriott stood there brandishing the Pernod bottle. Then he led the way to the lounge where the rest were gathering. 'Mrs Currie. The Chief Inspector would like...'

Before he could get it out, Mrs Currie had taken Littlejohn

in tow, upstairs, and to Mrs Beaumont. The old dragon looked better, almost herself again.

'Is it true, Inspector, you're giving up the case?'

'Yes, Mrs Beaumont, I've promised Dorange either to settle things or get out tonight. All I ask you, is to support me in anything I say. Don't be surprised at any turn in events. Let me have everything my own way without argument.'

'Very well, Chief Inspector. It's a bargain.'

'And I'd like you to follow the old custom after dinner, and lead off the ladies to the drawing room and leave the men to talk. Will you?'

'I don't know what you're getting at, but you can depend on me.'

'Thank you. And now I'll be off. I propose to leave about eleven. Could you see that the party breaks up about then? Go to bed almost at once after I've left and don't be afraid of anything that happens. You have a man from the local police almost outside your bedroom door and another posted in the garden, so even if you feel a bit nervous, you'll be looked after.'

'I'm not nervous. I can look after myself, Inspector, after what you've told me.'

When Littlejohn got downstairs again, all the company had gathered in the lounge, even the Curries, who were usually late. Young Peter was with them this time, a tall, dark, curly-haired boy, who gazed on Littlejohn with awe. To get him out of the atmosphere of *Bagatelle*, he had been spending his time at the villa of an English couple at Golfe-Juan, who had volunteered to take him as soon as they heard of the plight in which his parents found themselves. He had just remained behind to say how-do-you-do to the Chief Inspector at his own request, and immediately afterwards left with his new friends, who were waiting at the door in their car.

'And now we'll all have another appetiser and get on with our meal.'

Marriott was still throwing his weight about in a kind of false confidence in his own ability to handle matters.

The two large rooms on the ground floor were only separated by wide glass doors and these had been thrown back, making one vast room. The tables had been joined together, too, and the party were to gather at one long one, like a banquet.

'In honour of the Chief Inspector and a pity 'is good lady's not 'ere to join him,' said Marriott, explaining it all.

The arrangement made the rooms more imposing and Littlejohn found himself admiring the furniture for the first time. In the past, he'd seemed too preoccupied to notice the details of *Bagatelle*.

The long dining table was laid for twelve. The dining chairs were large and dignified and upholstered in *petit-point* tapestry. The carpet was a real Aubusson, but nobody knew it except Littlejohn, who had once had to study the subject in connection with a theft in Norwood, where a collector had used priceless carpets instead of paper on the walls, and had been stabbed to death in the middle of his choicest one.

To add a touch of lugubriousness to the proceedings, something had gone wrong with the electricity, which kept flickering up and down and now and again reduced the filaments to a mere red glow. It reminded you of travelling by night in an old-fashioned tramcar.

'They can't do anythin' proper here,' grumbled Marriott. 'Not even make electricity. You'd think we was runnin' it off batteries.'

They were all standing around, wondering what they ought to do. Three murders and a funeral. It was hardly the time for festivities, even if Littlejohn *was* saying goodbye to them. Besides, they didn't quite know how they ought to treat Littlejohn.

'Come to the table, everybody. Dinner's ready.'

Marriott was still throwing his weight about. Perhaps it was as well. Nobody else seemed to take the initiative.

'We've got a bottle or two of wine to cheer us up. You don't mind, do you, Mrs Bewmont? In fact, I must say I think a glass or two…as medicine, of course…would do you good, Mrs Bewmont. You look all-in.'

No answer. Instead, they all sorted themselves out and sat down to table; Mrs Beaumont at the head and Marriott at the foot. The loving couples kept together and Littlejohn found himself at Mrs Beaumont's right, with Mrs Currie on the other side.

The curtains were drawn and the room was lighted by a single large chandelier with a silk shade which threw a glow over the table and the heads of those sitting there, and left the rest in shadow. The cross-eyed maid who was serving, stood in the gloom with only now and then a brief illuminated view of her as she passed the dishes or changed the plates. She was not very good at it, and got mixed up now and then.

Hors d'oeuvres, roast veal, ice-cream and peaches, cheese… They followed one another to an accompaniment of small talk. The conversation was subdued, as though those assembled expected Littlejohn to start talking at any time and solve the crime before their eyes.

Four bottles of wine all jumbled up on the table and everyone drinking indiscriminately, except Mrs Beaumont, who ostentatiously poured out glasses of Vichy water.

Nobody proposed a toast. Littlejohn might have been one of the Turnpike party. In any case, on the night of Dawson's funeral, it seemed out of place.

Littlejohn watched Sheldon and Marriott putting down glass after glass of red wine.

'You've had quite enough.'

Mrs Sheldon had been watching the performance with distaste.

'Well, Chief Inspector? Any theories of who might have done these crimes?'

Marriott was getting impatient.

'Hardly, sir. That's why I've had to turn the cases over to the French police.'

'All the same, accordin' to what I gather, you think that one of us at this table is the murderer…'

Sheldon, bold from his wine, spoke loudly, almost truculently.

'Hush!'

His wife glared at him and plucked at his sleeve.

'No harm in gettin' to know what the Inspector thinks, is there, my dear?'

'Not here.'

Mrs Beaumont was on her feet.

'We'll leave the gentlemen to their coffee and the *dregs* of their *alcohol.* Do you mind closing the partitions, Mr Humphries, and we'll be quiet on our own till you've *drunk* your fill and care to join us.'

When the ladies had gone and the glass doors had been closed, Fonsine served coffee. The men sat down at table again. They could see the women through the glass, seated in a circle, throwing now and then anxious looks at the group of what looked like conspirators sitting with the empty bottles before them.

'Bring in that bottle of liqueur brandy I gave you, Fonsine.'

'*Pardon?*'

Humphries had to interpret for him.

'*Le cognac,* Fonsine.'

There was a fuss in obtaining clean glasses and then Marriott served the fine with a trembling hand.

'This is good. Spent all me life in the wine trade and I give you my word…'

They sat in silence, their faces lit by the glow of the chandelier; behind them the gloom of the room. Now and then the lights continued to flicker.

'Before you go, Inspector, you'd better tell us how far you've gone and what to expect next...'

It was Gauld this time, suddenly talkative after his wine. He threw a glance over his shoulder in the direction of Mary Hannon, also talkative in the drawing room.

'Yes. Let's know the worst and when we can expect to get home.'

Marriott helped himself to more brandy.

'If it will be of any use or comfort to you, we'll examine the case in detail. I say case, because it's all one...'

Littlejohn wiped his mouth and looked around. All eyes were on him. Marriott seemed sleepy.

'I'll not mince words, gentlemen, and you must be prepared to hear things you don't like.'

'Let's have the truth. We've been blundering in the dark for long enough.'

Currie said it with conviction. He was now the only dead-sober member of the party, with the exception of Littlejohn, but his face was white and strained. For the first time, the Chief Inspector noticed that Currie had a facial tic. A twitch of the nose when he was excited.

'Some of you joined this party because you'd drawn places. Others bought tickets from those who'd won them, because they'd reasons of their own for coming. I won't divide one class from the other, but you, Gauld, wished to be near Miss Hannon.'

Gauld looked daggers and put down his coffee cup very slowly and very deliberately.

'That's my own business and I'll trouble you...'

'Shut up! We all know it. Why pretend we don't. We asked for this. Now you're gettin' it. Go on, Inspector.'

Currie, his nose twitching, turned on Gauld, like a chairman silencing an unruly committee-man.

'Well, he shouldn't...'

'That'll do.'

'Mr Sheldon, too. He didn't want to come, but his wife insisted. She liked Dawson's company.'

Sheldon swallowed a mouthful of cognac and made a face.

'Resent that! But, as Currie says, everyone knows, so why get in a temper about the truth. Resent it, all the same. Might have spared me that, Chie' Inspector.'

It almost seemed that Littlejohn was deliberately choosing the most offensive aspects of the case. All the men began to look uncomfortable.

'Humphries took the chance of being conductor of the group because he speaks French very well. But that wasn't the prime reason. He is in love with Miss Blair and, although she doesn't or didn't love him, he hoped to persuade her during the trip.'

Humphries choked and tried to get up.

'Sit down. If you wish me to stop I can easily do so and go back to Juan. You asked me for a full account. If you don't like it, so much the worse.'

It might have been the brandy which made Littlejohn feel irritable. Or it might have been the way in which this motley crew of half-drunken holiday-makers had spoiled his own trip and kept him from the company of his wife. Now, he felt like facing them with all their petty motives and wringing from them, somehow, fresh reactions which would end the impasse once and for all.

'As far as I can see, the Misses Hannon and the Curries are the only members who came purely for a holiday. They drew tickets or bought them cheaply, and a trip of this kind was a godsend to them.'

'You're not suggesting that Miss Blair had any ulterior motive, are you?'

Humphries hastily drank off the dregs of his brandy and put down his glass with a bang.

'She came as company for Alderman Dawson, but I doubt that he was the main attraction. She rather likes your attentions, Mr Humphries, and I've no doubt a holiday with an agreeable companion like yourself finally made up her mind to accompany her uncle, who otherwise would, I'm sure, have been an old bore to her.'

'You're wrong there.'

Humphries wanted somebody to give him hope about Marie Ann Blair and cast his bleary eyes round for an answer.

'You want to stop dancin' round Marie Ann, Humphries, an' show her who's boss. She'll appreciate you better. Take it from me.'

Humphries turned on Marriott.

'You've a lot to give advice about. An old bachelor who's after a wealthy widow and can't pluck up courage to…' Marriott staggered to his feet and overturned his glass. 'What do you mean, you young whippersnapper? I'll…' Littlejohn paused in lighting his pipe.

'You know he's right, Marriott. You did pluck up courage, though, didn't you? She said "No"…'

'Who's bin sayin' things behind my back? Who's bin spyin' on me? Who told you? I want to know.'

Littlejohn finished with the match, blew it out and sat back.

'And every one of you had hardly a good word for Dawson, had you? Marriott, because he beat him to the post, proposed to Mrs Beaumont, and was accepted.'

There was a murmur of surprise from all but Marriott, who picked up his glass, mopped up the spilled brandy with his napkin, and poured himself another helping.

'And what if he did? No cause to wish him dead. More cause to pity 'im, marrying an old baggage like Bewmont.'

Sheldon wagged a tipsy forefinger at him.

'Now, now, now, Marriott. No runnin' down the ladies in the officers' mess. Besides, till we got 'ere, you were almost as attentive to Mrs Beaumont as is our young frien' Humphries to the charmin' Marie Ann. I see now why you suddenly changed and got scornful about Mrs Beaumont. She'd turned you down, had she?'

'You be careful what you're sayin', Sheldon. I know when I'm not wanted. You don't. Your wife doesn't want you. Makin' up to every man she comes across.'

Before anyone could intervene, Sheldon was milling round, clawing at Marriott, shaking him by the throat. The women in the next room were on their feet, too, making for the connecting door in a tight mass.

Currie hurried to keep them out whilst Littlejohn and Humphries separated the other two.

Finally, Sheldon and Marriott sat facing each other, panting and glaring.

'I'll see you pay for this, Sheldon. I'm not Dawson, you know. You know what I mean. You caught Dawson and your missus in a compromisin' situation at Avig'on, didn't you? You waited and killed him…'

Littlejohn hit the table with the flat of his hand.

'Be quiet, both of you. You'd all motives for wanting Dawson out of the way. Sheldon because his wife had betrayed him with Dawson and he heard about it on this trip. Marriott because Dawson had always beaten him to the post. Even at school, Dawson took the honours from you, Marriott. Be quiet, I say. You want to know what I know. You shall hear it. When you overheard Mrs Beaumont say she'd marry Dawson, you saw red, didn't you, Marriott? But not more, after all, than poor Sheldon, or Humphries, for that matter. Dawson didn't like Humphries for some reason and set out to stop him getting the girl he's mad about.'

The men were now so fascinated by Littlejohn's talk and each so eager to hear that everyone else had a motive as strong as his own, that they kept quiet and listened. Had they made a concerted effort to silence Littlejohn, it would all have ended, then and there. But they were too anxious to know about the rest.

'Even Currie. Dawson was a constant thorn in his flesh at the office. Currie is happy in his marriage and his home. But Dawson is a director of the concern he works for and in which he spends most of his life. Dawson, Dawson, Dawson, all the working day might be enough to drive a man off his head.'

'But not me. I didn't care a damn about Dawson.'

Currie had been drinking brandy and now his tone was growing truculent, too. A new Currie, this time.

'Anybody else you can incriminate?'

Humphries raised his face, which was flushed and spiteful, and almost climbed across the table to thrust it in Littlejohn's.

'Mrs Beaumont is, of course, a trustee of the Turnpike society. She thought she ought to come to see things straight and above board.'

Marriott sat up.

'Nosey Parker. Mrs Grundy…Eh? But that's not all. At first, she kept a sus…suspicious eye on friend Dawson. He was spendin' *her* money, you see. She'd invested in Dawson's bankrupt business an' he came to Cannes to blue it in. I overheard her givin' him the best tickin'-off he'd ever had in his life. An' then, Dawson shed crocodile tears, said he hadn' a friend in the world, and would she marry him. An', believe it or not, she said she would.'

He tapped the side of his nose.

'But don' you believe it. She was only kiddin'. Ask me, for what it's worth, when she thought it over, she got mad an' stuck him in the back with a rabbit knife.'

Littlejohn leaned quietly over the table.

'Who told you it was a rabbit knife, Marriott?'

'Who? Me? Why Madame…what's she called? Henri's mother. She was all over the place huntin' for it. Even said she was sure it had been used for the murder. So don' you try to catch me out.'

'The rest of the ladies have no cause to love Dawson. The Hannons... He brought about the downfall of their father, who was, we must confess, drinking heavily. But Dawson seems to have caused him a public disgrace. And Mrs Sheldon... But that doesn't matter. You all could have killed him. You'd all motives, more or less strong.'

'But we didn't kill him, Littlejohn. We were all here when he was murdered. All except Humphries and Marie Ann, who were out together. We've all got alibis. How can you crack those?'

Currie gave him a triumphant look.

'The alibis are all broken. Dawson was killed in a matter of minutes. Anyone could have simply left the room for three minutes, stabbed Dawson, hidden his body in the bushes in the garden, and taken it down to Palm Beach later. Any excuse. A box of matches from a bedroom, a visit to the bathroom, a stroll in the hall. Three minutes, just to pick up a knife, follow Dawson outside, and stab him. There he lay, unconscious, but alive...'

'And I suppose whoever did it, then shouldered the heavy body, and walked it down to Palm Beach in full view...?'

Humphries sounded nasty about it. All of them were smarting under the disclosure of their private affairs and peccadillos, and they all looked pleased at the question.

'No. He wasn't carried. He was driven down in the motor-truck which is in the shed in the garden. Another five minutes of a job. Three minutes from here to Palm Beach; shoot off the body; three minutes back. The house was shut up to keep out the mosquitoes. The windows are soundproof...plate-glass... Nobody heard. Then, whoever did it, strolled back. "I'd just forgotten my cigarettes in my room," or, "the air's a bit fuggy. Just take a breath at the door." It was done.'

They were quiet now, trying to cast back their minds to the

night of the crime. They eyed one another suspiciously. It was obvious what they were thinking. Now they were sure the killer was in the party, and it wasn't a pleasant thought.

'We mustn't forget Sammy, either.'

They looked surprised, as though the other murders were side shows, matters concerning somebody else.

'Whoever killed Dawson was seen by one person. Sammy. He was taking a stroll outside his café and saw the motor-cart on the waste ground at Palm Beach. He also saw the silhouette of whoever was driving it as he sat on the seat behind. When Sammy heard of the crime, he tumbled to what had happened. He didn't *know* or properly recognise the man at Palm Beach, but there was something about him Sammy was sure he'd know again. So he came to *Bagatelle* next day, hung around outside until his man emerged, recognised and challenged him, and demanded blackmail. That night, when he met the murderer to receive the spoils, Sammy got, instead, the knife. I wonder what it was that Sammy identified his man by.'

They all started and looked anxious. Now for it!

'I can't say…'

Relief.

'And Henri. He either saw the knife being stolen, or else one of the bodies being moved. But he was foolish enough to ask for the price of his silence. This time, it was a scarf, but the same vehicle. The funeral procession in secret…the motor-cart to *La Californie*, instead of Palm Beach. All the transportation done at the murderer's convenience, you see. No alibi needed. A quick kill and the motorbike and its grisly sidecar, all waiting for the next move at the right time. Only, in the case of Henri, there was a slip.'

The men held their breath. Through the glass doors of the partition the women were looking anxiously and Mrs Beaumont was making signs in the direction of the ormolu clock on the marble mantelpiece. Ten o'clock. The men were too spellbound to heed her.

'The murderer gave Henri a little on account. It was in small change, as though the victim could only pay his blackmail by scraping his pockets. It was presumably the first instalment. More to follow when he'd been to the bank. Henri changed two large notes for Mr Sheldon…or so Mr Sheldon says…'

'Damn it, man, don't you believe me?'

Marriott looked hard at Sheldon.

'Did you know the police were on this all the time and you didn't say a word to us…your friends? I think you've been damn close, damn close an' mean, Sheldon, holdin' out on us.'

Currie was too impatient for the rest.

'Shut up, Marriott. Go on, Littlejohn.'

'The small notes paid by someone to Henri were supplied by a bank in Bolchester. One of them bore the bank stamp. That's as far as we can go, yet. We shall pursue that further. Or rather, the French police will. As I said, I've finished.'

Humphries looked hard at the Chief Inspector.

'It looks as if you've nearly finished the case, as it is. Why pack up when you're so near the solution?'

'I'm *nowhere* near. I've had to find out all this the hard way. None of you has helped me. You didn't want to wash your own and other people's dirty linen, did you? You'd rather stay here for good! Well, the French police take over tomorrow and start where I left off.'

'You mean they'll question the women as well…in the French fashion?'

'Yes. You'll all get it. Particularly, I'm sorry to say, Mrs Beaumont. She's elderly, and in pretty bad shape. But she knows a lot she won't tell. I think she knows who committed the crime. Whether she saw one committed, or saw the knife being taken, or overheard something, I can't say. My view is that she won't betray a fellow Englishman or woman and leave them to the mercy of the French police and law. I can't shake her. She says she'd rather die than betray a friend to a foreign policeman and have him or her guillotined.'

'But, if she won't tell…?'

Sheldon's eyes were popping and he was sweating heavily.

'There's no question of that. The French police have their own ways. They'll break her down. They're not gentle, you know, with stubborn or stupid witnesses. She'll tell and I'm glad I won't be there to see the state she's in when she talks.'

'She's in bad shape, as you said. You ought to protect her, Littlejohn. She might kill herself. Does she know what she'll have to face?'

'Yes. That's the real reason why she ran away. I've talked with her. She'll have to be watched, you know. She mustn't be allowed to do anything desperate to save the life of whoever committed these crimes.'

'And yet, you're giving up…"

'She won't tell me anything. I'm no further use. Let those who can and will drag out the truth, do it.'

'I think you're damn callous about it, Littlejohn.'

Sheldon was redder than ever.

Littlejohn shrugged his shoulders.

'There'll be a French policeman under her window all night to see she doesn't try to get away. As for the rest, the arrangements are in your hands, gentlemen. Someone ought to keep an eye on her to see she doesn't do anything desperate before she tells what she knows.'

'I'll speak to my wife. We'll see to it.'

Currie nodded his head sagely.

'We'll see to it,' echoed Marriott.

Littlejohn rose.

'Shall we join the ladies? It's getting time for me to go. I'd like to say goodnight.'

On the way Littlejohn turned to Humphries.

'By the way, who sent for me, in the first place? You came to ask my help. Who told you to come?'

'Dawson, of course. He could hardly speak, but he seemed to remember you were somewhere around. He hated the French police. Marriott tried to persuade him to leave it and see how he went on, but Dawson insisted, so we came. A lot of good it's done.'

Littlejohn decided that he was no longer very popular at *Bagatelle*.

16

MELODRAMA AFTER DARK

Littlejohn looked at his watch as he left *Bagatelle*. Ten forty-five.

He had said goodbye to all the Turnpike trippers and promised to see them again later, in his unofficial capacity.

'I'm dreading tomorrow. Not many of us will sleep soundly tonight, I can assure you.'

Marie Ann Blair's sentiments were echoed by the rest.

'If you've an easy conscience, nothing can happen to you.' Marriott said it unctuously and got no reply, for they were in no mood for believing him.

'Shall we phone for a taxi?'

'No thanks, Sheldon. I'll walk to the cab rank. A breath of fresh air will do me good.'

But instead, Littlejohn walked fifty yards in the direction of Palm Beach, then turned in his steps, entered the garden of *Bagatelle,* found the shelter of a large palm tree, and hid behind it.

The man on duty in the grounds was busy talking to the cross-eyed maid at the kitchen door. Littlejohn could hear the buzz of their voices and see the glow of the police officer's cigarette.

The night was clear and cool. From where he stood, Littlejohn could see the lights of Cannes and the illuminated signs of hotels and restaurants in the town. Across the bay, the *Hôtel du Masque de Fer* on the island of St Marguerite was lit up. Noises of traffic, distant music, and frogs croaking in chorus. The curtains of the dining room of *Bagatelle* had been drawn back and Littlejohn could see the guests still talking in groups in the lounge, just as he had left them. Nobody seemed in the mood for bridge or even staying up long. The threat of the morrow seemed heavy upon them.

Fonsine had ceased her dalliance with the detective at the kitchen door, and was now clearing away the remains of the feast from the table in the dining room. Littlejohn saw Marriott enter, take away the brandy bottle, which had been half-empty when he left, and join the others again.

Fonsine finished her job and put out the lights. Littlejohn waited.

Lights began to go up on the first and second floors. The early birds were retiring. The Sheldons and the Curries. Then Mrs Beaumont. The shutters had all been drawn and the Inspector could follow operations by watching the slits illuminate. But first he saw the party slowly disintegrate down in the lounge below. Humphries and Marie Ann Blair left the room, the front door opened, and they strolled to the gate. They were smoking cigarettes.

From his post Littlejohn could hear the murmur of their voices.

'What about a stroll down to the beach?'

'I've got a headache. I only want a breath of air before I turn in.'

Their voices died down to almost a whisper. Humphries was talking earnestly, raising his voice a little now and then.

'…He said you didn't come mainly on account of Dawson, but because I was in the party.'

Humphries was cashing in on what Littlejohn had told him earlier in the evening. Marie Ann Blair laughed softly and provocatively. Humphries, apparently rattled, paused, and then with a quick gesture seized his companion, dragged her to him, and kissed her full on the mouth. There was a brief struggle and then she grew limp and flung her arms round him. They returned to the villa, pausing at every third step to kiss again.

One problem of Bagatelle apparently solved, thought Littlejohn.

They must have retired at once, for Marie Ann Blair's bedroom light went on immediately afterwards.

Gauld and Marriott were still talking in the lounge. Marriott seemed to be laying down the law, gesticulating and thumping his clenched fist in the palm of his other hand. Gauld was half-seas over and looked more cordial and sociable than ever before. Then he, too, left the room, followed by Marriott, who put out the lights.

The staff retired to the rooms in the basement soon afterwards. By half-past twelve all was quiet at *Bagatelle*. The French detective was still smoking under the eucalyptus tree near the kitchen, now and then strolling round to stretch his legs.

The clocks in the town struck one and the bell on St Honorat could be heard dimly announcing the offices of the night. Cannes below was just wakening up. Drunken shouts, distant music, the steady throb of traffic…

Alf Fowles appeared at last, unsteady, whistling to himself under his breath. He reeled up the path, round the side to the kitchen door, which he opened with a key they must have lent him. He entered noisily, the last of the Turnpike revellers.

Littlejohn crossed and tapped the man on watch on the shoulder. He almost jumped out of his skin.

'I'm going inside. Keep a careful eye on things…'

'Yes, sir.'

The Chief Inspector softly mounted the iron staircase to the first floor. The door at the top had been left unlocked and he passed through, finding himself between the bathroom and Mrs Beaumont's room.

From where he stood, the landing ran straight to a window on the front, with a balcony overlooking the town. The plaster figure of the naked lady holding an electric lamp made to look like a flaming torch, stood in an alcove near the window which had shutters, now closed, and a frame of heavy curtains in addition. The place was in darkness. Slits of light under three of the room doors. One vanished as Littlejohn looked at it, leaving Marriott's and Mrs Beaumont's still on. Then Mrs Beaumont's was extinguished.

Littlejohn tiptoed along until he reached the window and there, in the darkness, he made out the shelf of the alcove which held the nymph, and sat down at her feet.

Finally Marriott's light went out.

In the course of his career, Littlejohn had kept many vigils, but never one like this. Sitting outside the bedrooms of *Bagatelle,* waiting for something to turn up. If anything did. The seat at the feet of the naked woman was hard and cold and Littlejohn gently slid to the ground and sat on the thick carpet.

His thoughts wandered between Bolchester and *Bagatelle.* The extremes of the situation were comic. Bolchester and Cannes; Dorange and Haddock; Dawson, a model of aldermanic respectability, and Sammy, a twister and crook.

The ormolu clock on the mantelpiece downstairs was working overtime, striking the quarters. It sounded a lot louder in the stillness. A burst of chimes announced half-past two.

Upstairs someone had started to snore. It came from a far distance, like Fowles in his- attic. It probably *was* Fowles, sleeping off his debauch.

Littlejohn had got his eyes used to the darkness. Now, he could see the lady with the torch like a ghostly figure above him, and the pattern of the corridor and the doors, with the bathroom at the end and the faint hiss of water, as though somebody hadn't properly turned off a tap.

He must have dozed off, for the next time he heard the jingling clock below was half-past three. Someone was moving in one of the rooms. Then the faint crack of a door gently opening. Littlejohn tensed himself. A figure materialised in the dim light of the landing, slowly and silently travelling in the direction of Mrs Beaumont's room. Then it turned left, another door opened, and silence.

Littlejohn relaxed with a sigh in which there was a faint trace of a chuckle. He might easily have pounced and spoiled everything. As it was, by the light of the French window which gave on the outer stairs, he had made out Humphries, his shoes in his hand, tiptoeing back to his own quarters from Marie Ann's room! He thought of the reaction of the Turnpike trustees and what a lot they'd probably make of the sordid little interlude, if they knew. Probably even more than the *affaire Dawson*.

Then it started.

At first, Littlejohn was only instinctively aware that somebody was moving not far away. Then a pencil of light appeared under Marriott's door, which gently opened, revealing the occupant clad in pyjamas and dressing gown, carrying a small torch. He looked to right and left and listened for a second or two. The clock below jingled another quarter.

Littlejohn strained his eyes to see what Marriott was doing. In one hand the torch; in the other something small, certainly not a knife, or even a scarf. His behaviour was comic. A slow motion, tiptoeing gait, silent and grotesque, across to Mrs Beaumont's room. At the door he halted and then, with infinite patience, slowly turned the knob. It was locked. Marriott put his ear to the panel and listened. Then he drew back, paused, and came to a decision.

Littlejohn only just held himself back in time, for Marriott turned quickly, ran across to Sheldon's door, and knocked on it.

'Sheldon… Sheldon. Get up. Something's happened to Mrs Bewmont. Sheldon… Do you hear?'

Lights came on in the Sheldons' room and Sheldon appeared in the doorway, his fringe of hair dishevelled, his face bewildered and puffed with sleep.

'Mrs Bewmont… I'm sure somethin's happened. I thought I heard footsteps. Thought I'd better keep watch behind my door. You remember what Littlejohn said about her havin' vital information. But don't let's stay gassin' here. Break in the door.'

As they crossed the landing, Humphries appeared, and then Mrs Sheldon. On the upper floor they could hear the sounds of feet and voices. Lights going on everywhere.

The three men flung themselves at the door, which gave way at the second attempt, and the whole party rushed in the room.

Littlejohn hurried silently along the deserted landing to Humphries' room and looked around. The suit Humphries had been wearing was in the wardrobe on a hanger. Littlejohn searched it swiftly, withdrew something from the side pocket, and examined it briefly. It was a pair of long-nosed pliers.

'What has happened?' he said, appearing at the door of Mrs Beaumont's room.

Sheldon and Marriott had Mrs Beaumont held by the arms between them, making her walk about the floor. They were too busy to ask Littlejohn why he was there.

'She's taken an overdose of sleepin' tablets by the looks of things. If I hadn't 'appened to be awake and come across, she'd 'ave been a gonner by mornin'. As it is… They're gettin' a doctor.'

Below, in the hall, Mrs Sheldon was telephoning for a doctor with the help of the new cook, and Mrs Currie, who had hurried down, was making black coffee.

''Urry up and get that doctor, quick.'

Littlejohn looked round the room. It was all as tidy as Mrs Beaumont usually kept it. Her clothes neatly laid out, the fruit and candies on the table, flowers on the windowsill. On the bedside table, the small Vichy bottle she usually drank on retiring. Empty. Littlejohn opened the window and whistled for the French detective in the garden.

'See that nobody leaves,' he said when the man arrived.

He looked round again and mentally called the roll of the Turnpike party. Mrs Currie and Mrs Sheldon, below; Sheldon and Marriott. Humphries now on the landing telling Gauld and Currie what was going on. And Alf Fowles still snoring like mad upstairs. As he counted them, the two Hannon sisters arrived. They'd got themselves properly dressed and even powdered before making a public appearance.

Everybody busy and present, exccpt…

'Where's Marie Ann Blair?'

They all seemed to pause in what they were doing.

The key of the connecting door between Mrs Beaumont's room and Miss Blair's was sticking out on Mrs Beaumont's side. Littlejohn quickly turned it, put it in his pocket, and entered the room.

The shutters were closed and the room was dimly lit by the light from the door. Stretched quietly, too quietly, in bed was Marie Ann Blair. She, too, had had an overdose of sleeping tablets! At the side of the bed, a wine-glass with a few dregs in it. Mrs Beaumont had taken a similar drink, except it was Vichy water. Littlejohn tasted the lees just as he had done Mrs Beaumont's. Here it was a mere glass. In the case of Mrs Beaumont, it had been a whole small bottle of Vichy water.

So, it started all over again. Marie Ann was hoisted from bed, paraded round the room, her face and neck slapped with cold wet cloths.

'Where's that coffee?'

'Is anybody hurryin' up the doctor?'

The doorbell rang, the panic stricken, stupefied girl with the squint was letting in the doctor. It was Dr Molinard! He gave Littlejohn a strange look as he entered the bedroom of Mrs Beaumont.

Littlejohn strolled here and there with his hands behind his back. All around him, the crowd, giving coffee, chattering, some of the women half hysterical.

'God! I wish we were home. Never again!'

Elizabeth Hannon was giving way.

Miss Blair was coming round, but Mrs Beaumont was still unconscious. Molinard was very skilled. At his job, he looked a different man; keen, precise, tireless.

'She'll be all right. Only just in time, though. What has happened? Have the Cannes police been informed?'

'I'll see to it…' Littlejohn sent Gauld down to telephone to Dorange in Nice, which he did, again with the cook's help.

Littlejohn was listening to Marie Ann Blair, talking distractedly to Mrs Currie.

'It was Mrs Beaumont. She came in through the connecting door with a glass of wine. "You won't sleep tonight if you don't take something. Try this." It was bitter, but I thought it was some special stuff. "I'm taking some, too," she said.'

Then she started to sob hysterically.

'As she left the room, she turned and said, "I've caused this trouble and I'm going to put an end to it all." I'd drunk the wine by then, and I was falling asleep. She came across to me and looked at me with a terrible look. She always hated me. She was in love with Mr Humphries. At *her* age! How could I help it if he loved *me*? She did all she could to come between us and when she found she couldn't, she tried to kill me.'

'There, there, you must rest, Marie Ann. Don't get excited. You're safe now.'

'She's dead, isn't she? She said she was going to put an end to it. That's what she meant, I think.'

'No. She's not dead. They found her just in time.'

Marie Ann's eyes grew wide with horror.

'Don't let her get near me. She murdered my uncle and the rest. My uncle swindled her and made her poor. I heard her quarrelling with him about it. And the other two, Sammy and Henri, they saw her wheeling the body down the hill to where it was found on the shore. Keep her away from me!'

Molinard had given Mrs Beaumont an injection and she was now sleeping naturally. He entered Miss Blair's room to give her one, as well.

'Leave that a moment, doctor.'

Littlejohn spoke from the doorway.

'But…'

'Leave it a minute. Where's Humphries?'

'Who wants me?'

Humphries, hands in his pockets, sauntered in.

Littlejohn flung something down on the table. The crowd, now gathered in Marie Ann's room, recoiled.

'Ever seen that before, Humphries?'

'No. What is it?'

'The knife that killed Dawson and Sammy. I've just found it in the cistern of Mrs Beaumont's lavatory…'

'Well, I don't know anything about it.'

'It was a very obvious place, once we'd settled it from her apparent suicide, that Mrs Beaumont had murdered Dawson. It's *always* the place they plant such weapons, according to crime stories.'

Humphries turned red, then the blood drained from his face.

'What has it to do with me? Get her arrested when she's fit, and let us get home. All this is a supreme show of police incompetence.'

'I insist on the patient being left alone and quiet. Otherwise, I won't be responsible.'

Molinard, still caressing his hypodermic, stood between Littlejohn and Humphries.

'I don't think you'll find her as bad as Mrs Beaumont, doctor. She only had a few knock-out drops to lend verisimilitude to a very nasty piece of work. Between them, they tried to kill Mrs Beaumont.'

Humphries sprang across and thrust his face in Littlejohn's.

'Repeat that, in front of witnesses. I'll make you pay for this when we get back. You'll be a public disgrace and a laughing-stock. Chief Inspector Littlejohn of Scotland Yard, indeed!' Marriott looked completely in a dream.

'We're all bewildered, Inspector. 'Ow did anybody get in Mrs Bewmont's room and try to kill her? The doors were locked on the inside, both of 'em.'

'They got in to plant the knife and to dose Mrs Beaumont's nightly bottle of Vichy by using these.'

He took the long-nosed pliers from his pocket and flung them on the table.

'And this key. The scratches made on it by the pliers were rubbed out with something dark…perhaps burnt match and face cream or Vaseline. But when you wash the key, as I've done, the marks come back. That's how it was done. Then they sat up here together and waited for the overdose to work.'

A sudden scream from the bed and they all turned to see Marie Ann sitting up, wild-eyed, pointing at Humphries. Her lovely face had changed. Her features had a drawn, animal look, like a beast fighting for life. Her lips drew back, baring her teeth in a snarl.

'I didn't do it. *He* did it. My uncle interfered between us when we went for a walk at Lyons. My uncle called *him* names and *he* hit my uncle. Then, when he found us together on that night in Cannes, my uncle had a knife which he said he'd use if there was violence And he started to abuse *him* again. There was a fight… My uncle was stabbed… But I didn't care about my uncle. He told *him* and me before he was killed, that I was penniless. My uncle had invested all my money in his business, he said, and lost it. I hated him for that. I didn't care. I was terrified of *him*. *He* said he'd stop at nothing to get me.'

Suddenly Humphries spun round and the women screamed as they saw his revolver. There was a report. Marie Ann Blair first looked surprised. Then the light died from her fine eyes and she fell back. Humphries, too, was transformed. His small eyes shone madly through mere slits in his face. His nostrils dilated and his mouth contracted in the grimace of a maniac.

'So you didn't love me after all. Just wanted to save your own skin. As we fought, Dawson dropped the knife, and she stabbed him in the back. All the rest I did to save her. Don't move, any of you. I wanted us to die together, but she wouldn't, so now I've done it for her. Instead, she concocted this pretty little scene. Mrs Beaumont... Well... Don't move, anybody. When he was dying, Dawson called for Valerie and Littlejohn. But for Littlejohn, the case would have gone stone dead as an act of revenge by the French Underground. We'd have got away with it. I owe you a debt for this, Littlejohn. I think I shall shoot you, then myself.'

There was a second report, and this time it was Sheldon who held a gun, smoking in his hand.

Humphries opened his eyes and mouth wide in agony, spun half round, and fell on his face with his hands above his head.

Elizabeth Hannon fainted and Mrs Sheldon's voice was heard above the rest.

'Where did you get that gun?'

Sheldon looked bewildered and a bit bashful.

'Brought it with me. Was goin' to make an end of things here. One of the places I was truly happy in, long ago. Felt I'd be better out of your way. You see, you don't seem able to bear the sight of me any more...'

A new look came in Mrs Sheldon's hard face.

'Oh, Jeremy, I didn't know you loved me so much.' Littlejohn walked out to the landing. He'd had enough humbug and melodrama to last a lifetime!

Dorange was running up the stairs. He looked mad with everyone.

'What the hell's going on here?'

As if somebody had been letting off fireworks under his chair just to vex him!

17

RETURN TRIP

Two more appendages to the already swollen files of *l'Affaire Dawson. Dossier Humphries. Dossier Blair.*

M'sieur Joliclerc, knowing the solution to the crimes, was able to concentrate all his energies in compiling voluminous notes. He vented a considerable amount of spleen on Marriott for his red-herring of *Vallouris* when all the time he meant *Valerie*.

''Ow was I to know which he meant? I mentioned it to Humphries and he said it was the French word. No doubt about it.'

'You failed to mention that in your original testimony.'

'I forgot.'

'You forgot! Pah!'

Littlejohn interposed with another question.

'How was it you knew there was something wrong in Mrs Beaumont's room the night I caught you tiptoeing across and listening at the door?'

Marriott looked sheepish.

'I often passed the door on the way to the bathroom and I'd hear her…well… Well, if you must know, when she was sound asleep and all right, she used to snore. But for heaven's sake, don't tell 'er I said so.'

Since he'd rescued her, Marriott and Mrs Beaumont had become buddies. She thought she owed her life to him, but her gratitude extended simply to warm friendship. Marriott's chances of successfully popping the question were as remote as ever.

'She snored!'

M'sieur Joliclerc snorted and recoiled. The Englishman's idea of romance! Happy because the woman snored!

It took them two days to get the whole matter squared-up, and every morning Alf Fowles brought his charabanc to the door of *Bagatelle* and polished it furiously to keep up the morale of his clients and let them see that it was ready to take them home.

Humphries was shot in the chest and died an hour afterwards. Between spells of unconsciousness, he recovered sufficiently to repeat that Dawson had followed and started to abuse him and Marie Ann Blair when they took a walk at Lyons. Humphries had lost his temper and there had been a scuffle, after Dawson had revealed, in uncontrolled rage, that he'd used his niece's money himself; so Humphries would marry a pauper. The same had been repeated after dinner at *Bagatelle*, but this time, Dawson had produced a knife and told Humphries to keep off. Humphries, the gymnast, had knocked it from his hand and they had scuffled again. Marie Ann, distracted with temper at the revelation that her uncle had dissipated her fortune, had picked up the weapon in a frenzy and struck wildly. They had thought Dawson dead and, in seeking a place to hide the body, had come across the petrol-cart and used it to get Dawson to the shore, where they hoped to get rid of him in the sea. Someone had appeared and they had fled.

Next day, Sammy had accosted them outside *Bagatelle*. He recognised them through Marie Ann, the only shapely woman of the party…*Svelte*. Humphries smiled as he gasped out the word.

Henri, spying from his attic window, had seen them returning the petrol-cart after disposing of Dawson, and the next day watched them as Sammy approached them in front of *Bagatelle*. He had asked for ten thousand francs, Humphries' wristwatch, Marie Ann's diamond clip. As the first instalment.

Humphries, driven off his head with panic, love and anxiety for Marie Ann as well as fear for his own skin, had killed twice.

'She didn't love me, after all.'

'My big mistake was,' said Littlejohn to Dorange, 'that I didn't check the statement that the bank, as well as Dawson, was Miss Blair's trustee. It seems Dawson alone had control of the money and spent it, but talked about the bank as co-trustee just to prevent suspicion and make things seem above board.'

A telephone call to Haddock, who at once spoke to Miss Blair's lawyer, proved the fact.

'Hearty congratulations,' said Dorange as they lunched with easy minds after the dossiers had finally been completed, signed and attested.

'Don't congratulate *me*! It was a pure stroke of luck. I began my vigil expecting Marriott to try some funny work. I sowed the seeds of it. I said Mrs Beaumont had some secret she wouldn't reveal and I thought she knew who killed Dawson. I painted a very lurid picture of French methods of police interrogation. I scared the lot of them.'

Dorange raised his happy face from sniffing a bowl of *Bouillabaisse Flambée*.

'You dwelt lovingly on a *passage à tabac*, your favourite torture?'

'I was dumbfounded at Marriott's response. He'd evidently constituted himself as a kind of sentry over Mrs Beaumont's welfare. When he gave the alarm, it suddenly struck me that what I thought was a sordid little affair going on in Miss Blair's bedroom, might have been something much more sinister. I remembered the key on Mrs Beaumont's side of the lock of the communicating door and I took the opportunity of searching Humphries' room for a means of turning it from the other side. I was lucky. They made one big mistake, too. Marie Ann pretended Mrs Beaumont had given her sleeping tablets in *wine*! Mrs Beaumont is rabid teetotal, if you know what that means. She wouldn't touch wine on any account. We'd have used Vichy as a matter of course.

'I suspected Marriott until then. He'd motive, because Dawson had done him so many dirty tricks, culminating in persuading Mrs Beaumont to marry him under Marriott's very nose. And I thought the sure phenomenon by which Sammy recognised the person dumping Dawson's body in the dim light, was that atrocious white cap of Marriott's. There's not another cap like that in the whole of the Alpes-Maritimes!'

One thing Littlejohn did not reveal to Dorange was his strange interview with Sheldon after the death of Humphries.

Littlejohn had thanked Jeremy Sheldon for saving his life. Sheldon had looked very crestfallen.

'When I heard the alarm, I took the gun out of my hip pocket and put it in my dressin' gown. Good job I did. But I didn't mean to kill Humphries. Only wing him. Fired for his legs. Always have it on my conscience.'

Littlejohn had patted Sheldon's shoulder in comforting him.

'You saved me and you certainly saved Humphries from a worse fate. Death, or a penal settlement.'

Sheldon had nodded, better pleased.

'Don't tell my wife, sir, please. If she knows I fired at his legs and hit the poor blighter in the heart, she'll only go for me. Always used to say I bungled everythin'. Now, she's better disposed towards me. In fact, the little gel's quite cut up to think I was contemplatin' blowin' out my brains on her account. We've made a fresh start, Littlejohn, and so long as I keep the revolver as a kind of menace, I think we'll make the grade, sir.'

She didn't deserve the man, really. Anyone so naïve and childlike merited somebody to take better care of him.

There was little trouble with the French police afterwards. Littlejohn's statement about the circumstances of the shooting of Humphries made Sheldon more of a hero than a malefactor, and two days after the event, the *Parquet* gave the charabanc and its depleted load a clearance.

Littlejohn, his wife, Dorange and a more amiable M'sieur Joliclerc saw them off from *Bagatelle*.

'I shall recommend the trustees to close this place after what has happened here.'

Mrs Beaumont, as resident representative of the Turnpike charity, spoke an official word as Alf Fowles started the engine of his bus.

'Get away!' commented Marriott with vulgar familiarity. 'After what's gone on, the place'll be a sensation, Valerie. They'll be fightin' for tickets in Bolchester and there'll be rackets in buyin' and sellin' 'oliday vouchers.'

They were sitting side by side in the motor coach and Marriott was still wearing his atrocious white cap.

The Curries, a happy family again. Gauld and Mary Hannon, sitting together going back home to heaven-knew-what, and Elizabeth Hannon bidding goodbye to a man she'd met at the casino and promising to write to him. He was elderly and wore a white suit, a snakeskin belt, a panama, and white shoes with cloth tops. He had borrowed Elizabeth's last two thousand francs, because he said he'd left his wallet by mistake in his bedroom at his château.

Sheldon and his wife, happily talking together about the journey home. She wore a necklet of artificial jewels to which she'd taken a fancy, and which Sheldon had bought with the last of his francs, including some of the small currency exchanged by Henri.

They all put on their sunglasses. Handshakes, exchanges of addresses, thanks again, farewells. Alf Fowles let in the clutch and the coach, with BREWERS, BOLCHESTER large on its rear, slid away to the Corniche d'Or, and home…

Dorange handed a cheroot to Littlejohn and lit it for him.

'Now, let me take you for a pleasure ride.'

He indicated his small car, which now looked larger with the charabanc not there for comparison.

Along the noisy main road again, through Cannes, Juan, Antibes, to St Laurent-du-Var, and there Dorange turned left.

Fields of flowers, groves of orange, lemon and olive trees, with the bastion of the Alpes right ahead. Near St Jeannet they ascended into the hills, through huge plantations of roses, carnations and mimosa until they reached a white house with a broad courtyard, where workmen were loading lorries with innumerable flowers.

An elderly couple stood in the porch of the villa. A stocky little man with a strong, clever face shrivelled by the sun and shaded by a straw hat with a wide brim, and a gracious lady who must have been a dark beauty in her youth.

'Jerome!'

The waiting pair said it almost together. It was the first time Littlejohn had heard Dorange's Christian name.

Dorange embraced them both.

'My father and mother… Chief Inspector and Mrs Littlejohn.'

It was then that Littlejohn fully realised how much Dorange thought about him. He had bestowed upon him the highest honour a Frenchman can give to a foreigner. He had brought him to his own people and his home.

ABOUT THE AUTHOR

George Bellairs is the pseudonym under which Harold Blundell (1902–1982) wrote police procedural thrillers in rural British settings. He was born in Lancashire, England, and worked as a bank manager in Manchester. After retiring, Bellairs moved to the Isle of Man, where several of his novels are set, to be with friends and family.

In 1941 Bellairs wrote his first mystery, *Littlejohn on Leave*, during spare moments at his air raid warden's post. The title introduced Thomas Littlejohn, the detective who appears in fifty-seven of his novels. Bellairs was also a regular contributor to the *Manchester Guardian* and worked as a freelance writer for newspapers both local and national.

THE INSPECTOR LITTLEJOHN MYSTERIES

FROM OPEN ROAD MEDIA

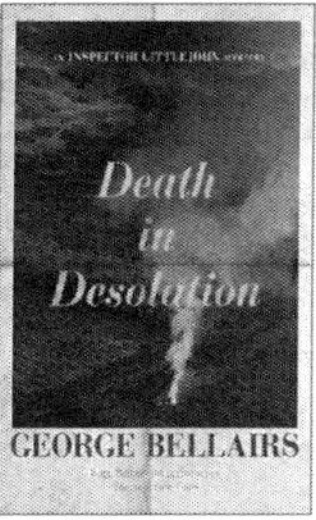

OPEN ROAD
INTEGRATED MEDIA